VALERIE PEPPER

Cover Design: Sarah Hansen, Okay Creations

Editor: Jennifer Sommersby, SGA Books

Published by Stafford Lane Publishing LLC

This one's for the readers: Grab a fan. Maybe some water. You're gonna need it.

TORI

I HAVE MADE a terrible mistake.

Huge.

And while I could, perhaps, be talking about the past twenty years of my life, I am in fact talking about the past ten seconds.

Note to self: do not *ever* walk unannounced into Mom's house again.

Plastered against the front door and wanting to bleach my eyes after what I just saw, I try to shake the vision away. No child should be subjected to seeing her mother getting it on with some guy on the couch, no matter how old she is. We're not talking some casual making out, either. Quite the opposite. I stumbled into a very much *not* casual, very much clothing-optional situation when I burst through the front door.

And listen, at the ripe age of thirty-seven, I know that people of all ages are sexual beings, and I heartily approve of each person getting theirs. Pleasure knows no bounds and all that. But I could have gone to my grave without seeing that.

I suppress a full-body case of the shivers and get back in my trusty little hatchback, aiming for anywhere that doesn't feature a couch with wrinkled old man butt on it. But something is off. There aren't any cars on the road, and the whole place seems desolate, which is not helping me feel great about my decision to surprise my mom with the news that I've come home to live with her.

I crack my window to let in some cool air, still a little flushed, and hear the unmistakable sounds of a marching band. Then I realize it's December 1, which means the Talladega Christmas Parade is in full swing a couple of blocks away. I turn my car in its direction to get as close as I can, wincing at the love tap I give the Jeep in front of me as I parallel park.

After I make sure the Jeep is fine, I make my way to the town square. By the time I arrive, the parade has finished and the square is filled with people full of the holiday spirit. Every available space has been decorated with wreaths and garland, and warm white lights are strung along to give off the perfect amount of cozy light. Chief Suarez is dressed as Santa, like always, though he's a little grayer and a little thicker than the last time I saw him. And like always, he beams with pride as he lights the tree in the center of the square. I'm on the edge of the crowd, but I swear I see the man's eyes twinkle in delight.

My stomach growls, clearly over the scene at my mom's and finally seeming to realize it's been a long time since I've eaten. Twelve hours? Fourteen? Sometimes I forget because I get busy with other things, and it's safe to say that today has been full of "things." From chucking the last of my possessions into storage with my best friend Conner and delivering apartment keys to a more-than-disgruntled building manager, to shoving way more boxes than was probably safe into my hatchback to make the two-hour drive home from Atlanta, I've been busy. I find a cute little coffee shop, but when I tug on the door, it's locked.

"Coffee and hot chocolate are over there," a voice warbles near me.

I barely manage to keep my expression in check as I take in

the older woman to the right of me. She's wearing a knitted purple beanie with a hot pink pompom waving jauntily on top, her scarf is striped like a candy cane, and she's nearly engulfed in a pink puffer coat. She's a technicolor elf of sorts, and I grin. "Good to know, thank you."

She peers closer, her eyes narrowing behind thick lenses. "Tori?"

I blink and try to remember how I would know her. "Y-yes. I'm sorry, I don't—"

She waves me off. "Pfft. I'm Mrs. Withers. I was your neighbor a long time ago—you were a little scrap of a thing, maybe ten, when you had to move."

The statement is an unintentional wallop of pain against my chest. It may have been well over two decades since we lost Dad, but sometimes the ache of it still takes me by surprise. I struggle against the emotion in my throat as I manage to say, "Ah. Well, nice to meet you again, Mrs. Withers."

"Are you visiting your mother or are you home for good?" she asks.

I'm almost put off by such a direct question, but this is a small town, and people make it their business to know all there is to know around here. "Too soon to tell," I smile.

"Well, it's good to see you. Let your mama know I'll bring those overdue books back this week."

I grimace as she pats my arm and toddles off, waving her hand at people I vaguely recognize. My mother is the opposite of who I want to think about right now.

I make my way to the coffee and hot chocolate booth, my head down as I root around my tote for my wallet. Keys, sunglasses, lipstick, regular lip moisturizer, tinted lip moisturizer, phone, book, silk hair tie...where the hell is my wallet? Digging deeper in the dark bag, I manage to trip over my own two feet. I jerk my head up, flinging my arms out for balance in a practiced move.

"Ow!" someone yelps beside me.

"Oh no, I'm so sorry!" The words are out of my mouth before I even see who I've hit.

"It's okay," the blonde mumbles, holding her cheek and raking her eyes over me. "Just, be careful? There are kids and dogs all over the place, and let me be the first to assure you that they're all deadly in one way or another." She's smiling by the end and holding a gloved hand out. "I'm Ceci. You new here?"

I shake her hand, pleasantly surprised by the grip. "Tori. Not new, just…returning. For an unknown length of time." May as well get that part out of the way.

"Well, welcome back," Ceci says, then gestures ahead of her. "Were you heading to the Daily Dose booth?"

"Um, yes. Just need to find my wallet," I say, looking back into my tote and wishing that I could be a little less scattered. But that ship sailed a long time ago.

"You mean that wallet?" Ceci points to the ground.

I look and sigh. "Yep. That wallet." I bend to grab it, then get knocked all the way over by someone as they walk by. My knees hit the ground, soaking in the muddied dirt and grass before I manage to straighten myself. This has to be it. My luck happens in threes, and since I've seen my mom in a way I'll never recover from, given a Jeep the teensiest, tiniest love tap imaginable, *and* stained my white jeans, surely I'm done for the day.

Ceci laughs. "The drink's on me." She helps me up and loops an arm through mine, then hauls me forward without another word.

I stumble again but manage to keep my feet under me as I wonder exactly what kind of superhuman power this woman has, because I am not the person who lets herself get *handled* by someone. And Ceci is most definitely handling me.

"Darius!" Ceci yells as we approach. "A drink for our new friend here."

I wince at him, but relax when I see the understanding smile on his face.

"Ceci, maybe ask your *friend* if she wants to be attached to you like that," Darius says, laughing. Then he looks at me, amusement in his dark brown eyes. "Don't mind her. She's aggressive, but it's out of kindness and a deep need for all your gossip."

I nod and try to rub the feeling back into my arm now that Ceci has let go of it. "Got it. Aggressively kind and nosy."

Ceci levels a glare at Darius that I'm not sure is entirely playful, but he doesn't seem fazed. He blows a kiss at her and looks back at me. "What'll it be? We're rolling straightforward tonight: drip coffee or hot chocolate, with or without marshmallows. Both are good, but the hot chocolate is legit."

"In that case, hot chocolate, please. With marshmallows." I look around the booth. "Do you have anything to eat?"

"You mean other than the marshmallows?" he laughs. "No, but the restaurant over there is open," he says, pointing diagonally across the square.

I take a sip of the hot chocolate and my knees actually buckle a bit. "Oh. Wow," I say. "That's…"

"Told you," he says and winks. "Ceci, that's five bucks."

"Highway robbery," she sniffs, but hands over a ten and waves him to put the rest in the tip jar.

Immediately I like her even more. "Thank you, Darius, and Ceci, thanks for the hot chocolate."

She swings her gaze back from where she'd been searching the crowd. "Not a problem. And if you happen to see a smoking-hot, slightly growly man with two little gremlins with him, will you tell him his wife is ready to go?"

I grin and tip the cup at her. "Absolutely." Then I head towards the restaurant Darius mentioned, weaving through a still-thick crowd and holding tight to my cup.

WILL

I LEAN AGAINST the bar and watch the crowd like I always do. The usuals are here, along with some families grabbing a bite to eat after the parade, plus an increasing number of people I don't recognize. The town keeps growing, and that's good I guess, but it doesn't mean I have to like it.

I chug the ice water and refill it with the pitcher that Sarina knows to always give me. Saves her from constantly coming over here.

"Want a beer? It's on me," the guy next to me says. "As thanks for being a firefighter and all that."

I fight the scowl and shake my head. "No." I'm not a big drinker anyway, but it's one hundred percent water, one hundred percent of the time when I'm on-shift.

He shrugs, says "okay," and turns back to his buddy.

I hate that kind of stuff. Being a firefighter is a job. It's not the one I want, it never has been, and even if it was, I sure as hell don't deserve special treatment for being one. This guy is definitely new to town, or he'd have already known not to bother offering.

Sarina swings over and starts making a couple of drinks in

front of me, moving on auto-pilot as she grins up at me. "Want your usual, Will?"

I grunt. She knows I do, or I wouldn't have come in here. "To go. I need to get back to the station."

"Sure thing." She turns away, all business, and enters my order. Steak salad, extra steak, medium rare, hold the cheese, double cucumbers, double tomatoes, no dressing, no bread, and a side of quinoa.

I check my phone to make sure I haven't missed any alerts from the station. None. I see a notification for a text from Mom, but ignore it for now and tuck the snag of guilt down tight. She treats me like her go-between for both my brothers, and usually I don't mind. Hell, I'm the one who made it happen, even though I didn't realize it at the time. But it's late, and I've spent the day talking to everyone. I'm done interacting with people more than is strictly necessary.

I know my limits.

I down another glass of water and fill it again, content to study the dark swirls of the bar's wooden grain and let myself float for a few precious moments of solitude. I let the world around me get fuzzy and quiet, a technique I taught myself as a kid to block out the sounds of my parents arguing, and it hasn't failed me yet. It's nice and calm in my head, almost like sleeping in the darkened cool of a house during summer, no sounds but the box fan to lull me to sleep.

A tingling sensation at the nape of my neck tugs me back to awareness, and I blink up at Sarina as she hands me the salad, already packed in a to go box and tied in a plastic bag. She's smiling at someone behind me, and as I turn and slide off the stool, the tingling races down the entire left side of my body.

And my heart nearly stops.

Because not two steps from me is Tori Welch. She's unmistakable, even if it's been almost twenty years since I've laid eyes on her. *Beautiful.* Her coily brown hair hangs past her shoulders and bounces as she heads toward me and looks everywhere other than where she's going. Her light brown skin, supple and perfect, is highlighted by the bright red puffer coat she's in. All around her is the same frenetic energy she's always had, a warning beacon to protect one's self against her at all costs. Or maybe that's just me.

Either way, there's no escaping her.

She finally looks up and stutters to a stop as liquid sloshes in her cup. "Oh, crap."

The world stops spinning when our gazes collide. Her dark brown eyes catch the light as they flare in recognition, and in the millisecond it takes her to process the fact of me, I let the memories flood my system: the five dates we went on, the way I fought for control of myself around her and lost repeatedly, the way her lush lips felt beneath mine, pillow-soft and generous, and the way she dropped me to go to prom with the quarterback, crushing me more than I ever thought possible.

Blinking, I shove those thoughts way, way down, locking them back in the vault where they belong, and mentally incinerate the key.

"Will?"

I raise an eyebrow and grip the plastic bag like a goddamn life raft. "Tori."

"Hi," she says, her eyes wide. Then she recovers. "Sorry. Hello. You are the *last* person I expected to see."

I could say the same. I stare.

"You're...huge," she says, then blanches. "I said that out loud, didn't I?"

I feel the tiniest muscle tick at the side of my lips.

Her glossy lips twitch. "That mustache is...something. Knowing you, there's some bet you're entrenched in that only you remember by now, and even though everyone else has moved on, you're still stuck in seventies facial hair hell."

The fact that she almost nails it pisses me off.

She waves a hand at me, a smile tugging at her mouth. "Still a big talker, I see."

I grunt.

She laughs, her eyes soft as she takes me in. "Will Joseph, never change." A beat passes, then another, and her bright smile begins to falter. "So…"

I manage to find my voice. "Why are you here?" The question comes out harsher than I intended.

A shadow of sadness flits across her face, and I curse myself for noticing. It's gone in a millisecond, but this time, her smile doesn't reach her eyes. "It's the holiday season—can't a girl visit her mom without being given the third degree?"

"It's December first."

"Like I said: holiday season."

It figures that she's one of those people who launches a Christmas offensive the moment the calendar says November. But even still, none of this tracks.

"Did that bag hurt you?" she asks with a pointed glance.

I've got my salad in a death grip. "No." I force myself to relax, growing more and more irritated that I can't manage to act like a functioning adult around her. She is the only woman who has ever done this to me. The only woman who can shatter my sense of normalcy. She came close to ruining me in high school, and I don't intend on letting her do it again. "Enjoy your visit."

Ignoring the look of hurt on her face, I step around her and force myself to maintain a regular pace as I leave the restaurant.

Outside, I lengthen my stride, unzipping my jacket and taking deep gulps of cold air, desperate to quell the burning heat that's coursing through me.

Tori Welch. *Tori Welch.*

She absolutely cannot stay.

Tori

IS LIPS ARE an inch from mine, his breath sweet and minty, and I surge up, closing the distance between us as I finally kiss Will Joseph. It's everything I thought it would be, his lips firm but soft as he immediately takes control of the kiss. One of his hands, huge and strong, grips my waist hard enough that I think it might leave bruises, and the idea absolutely thrills me.

I jerk awake, my pulse hammering, my breathing erratic, and blink as consciousness comes. Crap. Was I actually *dreaming* about Will? I close my eyes and force a deep inhale and exhale, again and again, taking one cleansing breath after another until my brain and body quiets.

There.

I will not think about how my entire being lit up last night with the kind of euphoric energy that he and he alone could pull out of me. And I will definitely not think about how much bigger he was than I remember, a freaking *beast* of a man, his broad shoulders nearly blocking the light as he stood in front of me. He looked like he had muscles stacked on muscles beneath that enormous jacket.

That enormous *firefighter* jacket. Because of course he's a firefighter. I knew that—I really have visited my mom after I fled post-high school—but seeing him in the flesh, was…a lot.

To say he has filled out would be the understatement of the century.

And he looked so growly and yummy.

Real talk: High school Tori was an idiot. Because high school Tori had a chance at Will, and she pushed him to the side because she was scared of the way Will made her feel. It'd been too much, too soon. *He'd* been too much, the way he could look at me like he actually saw me, and give me the elusive peace I was always searching for. Our connection was instant and overwhelming, and whether it was built on the shared experiences of growing up in a small town or something deeper, it scared the shit out of me. So I dumped him and went out with the jerk quarterback instead. It could not have been more stupid. Drew ended up being a total waste who treated me like shit and thought he was entitled to get down my pants just because he was QB.

Honestly, my choices in men ever since then have been questionable. But I'm a mess. Messy Tori with messy feelings that always, *always* get me in trouble.

Sighing, I sit up and get out of the bed, letting the familiar groan of the floorboards ground me in the present. It's the only thing that's remained the same in this room; Mom changed everything else after I left. She's never been one for sentimentality, but I gotta say, it hurt that first time I came home from college.

Honestly, I think half of it was driven by the good-natured grudge she held against me for choosing to go to the University of Georgia instead of the University of Alabama. Roll Tide and all that. But I needed out. I was tired of being the person everyone knew in Talladega. I needed a new start. A chance to be someone new. Start over in a place where nothing about me was different or interesting.

It didn't work. I was still a walking bottle of chaos that spilled on literally everyone and everything. Friends were made and lost. Mistakes happened. Some were small, some were big, and some were named Eric Kane.

Not that my losing it and deciding to quit my career and move home was his fault. No, Eric was only the latest in a more than twenty-year line of boyfriends who were happy to enjoy my no-strings-attached approach to relationships and sex. Sometimes it was good sex, and sometimes it wasn't. Safe to say I'd been around the block and around the world with all kinds of men, doing all kinds of things. The French were sensuous, Serbians were downright delightful, and the Scots...have mercy. Truly haven't lived until you hear a deep Scottish burr in your ear while a hand squeezes your throat *just* enough.

Anyway. I'd been called into the boss's office that morning and given a bonus for landing a new account for our company's most expensive drug. It was a massive amount, nearly as much as my annual salary. Which I'd freaking earned by enduring four damn months of the company's CFO making more and more aggressive passes at me, and I'd already promised myself I wouldn't do that shit again.

Except I wasn't sure I'd be able to keep that promise. Not in my line of work.

I'd gone home, and there was Eric, watching ESPN and waiting on me for a round of mediocre sex. His glossy brown accountant hair was still perfectly in place after a day at the office, and he had one arm flung casually over the back of the couch, his sleeves rolled up. He took a swig of Heineken and tossed an easy "hey, babe" at me without so much as looking my way.

I stared at him, mouth agape, and tried to reconcile what the hell had happened in my life to get me there. And without any warning, I cracked. Utterly lost it, yelling about morals and choices and mistakes and roads not taken, then demanded my key and screamed at him to get out. The worst part—at least, I guess it was the worst part, but the more I think about it, the more I'm really not sure—is that he shrugged, smiled, and told me to text him if I changed my mind. Dude had not given two shits that I was clearly not in a good mental place. But I shouldn't have expected him to; I'd been deliberately picking men who swam in the shallow end of the feelings pool to have "relationships" with for a reason.

That was two days ago. I quit my job, broke the lease on my Atlanta apartment, shoved all my worldly possessions in storage for Future Tori to deal with, and came home. Conner thought I was nuts. I'm sure he still does. As for me? I have no idea what I'm doing next.

Well, scratch that. I *do* know what I'm doing next: Coffee.

I throw a robe on over my shirt and sleeping shorts, both to ward off the chill of the morning air and to avoid giving Mom's guy friend a show if he happens to be here, and pad into the kitchen.

Mom's already there, and she looks up from where she's leaning on the island, her favorite cup in one hand and her phone in the other. I swear, the woman doesn't age, and at thirty-seven, I'm showing strong hints that I inherited that part of her in the biracial lottery. I'm actually a pretty solid mix of my parents, but the older I get, the more I see my mom in the mirror. Some days I wish I had more of my dad, if only so I could *see* him. He died of an undetected heart condition in his sleep when I was ten.

My mom plans to live until she's one hundred, to "piss off Satan," as she puts it. The only hint that she's in her early sixties are the fine crow's feet at her eyes and the short, graying dreadlocks she's been wearing lately. "Good morning," she says, then gestures with her cup to the coffee pot on the counter. "Made enough for you."

"Thanks," I say, grabbing the biggest mug she has and pouring. Then I grab the mocha peppermint flavored creamer that Mom favors to top it off.

"Come sit," she commands when I turn around, sliding onto the barstool and waiting for me to do the same. When I'm settled, she peers at me over her reading glasses. "Want to tell me why you thought it was a good idea to come barging into the house without so much as giving me a heads up that you planned to visit?"

I cringe. "I really don't need the reminder of what I saw, Mom."

She clicks her tongue. "Serves you right for not telling your mama when you're coming home." Then she chuckles. "Damn near gave the man a heart attack. And at my age, that's a real possibility."

I take another big sip of coffee and try to flush the image away. "Sorry," I mumble.

She waves her hand. "You should be. But I sent him home. Figured I didn't need you two meeting so soon after that."

I sigh in relief. At least I won't have to meet whoever he was. Not yet, anyway.

"Want to tell me why you're here?" She pins me with the same look she's wielded to perfection my entire life, her deep-set eyes missing nothing.

"I quit my job."

She stills. "You what?"

"I quit my job."

"Victoria Athena Welch, you did *what*?"

I tilt my chin up. "I. Quit. My. Job. I have savings." Including a big-ass bonus that feels a little tainted, if I'm being honest, but I worked too damn long and too damn hard not to keep it. "I'll be fine, Mom."

"I thought you liked it."

I shrug. "It was fine."

"It was *fine*?" she repeats. "You consistently outsold everyone in your region. You won so many damn awards we joked about having to rent you a bigger place just to hold the things. And it was *fine*?"

I shrug. I'd loved my job as a pharmaceutical sales rep for a long, long time. It was the one thing I was good at. Well, that and Pilates. The thrill of being given a goal by the crusty old white guys who thought I couldn't hack it, and then crushing that goal and lording it over their shriveled asses, was a high I never tired of. I was so good at it that I could choose the drugs I sold, and that was its own reward. But the past couple of years hadn't been as fun as all the ones before, and no amount of vacations in swanky places with hot guys was enough to keep away the inevitable realization that my job was absolutely and completely soulless and filled with too many people with questionable morals around damn near every-thing. I'd finally grown weary of dragging my bag of tricks into practice after practice, clinic after clinic, pushing and wheedling.

"I wanted a change," I say.

"How can you sound so cavalier about it?"

"Because it was just a job, Mom."

She rolls her eyes. "Millennials."

I roll mine right back. "What do you want me to say?"

"I want you to realize it wasn't 'just a job,' Victoria. It's a career. One that you shouldn't just toss away on a whim."

"Yeah, well, it sucked."

Her eyes widen. "Is there more to this that you're not telling me? Oh god." She places her hand on her chest. "Are you pregnant?"

"What?" I screech. I feel my face go into cartoon-like contor-tions, with my jaw hitting the counter, my eyes popping and my brows going every which way. "No!"

"Then what has caused all this?"

"A lack of good sex, okay?" I shoot back.

She opens her mouth to retort, but then she seems to actually realize what I've said, and she starts laughing.

I smile into my coffee cup. "Honestly, it's partially true."

She wipes the tears of laughter away as she gets control of herself again. "Okay, fine. You win."

"Good. Seeing as how it's my life and all," I say, twisting my lips.

"Okay, Miss Thing, and you plan on doing what, exactly, with this life of yours?" she prods.

Pilates studio. The idea roars to life inside my head, fully formed and entirely unbidden. And that's the answer. Boom! Done. But I know better than to get into yet another discussion about my life choices with Mom, so I say, "I don't know yet. I figured I'd stay with you—"

Her bark of laughter cuts me off. "Stay with me? Oh child, no. No, no, no."

I gawp at her. "Why not? You're always saying how you miss me, so I thought I could stay here while I figured out my next move." Was she honestly not going to let me stay here?

Mom levels her *I mean business* look on me. "I sent Stanley to stay at his house last night, but only because I knew you'd be coming back. He usually stays here. We're usually busy."

I don't miss the way she says *busy,* and I struggle to keep from shuddering. "But where am I supposed to stay?"

She shrugs and finishes her coffee. "One minute you're grown and 'it's my life' and 'I'll date who I want' and 'no you're not getting grandkids,' the next minute you want me to fix it for you." She slides off the stool and puts some bread in the toaster. "There's a new bed-and-breakfast that opened up. Other side of the square. I heard it's cute."

I narrow my eyes at her back. "Cute is code for expensive."

She raises a shoulder. "Should have thought of that before you barged in on me and Stanley."

I will the visual to stay away and concede defeat, because

there is no use arguing with my mother. "Yes, ma'am. Can I at least stay here a couple of days? Spend time with you?"

She turns around and beams, having won this round. "I'd love it. I've been stockpiling new puzzles for one of your visits."

I smile behind the coffee cup, but temper my excitement. Maybe quitting my job and leaving Atlanta wasn't the best idea.

I let that thought slide away. No negative self-talk. I have always leaped first, and I'm not stopping anytime soon. Life figures itself out.

Besides, now that I won't be paying Atlanta rental prices, I can relax and figure out next steps. Like what all it takes to open a Pilates studio. How hard can it be? Find the space, sign the lease, slap some paint in there, get some machines, and voila: Pilates. And yoga. Definitely Pilates and yoga.

Mom starts rinsing her cup. With her back to me, the water running, I barely hear the words. "The Joseph brothers own it."

I still. "Sorry, what?"

She turns the water off and turns around, drying her hands on a red-checked tea towel. "The inn. It's owned by the Joseph brothers."

I nearly choke as the bread pops out of the toaster. "Will?"

She nods, completely oblivious to my shock. "And Price. I don't think Aaron has anything to do with it, but my gossip skills aren't what they used to be. Didn't you date Will in high school?"

"Um, yeah," I say, pouring more coffee and wishing I had some Bailey's to put in it.

She hums. "You see him yet?"

Where is she going with this? "Ran into him at the burger place on the square last night." She hums again as I gulp hot coffee.

I turn with the pot in my hand and bang it into the counter.

"Tori!" Mom chides.

I hiss in a breath and inspect the glass. "Sorry. Looks like it's fine, though."

"I swear, child..." she doesn't bother saying the rest. She doesn't need to. My penchant for clumsiness is legendary.

It's only when I know she's left the kitchen with her toast, humming a song that could honestly be Beyoncé or gospel, that I finally exhale.

Guess I'll be finding a room at Will's inn.

WILL

TORI WELCH. TORI Welch. Tori Welch.

It's not even six a.m. and I'm already pissed, because the only woman to ever get under my skin has managed to climb right back under it with a three-minute conversation.

Why is she here? How long is she staying? Will I see her again?

I mutter a curse and turn the water off, barely managing to avoid knocking over one of the five million bottles of girl products in the shower caddy in the process. I'll be glad when my brother Price and his girlfriend Jodi are firmly ensconced in the house he bought across the street, because I'm tired of sharing a bathroom with two people. Not to mention a mattress.

That's why I sleep in an unoccupied guest room whenever possible. Price and I swap out the bedsheets on our last morning before heading to the fire station, but that doesn't make up for the fact that I know the kind of stuff they're doing in it.

Stepping out of the shower, I wrap a towel around my waist and palm the condensation off the mirror. Time to shave this godawful mustache and pay up, because if I have to see myself with it one more day, I might really turn into the giant green character that Price calls me on a near-daily basis. In minutes, it's off, and I'm back to the clean-shaven look I've sported my entire life. Well, clean-shaven until it starts to grow back, which happens damn near instantly.

Having it gone makes me feel physically lighter. How the hell does Chief live with the walrus of a mustache he has?

Shaking my head, I finish up in the bathroom and get dressed. Then it's out to the kitchen to prep for the guests: coffee, some pastry, a breakfast casserole, fruit. They eat better when I'm here, so Price and I have taken to marketing it as though it's a good thing: continental breakfast with Price, and full breakfast with me.

I love it in the kitchen. When we redid the place, it was the one room I insisted was mine to oversee, and it turned out beautifully. Restaurant-quality stainless steel appliances, plus an island for storage and prep two steps behind me when I'm cooking. We finally got the farm table I special-ordered from an old friend in Fairhope, a simple, golden oak shined to perfection, and seats twelve. Fresh-cut winter bouquets sit in two fat, low-profile vases on the table, the waxy green and bright red of the arrangements hinting at the holiday to come.

I've just pulled the egg, spinach, mushroom, and hash brown casserole out of the oven when the first couple appears, ready to take on a day of hiking. They're older, retired, and perfectly content to let me speak as little as possible. I'm not a people person and I know it; that's Price's forte. But I make up for it with my skills in the kitchen and a binder full of information on the town and surrounding area. Another couple appears a bit later, getting ready for a day at the racetrack. We've gotten more of those types of guests than I'd counted on, people who pay an outrageous sum of money to drive a NASCAR car a few times around the track.

The morning activities are over by ten, and I've cleaned up

and have a load of sheets in the industrial washer going when the front door opens. "Can I help y—?"

But the words die on my tongue.

Because she's here. In my inn. And in the rays of the morning sun, the crisp air rushing in with her, she's even more stunning than last night. Radiant. Her light-brown skin is flushed with the cold, her lips glossed and smiling, and her hair. Hair I never allowed myself to touch because I knew it'd be my undoing, fanning out from her head like her personal halo. Or warning signal.

Definitely warning signal.

After an almost uncomfortable beat of silence, Tori forces a smile. "Hi!" She barrels toward me with the same kind of willful confidence that brought me to my knees all those years ago. "You shaved."

I swear her eyes darken as she says it, but they're already such a deep brown that this far away it's impossible to tell. Those eyes were my undoing when I was a stupid teenager.

Talk, asshole. "Welcome to Shirley's Inn," I manage to grit out.

She brightens, her smile knowing. "Ah. So we're *not* talking about the mustache? Got it. Hope I wasn't what finally tipped you over the edge."

She was...not. She was *not*.

Dammit.

She looks around, and I take the second that her back is turned to gather my wits. I can't let her fluster me like this.

"So, this is your place? I heard you and your brother were running it. Plus the firefighter gig? How's that work?"

It's too many questions. "Still do it. I do this, too." I shift in the chair that's suddenly too small, trapped behind a desk I want to turn into kindling. She's *heard* about me? What did she hear?

I shut that line of thinking down. Of course she heard. This town may be growing, but all it takes is one trip to the Piggly Wiggly or Daily Dose, and a person will hear everything that's going on in under five minutes. Especially if that person used to live here and is visiting.

And I am counting on "visit" being the case for Tori.

Her deep brown eyes assess me and probably find me just as lacking as they did in high school. Fucking Drew. Guy was a dick then and is a dick now, still living on his quarterback glory days like anyone cares. Tells anyone who'll listen that he played for Alabama, but it's the biggest crock of bull because he was a walk-on for third string long snapper and he never saw the field once during games.

I shift again, growing more uncomfortable under her scrutiny with every passing second. Finally, I ask, "So, is there something I can help you with?"

She jerks to attention, seeming to come back from wherever she'd gone in her head, and smiles even wider. It's a fake smile, and it's hiding something, and again it's more than irritating that I can see that. Over twenty years have passed. *Why* do I still notice?

"I need a room."

"You what?" I didn't hear that correctly.

She tilts her head. "I need a room, Will. This is an inn. I need a place to stay."

No. Clenching my jaw so hard it pops, I ask, "For how long?"

The smile on her face is bashful now, but genuine. "I don't know. I kind of...imploded my life last week. And my mom won't let me stay at her house."

"She won't?" Is it possible her relationship with her mother is even worse than mine and my brothers' with ours?

She laughs softly. "Let's just say that my mom has a new friend, and he's very, um, attentive."

I try to school my face, but I must do a shit job of it because her eyes sparkle. *Sparkle.* Dammit.

"Exactly, Will," she says. "So…can I stay?"

This is bad. If she's here, then I can't get away from her. Can't pretend she doesn't exist. And I need that. Need her to disappear back into nothingness, back where teenage Will and his hurt stay buried.

"Will?" she prompts.

I sigh. Rules are rules, and the rules are that if we have a room and a paying customer wants it, they get it.

Resigned, I nod.

TORI

WILL IS ABSOLUTELY beside himself about me staying here, and it's hot.

He's hot.

Seeing him last night at the bar was one thing, but here? When he's shaved his mustache and already has a five o'clock shadow at ten in the morning and is in a black henley, glaring at me like everything wrong in the world is my fault?

Have mercy.

I shouldn't be turned on by it—by *him*—but here we are. And I've lived long enough on this planet to know that there's nothing I can do about my continuing attraction to him except to simply go with it. Lean into the chaos, because fighting it never works out for me. Besides, where's the fun in fighting something as hot as Will Joseph?

I refocus on what he's saying.

"...only room is our largest."

I nod. "That's fine. Can I see it?"

Wordlessly, he stands, and I try to keep my face neutral as I'm reminded again of just how big he is. He rounds the desk in three strides and inclines his head toward the stairs. I follow, taking him in as we go. He'd been tall in high school, and I'm 5'9", so it's not the height that's doing it for me. No, it's the nearly door-frame width of him, how the fabric of his shirt strains against his chest and biceps, the way his shoulders taper down to an ass that is fine as hell and probably hard as steel, and tree-trunk thighs that strain against his joggers. Thick thighs save lives, but his might make me pass out. There's something primal in the way I want to climb him like a jungle gym. As though evolution itself has set its hand on top of my head, swiveled it to Will, and said *That one.*

Honestly, there's no other explanation for it. I will not allow it to be any kind of residual feelings from high school. Sure, he was the only one who made me think that love might be possible, but I'd already sworn love off by then. I saw what losing my dad did to my mom, never mind what it did to me, and no way was I putting myself through that. I never have, and never will. Whatever this is, it's purely physical. So I swallow the drool and follow him to the room he's stalking towards.

"This one." He waves at the open door, but doesn't move.

And, okay, maybe it's a little wrong of me to brush by him so closely as I step in to get a better look at the room, but he *is* standing in the doorway, and he *is* basically filling the space. He stills as I brush past him, and it takes every ounce of willpower to not nuzzle against him like a cat as I go by. Rub my head against him to leave my scent on him and everything.

"I'll take it." The morning sun slants into the two eastern-facing windows, showing off a bright and cheery room. A king-size bed dominates the space, and is covered with a beautifully patterned yellow and white quilt. There's a big swath of open, bare floor between the bed and dresser, perfect for my Pilates and yoga practice. The walls are a light yellow and are graced by framed photos of flowers and birds. The combined effect almost makes me feel calm.

Then I turn and hot-as-hell Will is still glaring at me, and I have to clench my thighs together. "How much?"

He grunts out the price, and honestly, I have to fight not to laugh at how inexpensive it is.

"What." The way he says it is more of a demand than anything.

"I never apologized for how I treated you in high school," I say, then immediately want to shove the words back in my mouth. Why am I opening up this can of worms? It's dangerously close to admitting things he never needs to know.

His eyes flare, and in my periphery I catch the way he clenches his fist. "Doesn't matter."

My heart squeezes. *It doesn't?* What about the way he cradled me as I bawled into his chest on the anniversary of my dad's death, kissing my tears away and murmuring he'd always be there for me? Or the times I caught him glaring at racist idiots who stared at the two of us together?

He can't know how much I regret everything. So I double down. "I was stupid. I wanted the prestige of going to the prom with the quarterback. And it backfired." I laugh awkwardly to cover the lie. "Kid could not kiss to save his life, and he actually thought he was going to get in my pants. *Big* mistake."

Will swallows audibly in the silence that follows, his eyes searing into mine. I'd forgotten about those eyes. Dark gray and shot through with a light blue, so the effect makes them look almost silver. I suppress a shiver.

"He was a dick," Will finally pronounces. "Still is."

Why does he look so good? I can't possibly stay here without wanting to touch him, to feel his arms around me. But after the way I treated him? "You should sleep with me," I blurt.

At this point, everything goes into slow-motion, and it's as if entire worlds are born and cease to exist in the amount of time it takes him to blink.

When he speaks, his voice is impossibly low, and the sound

of it scrapes against a craving deep inside me. "What did you just say?"

Ignoring the clanging of warning bells going off in my head—the ones that are screaming *You literally left Atlanta to start over and this is* not *a good start!*—I repeat myself. "Sleep with me."

The range of emotions playing across his face is almost comical. "You," he grits out, "want to sleep. With me." Another statement.

I can't stop the smirk on my face. "You're still not one for questions, are you, big guy?"

He takes a step back, his face paling. "No."

Now I'm full-on grinning. I'm dancing on the edge here, no clue if it's going to work, and it's exhilarating. Instead of feeling like I'm doing something reckless that I'll pay for later, I actually feel more serene than I've been since…well, since I kicked whatshisface out of my apartment and decided to come home. None of it makes sense, but here we are.

Meanwhile, it appears I've thrown Will for the loop of his life. So I say, "No, you're still not a questions kind of guy, or no, you don't want to sleep with me?"

"Yes." He shakes his head. "I mean, no." He backs up again and curses under his breath. "I don't—no. No," he repeats, as though he's trying to convince himself. "No, I don't want to sleep with you. I mean, I do, Jesus, *look* at you, but no. You're a guest. And I don't sleep with guests."

My smile gets even bigger. I can work with this. "So if I weren't a guest…?"

He reddens, the spots of color on his cheeks standing out like deep red cherries against cream. Both of which I'd enjoy tasting.

"No!" he yelps. "Just—will you just give me a minute?" He runs his hand through his hair, clearly distraught, and the way he does it reminds me of the boy he was in high school. It's vulnerable. And it kind of makes me want to put him in my pocket and keep him like a pet. But it also increases my desire to have him rail me.

Good and hard.

But I'm a big girl, and I can take no for an answer. I wait, taking my fill of him as he looks anywhere but at me, his body tense. Good *lord*, his body. Meaty and thick and ripped and just, *damn*. I can't imagine the time he spends on it, and I'd like to thank him on behalf of people everywhere for his efforts in that regard. Those *thighs*. I could cuddle them.

"Tori."

I snap my gaze back up to his. "Will."

His expression softens for a millisecond, and I want to freeze time. Because there the boy is again, the boy who made me feel things far too deeply. The boy who clearly had those deep feelings for me, too, and would have done anything for me before I crushed his heart. But almost instantly, fuck-hot Will is back, and neither one of us are kids anymore. I have to remember that.

His voice is strong when he says, "I accept your apology from high school. Even though it's not necessary. And I appreciate the offer to sleep together, but I will pass. When you're ready, I can enter in your payment details for the room back downstairs. Thank you." He swivels on his heel and leaves the room.

And all I can do is smile, because fair enough. If Will Joseph says no, then Will Joseph says no. But I'd love to turn that *no* into a *yes*. Not for anything other than sex, obviously, because when it comes to men, it's all I've ever been good for. And with Will? That's all it can be.

TORI

WITH MY LIVING situation settled, I toss a final lusty smile at Will and head to my car to drive to the coffee shop. But I can't find my keys. After five minutes in which I rummage through everything in my massive tote and come up empty-handed except for that one Tarte gloss I'd been searching for over a month, I walk back into the house. Ignoring the confused look on Will's face, I go up the stairs and back to the room I'll be calling home.

There, on the dresser, are my keys. "How?" I ask the room.

No answer comes.

Back in my car with my keys, I make the short trek to the coffee shop. I'd wanted to go in that first night I was here, and now that I've got a little time on my hands, I want to see it.

I read the sign hanging above the shop. Daily Dose. Cute. The whole square is cute, always has been. A bell dings over my head as I enter, and the barista, a strawberry-blonde in a chambray polka-dot apron, looks up and smiles.

"Welcome to Daily Dose," she calls brightly.

I startle, not ready for that kind of greeting. I am *not* in Atlanta anymore. No disrespect to the A-T-L, but anonymity was the name of the game whenever I got my caffeine fix there. And that's part of why I loved it. That and the ability to do whatever caught my interest at the time, whether that was pottery (short-lived) or learning how to make charcuterie boards. Plus, Atlanta was glitzy. Parts of it anyway. And I loved dressing up and being glitzy right alongside the men I dated. Approaching the counter, with a shop full of decidedly *not* glitzy people in it, I realize I don't miss that aspect at all.

"What'll it be?" the woman asks.

The menu has the standard fare, along with a board of more localized drinks. The *Dega, Baby* looks like it's intended to put someone into a sugar high, and there's even a Ricky Bobby-inspired drink called the *I Wanna Go Fast Espresso Blast*. "Can I have a pumpkin spice latte, please?"

Sue me. I'm half white, and the basic in me has to come out sometimes, okay? I own it.

"For here?"

I nod, and the barista smiles, takes my payment, and gets to work while I scan the rest of the shop. It's cozy and busy. A table of women and kids are off to the side, and I swear I recognize at least one of them from high school. There's also a couple cuddling over a notebook, and two separate people buried in their laptops.

I will definitely make this my usual coffee shop.

"Here you go," the barista says, smiling warmly as she hands a beautiful, dark blue and purple polka dot cup and saucer to me over the pastry-filled display case.

"Thanks," I say, inhaling the spicy scent. "It smells incredible."

Her smile broadens. "Wait'll you taste it. Much better than the chain places. I'm Jodi, by the way, and you look super familiar."

Smiling, I answer. "I grew up here. I'm Tori; my mom is the librarian."

"That's it!" she says. "Were you on the dance team at the high school?"

"Wow, taking me back." I try to place her. "Yes—but I don't remember you."

"I was way behind you," she says. "In middle school when you were in high school. But I remember you from the football games. You were the best dancer there was."

I raise an eyebrow but thank her, because she's right: I was. And it was a good way to use all the excess energy I could never seem to get rid of.

She laughs. "So are you just visiting your mom? Or did you come back to coach the dance team?"

I take a sip of the latte. "Oh, wow, this *is* good," I say. "First the hot chocolate, and now the latte."

"Thanks. So...dance team?" she prompts.

I quirk my lips at her. "Definitely not. I was in Atlanta but I'm here for the duration now, while I figure out next steps."

"Well then, welcome home!" she says. "We're glad to have you back. We need more cool chicks around here."

I snort a laugh. "I'm hardly cool. But I do have a question for you. Is there a Pilates or yoga studio nearby?"

Now it's her turn to snort. "I don't think so. I might be wrong, but I'm fairly certain the closest is about half an hour from here. Which isn't *that* far, but far enough that locals aren't inclined to go."

I nod thoughtfully.

She narrows her eyes. "You look like you're up to something." She turns to the man who's joined her from what looks like a storage room. "Darius, doesn't she look like she's up to something?"

We throw each other inquisitive looks. "You gave me the best hot chocolate of my life the other night." Today, he's rocking some serious make-up over smooth skin that, in the daylight, is a gorgeous teakwood color, and his edges are flawless.

He smiles and bows. "I most certainly did."

Delighted, I lean forward as a fun little thought takes shape. "Are you single?"

He raises an eyebrow. "You're cute, bae, but you have one too many X chromosomes."

I laugh and set my latte down. I love meeting new people, and I love it when I can make a match happen. And the vibe I'm getting from Darius is absolutely perfect for who I have in mind. "Not for me. But I have a friend."

His glossy lips widen. "Shouldn't we at least know your name before you try to go all gay boy gal pal on us?"

I raise my hands in surrender. "I'm Tori. My friend is Conner."

"Sounds white."

"He is."

"Local?"

"Atlanta."

"Interesting. Age?"

"Thirty-five."

"He is *twenty-six*!" Jodi says.

"So?" Darius and I say together, and I know my instincts are right.

Before we can continue, the bell dings again and a voice says, "How is my drink not ready? I texted!"

I turn to see the woman I met the other night, and she smiles.

"You again! At least now you get the full version of Jodi's amazing coffee shop."

I nod, realizing Jodi is the owner. "Me again," I answer.

"Here indefinitely, right?"

"Nailed it," I say, feeling nothing but warmth that she's getting everything correct. "And you have kids and a hot husband—although I didn't see either the other night, so I'm just going by what you said."

Her eyes light up. "Oh, he's definitely hot. And yes, twins, Luke and Eva, god help me." She reaches for her drink and turns back to me. "Wanna sit?"

My answer is immediate. "Absolutely. And your drink is on me." I pay for both, and before I walk away, I look at Darius. "We're not done."

"We're definitely not," comes his response.

As Ceci leads me to a set of over-stuffed chairs in the back, I'm wondering why I craved anonymity so much. Because the sense of family and love they have for each other makes me want to curl up in it. Then my toe catches on the rug and I stumble.

"You good?" Ceci asks.

Cheeks burning, I say, "I'm fine." But as I look closer at her, I see nothing but open acceptance on her face. Not the scowling judgment I seem to get from others when something like that happens. Maybe it's because she's a mom? Or maybe she just doesn't care that I tripped, and honestly, that would be amazing.

"This is where we relax and gab," she says. "We're far enough from the Mom Table over there, and we can sit and judge and gossip about everyone without them hearing us. Most of the time."

I grin as we settle in. "Sounds perfect. Pretty sure I went to high school with one of them."

"You probably did. I didn't because I went to a private school. But we're not talking about me yet. Spill it, sister. Who are you, where you from, why are you here, the whole thing."

I can't help the smile that's spread across my face. "Are you always this intense?"

She shrugs. "I don't see the point of wasting time."

"Well, I'm all for it."

"Good. Then answer my questions," she prompts.

I laugh. "Got it. Tori Welch, grew up here and went to Georgia for college, back because I accidentally-on-purpose imploded my life, thought I could stay with my mom until I walked in on her and her boyfriend the night of the Christmas parade, so now I'm staying at a little bed-and-breakfast down the street while I decide if I can pull off a Pilates and yoga studio in this town as a new career."

Ceci nods and purses her lips. "I like you."

I laugh. "Right back at ya."

"The bed-and-breakfast," she says. "You mean Shirley's Inn?"

I nod.

"Ooh, that's delicious. Which of the owners have you met?"

I sit back, able to see a trap when it's laid out before me. "Oh, no. I can tell you're holding out on me. You first."

She sets her drink down and pulls out her phone. "Hang on. I'm telling my hot husband that I'm taking a longer than normal coffee break, because I've just found a new best friend." When she finishes, she puts her attention back on me. "Okay, Miss Takes Everything I Can Dish At You And Throws It Right Back, I know a fellow chaos-bringer when I see one. And you must have dropped your crown on your way into town, because all of this," she waves her fingers at me, "has a story. And I'm willing to do what it takes to get it."

I laugh. She really *is* fun, and warm, and open. "We can absolutely trade stories. But the fact that you referred to me taking a room at Shirley's Inn as 'delicious,' and asking me which owner I've met, tells me that you know the owners well. Am I right?"

She takes a sip of her latte. "Yes."

My lips tilt up. "Do tell."

"But you know them, too, right? You grew up here."

I wave it away. "I do, but I've been gone for twenty years. Enlighten me with your version."

"Three brothers: Will, Price, and Aaron. Jodi over there is

hot and heavy with Price; she owns this shop and Price is a firefighter at the station down the block. Will is also a firefighter down there. He and Price own the inn. Aaron is a paramedic, also at the station, and is engaged to a woman named Devon. Devon is my hot husband's sister, and she used to be married to Jodi's brother, another firefighter, who died in a terrible accident fighting a fire almost seven years ago. She took off after the funeral and didn't live in town for five years. Shirley, also known as Gigi, was Rick—my hot husband—and Devon's grandmother, and when she passed away, she wrote in her will that Devon needed to come back and take care of the house, but she had to live in it for six months before she could do anything with it. Those six months gave our boy Aaron the time he needed to get Devon to fall in love with him. They're engaged and haven't set a date and it's driving me crazy. Devon, Jodi and I are thick as thieves and I'm dragging you in with us. There." She leans back against the chair and takes a deep drink of her coffee. "Your turn."

My head spins. "Wait, wait, wait. You just dropped a ton of information on me." I take a sip of coffee while I process. "Devon and Rick. Hang on. Is your husband Rick Rayne?"

Ceci nods. "Oh wait—you know them?"

I nod and grin. "I do, but just in passing. Will and I were in the same grade. We dated until I dumped him to go to the prom with Drew Ackerman. Drew was a dick—"

"Still is," Ceci says, her eyes full of mirth as she clenches her hands in what appears to be outright glee.

"After college, I moved to Atlanta and started a career as a pharmaceutical sales rep, and last week I decided I'd had enough. So I kicked out my current flavor of the month, quit my job, packed my apartment, and thought I'd come home and stay with my mom while I figured my shit out. But I walked in on my mom with her boo, which I'm trying to forget I ever saw. And that's why I'm at the inn."

Ceci leans forward. "Can we go back to the part where you dated Will? Was he just as growly then as he is now?"

I snicker. "Mostly." No way will I tell her that with me, he was a teddy bear. That when it was just the two of us, he made me feel like I was the center of his world. But we both had our own demons to battle, and instead of battling them together, I ran.

She nods and toasts me with her latte. "Welcome home, Tori. We're about to have ourselves a grand time."

WILL

I'M BY MYSELF in the sad excuse for a weight room at the station, hoping to sweat thoughts of Tori and her proposition out of my head, when Price walks in. I don't bother stopping the dumbbell lifts I'm doing, and instead meet his eyes in the mirror and wait for him to speak. It's not like he needs an invitation, and even if he did, I'm certain he'd ignore it.

"Broseph!" Price says, smiling his standard grin and looking at me like the cat that ate the canary. "Why didn't you tell me that you had a history with our *guest*, hmm?"

I grunt. It's not his business, that's why.

He leans against the door frame. "Just kidding. I've known that since it actually happened."

I shift the barbell to my other hand and try not to let the surprise show on my face.

Price laughs. "C'mon, man, you think Aaron and I don't know *allll* about Tori? We placed bets the first night she was back in town."

"Don't." I don't want my brothers so much as thinking about her. I'm not jealous, I'm just...fuck, I don't know what I am. Confused. Irritated. Tempted.

He pushes off the frame and steps into the room. "Hate to tell you, but there's no stopping a friendly wager between brothers about the other brother."

I scowl at him, and he ignores it.

"Anyway, seems our *guest* is now buddies with Ceci, and Ceci told my sweet Jodi that Tori told her you two used to date."

"Quit emphasizing the word guest," I say.

Price's grin widens. "Where's the fun in that? No, I like knowing that for once, *I* have the moral high ground here. Because you've been more growly bear than usual these past two days, and I know it's because our *guest* is rattling your cage."

I finish my reps and face him. "What do you want, Price?"

He chuckles. "Just giving you shit, man. It truly brings me joy."

I shake my head. "Dumbass."

"So, listen." His grin disappears, and he gets serious. Well, as serious as he can get.

I grunt.

"I'm closing on the house next week." He looks at me expectantly.

"And?" I finally prompt.

"*And*, isn't there anything you'd like to say about that?"

I turn away from him, needing to continue my workout. I swear he knows I don't want to be a firefighter anymore, but I can't stop. Not yet. My savings aren't nearly enough. Because what if something happened to him or Aaron? They're my responsibility and always have been, and now they have Devon and Jodi relying on them. Which means I have to think of them, too.

I pick up a kettlebell and try to ignore the way it feels heavier than usual.

"Will," Price starts.

Nope. Not doing this. "Shouldn't you be at the house? What if someone needs to check in?" *What if Tori needs something? Or hurts herself?* I shake my head, desperate for thoughts of her to exorcise themselves. Her accident-prone ways aren't my concern.

The alarm blares, indicating we've got a call. I catch my phone as Price tosses it to me and steps out of my way. He's not on shift since we trade them out: he works at the inn while I'm here, and vice versa. I'm sure he only came by to do exactly what he said: give me shit.

I read the alert on the screen as I cover the quick distance to the bay, and see it's not a fire. Assuming Aaron and Mike get to the scene in their unit first, my team will function more as support for Aaron and Mike, but knowing that doesn't decrease anyone's level of urgency. Besides, if our rig gets there first, we handle the call. I shuck my running shoes and pull uniform pants on over my shorts. Price constantly makes fun of me for the tiny shorts I wear, but needing to get in the rig quickly is exactly why I do it. I shove my arms into the button-down and make my way to the passenger seat of Glenda right as Buck swings into the driver's seat. Zach is already in the seat behind me; he's one of the probies and will stay in the back until someone retires. Doesn't mean he's not valuable; just means he's newer.

Mike and Aaron pull out of the bay and turn on the siren, making a left and heading toward the race track. We follow as I finish buttoning my shirt and tucking it in.

"Anything else?" Buck asks.

I look down at the screen. Nothing has changed, but I know Buck wants the full run-down just in case he missed something on his first read. "We're heading to the long-term care facility. Caucasian male, seventy-six, appears to be a stroke. Dementia. Found him on routine check."

Buck nods tightly as he brakes through an intersection. Mike and Aaron's truck is already a block and a half ahead of us, and I know Buck is determined to not let the distance increase.

Drivers barely seem to notice us thanks to their loud-ass car speakers and ear buds, and Buck's not shy about using the horn, but Talladega residents will usually stay pulled over if we're close enough behind the ambulance.

"Hate these calls," Buck says a minute later, even as we all smile and wave at the group of kids on bikes outside a Dollar General.

I glance over, surprised he's showing sentiment. Then again, I'm one of the older ones at the station, and he's the oldest of all of us, so I get where he's coming from. "We're not flower delivery guys," I say. "No call is a good call."

He grunts in response and I stay silent. Zach says nothing.

Aaron and Mike are already jogging toward the front doors with the stretcher, their gear bags resting on top, when Buck kills the siren and pulls us into the semicircle driveway. I grab the med kit and we're out of the apparatus and in through the doors a moment later.

I nod at Mrs. Davis, the receptionist. For better or worse, we all know each other here.

"It's Mr. Luther," she says. "Down the hall and take a left."

Coach. I fight through the gut punch she's just delivered and keep moving.

We get to the room right as Aaron and Mike are evaluating Coach. Staff are fanned out in the hallway, knowing they need to stay out of the way but also nearby in case they can provide any needed support, which can be critical if the patient is conscious and scared or confused.

Coach is lying on the bed, eyes closed, a heart monitor beeping as Aaron and Mike evaluate him. Thin and shrunken, he's a far cry from the intimidating hulk of a man he used to be all those years ago, when he stood on the sidelines of the football field and yelled at us until his face was purple.

"He's stable," Mike says.

"Let's move him," Aaron answers.

That tells me they're taking him to the hospital. Buck and I wordlessly wait as the other two work, and when Aaron's eyes meet mine as they wheel Coach out, I know he's just as shaken as I am.

Coach wasn't a warm and fuzzy man. Not by far. To my knowledge, he never married or had any kids, and I'd bet he gets little to no visitors. These kinds of places are dreary on their best days, but to not get any visitors would make it downright bleak.

Mrs. Davis waits with the paperwork at the front, and Buck and I make Zach take care of it. As we haul ourselves back up into the apparatus, Buck lets out a thoughtful sigh.

"Never thought I'd see the day Coach Luther looked like that."

"He coach you, too?" I ask.

Buck steers us onto the street and chuckles. "Nah. I was in the marching band. Tuba. But Luther always seemed like a miserable bastard."

I grunt a concurrence. That he did. "No family?"

"Don't think so. Felt like someone walked over my grave as they wheeled him past."

Without warning, Tori drops into my thoughts. I mentally curse. I'd finally managed to get her out of my head for more than five minutes, and had been better for it. I couldn't get past what she'd said the other day. *Sleep with me.*

God, I wanted to. Wanted to splay her out and feast on her. Make her come so hard that she'd see stars and never be the same again.

That woman turned me inside out and flustered me more than anyone. Always had, and apparently always would. And when she'd propositioned me, I'd stammered and stuttered like a damn teenager in the face of his first sexual encounter.

The nerve of her. Who does that? Just blurts out something that could change the course of a life like it's not a big deal? Tori. Tori Welch does that, and she's driving me to distraction.

I need her to leave. Need her to get out from where she's nestled back under my skin like a cat next to a fireplace. If I'm not careful, she'll be right back where she was in high school, holding my heart in her hands right before she crushes it.

An hour later, I'm in the kitchen making a smoothie when Aaron walks in and leans against the counter. My stomach drops at the look on his face, but I ask anyway. "How is he?"

He shakes his head. "Coded right when we handed him off. They couldn't revive him."

I blow out a breath. "Damn."

"LaToya at the hospital said there wasn't anyone to call, either. Coach had no family."

A cold sense of unease settles over me. I can't be like him. Can't be a seventy-six-year-old man alone in a long-term care facility, my only legacy being how much of a controlling jerk I was. Can't be a burden to my brothers, either. I need to find someone. The thought is overwhelming and every instinct in me rears back in horror at the thought of it, but I push ahead. I can make a list. Lists are infallible.

"I'm sorry, man," Aaron says. "I know he was important to you."

Focusing back on my brother, I shrug. "He was my football coach."

Aaron looks at me, assessing, like he sees more than he lets on.

I stare back at him. Why are both my brothers paying this much attention to me? It's unnecessary. And unnerving.

"They're not having a funeral," he finally says. "Mrs. Davis said he'd already made arrangements for a cremation. He wants to be scattered at Bryant-Denny. Apparently being told repeatedly that there were rules specifically against it didn't sway him in the slightest."

I grunt. Of course the old man wanted his ashes spread at the University of Alabama's football field. Memories of him yelling at us from the sidelines, purple-faced and pissed off to high heaven, swirl around in my head. At practices he'd pace back and forth, a clipboard in one hand and a bullhorn in the other, spit flying as he went on and on about how we needed to do it better, do it faster, and finish what we started.

Aaron leaves me to my smoothie and memories. Memories of not just Coach, but Tori, and the women in between. It was pathetic, the way Tori had unknowingly set the bar for every woman after her. I've always been a moody, controlling asshole, and that, plus the way I look, has been enough to keep most people away. Certainly no one stuck around long enough to get to know who I really am.

But Tori. She was different from the very beginning. Wasn't put off by my silence or my moods, and took what I now know is some serious fucking anxiety on my part in stride. She pushed me out of my head—hell, she *yanked* me out of it because of my need to keep her safe—and when she broke up with me, I thought my world had ended.

Not that I let her or anyone know that. As far as everyone knew, we'd gone on some dates and that was it. But not to me. No, Tori had whirled into my vicinity, blew up everything I thought I knew, and whirled right back out. I vowed never to give my heart so easily after that, and no one has ever tempted me to think otherwise.

And now she's returned, throwing my life into yet another spiral by her very presence, wanting me to sleep with her.

I can't.

But maybe...maybe I can. I could certainly use the release, and I'll just keep my heart out of it. The way she so easily suggested we sleep together, it's clear she doesn't want me for anything other than an orgasm. Once we're done, I'll start my search for someone permanent.

By the time I've cleaned up and polished the smoothie off, I've come to a decision. *Finish what you started*, Coach had said. All respect to the dead, it was the only thing the old man said that was right. And while it's a roundabout way of finishing things, I figure I can do this. I'll finish my Tori Welch experience and then find someone who wants me. The real me. No idea how I'll do that, but that's not worth worrying about yet.

I let myself smile. This is a perfect plan. I'll sleep with Tori once, and we'll both get it out of our systems. As long as I lay some ground rules, I'll be fine.

TORI

MOM LOOKS OVER her cup of tea at me. "Pilates studio?"

I nod. "Yep." Even though I wasn't sure what her reaction would be, waiting three days to tell her was torture. The woman knows *everything* about me. Well, almost.

She waves her fingers around, indicating the shop and town. "Here?"

I nod again, hoping that I look and sound more confident than I feel. "Just have to find the space." And that can't be too hard. A small town like this is bound to have a few closed-up shops, maybe even one here in the square.

Mom isn't impressed. "I know you're into Pilates, but do you know what it takes to do something like this? Run a small business?"

I smile. "I do." Sort of. I read some stuff this morning. But first things first.

"But your career…" she says.

"Wasn't great. It was empty, Mom."

Her brows knit. "I thought you loved it."

"I used to, but then I didn't."

She pins a stare on me. "Victoria. What aren't you telling me?"

I sigh, not wanting to get into this with her, but also knowing she won't let it go until I do. "I was tired of the hustle and the sexual harassment. I didn't feel like peddling drugs anymore. I was good at it, but the effort to tap-dance around those nods and winks, the flirty doctors, the constant grind and chasing the sale…I was done."

Her face falls and she reaches for my hands. "I didn't realize it'd gotten that bad."

I wave her off. "Yeah, well, you taught me that it never helped to complain."

"But harassment? Tori, you should—"

"I *quit*, Mom," I say gently. "And I want to leave it all in the past. Okay?"

She squeezes my hands and nods, but it's obvious she's not happy.

"So how's the library?" I ask, changing the topic.

Mom grunts a laugh. "Oh, fine. Mr. Buchanan keeps insisting I buy more James Patterson, but between me and Brook at the bookstore, we've got more than enough of that crusty old man's titles."

I grin. Some things never change. Mom's the head librarian, and she's gone toe to toe with citizens about all kinds of things. Mr. Buchanan is a kitten compared to some of the stories she's told me over the years. And woe to the person who tries to get her to remove a book from the shelves for one misguided reason or another. That woman practically walks around with a soapbox in her tote.

She leans forward and drops her voice. "I did just buy a whole new stack of romance books, though. The ones with Price Joseph on them."

I can feel my eyes widen. "Say what?"

She titters as she drinks the last of her tea. "You've been

home nearly a week, *and* you're living at the man's bed-and-breakfast. You hadn't heard this yet?"

"Apparently the gossip train is slacking," I say and shrug. "What do you mean *on* them?"

"He's a romance cover model," she says, her voice staying low.

"He's a—" I stop. Because of course he is; it's just crazy enough to be true. He's no Will Joseph, but he's cute. I bet he's got some muscles, but again: he's no Will Joseph. Who I should get over. He said no, and no means no.

"Whole thing went down in this very shop," she continues. "You know he's dating the owner?"

I snap and point at her. "At least I know that much." I make a note to ask Ceci what else she left out from our gab fest the other day.

Mom checks her watch. "Lunch time is over," she says, then stands. "Back to the library I go. Come over on Sunday. We'll have lunch and you can meet Stanley."

I give her a hug. "Sure thing."

I'm in my room at the inn, music streaming into my ears while I sweat my tits off in downward dog, when I can feel Will coming down the hall. He's got a very particular cadence, his feet hitting the floor like it's offended him on a personal level, and the vibrations pound into my palms and soles.

I flick my eyes open as he comes to a stop in the doorway. My brain must be short-circuiting, because he's in running shoes and all I see are bare legs. They're gorgeous and tan, with a perfect amount of dark hair. Thanks to me looking through my own legs, my view of him cuts off right above his knees. I bet his thighs are tree-trunk delicious.

After a moment, I realize he's getting his own eyeful of my

ass—*you're welcome, sir*— and for all I know, he's talking. So I rise up on my toes, then bend my knees and hop into a squat position. Exhaling, I come to standing, flowing my arms up, out, and down as I breathe out. I pluck the earbuds out and turn to him, and honestly, thank god I was already breathing hard, because holy shit.

I was right. His thighs. His *thighs*. They're muscle on muscle, and they twitch as he shifts. I keep moving up, not caring that I'm ogling him, because again, he got an eyeful of my gluteus maximus, and I clock what must be five-inch black shorts, followed by a black tank top that clearly must have been designed by a woman because it covers just enough of him to make it almost more revealing than if he wore nothing. He has freaking rib muscles, because of course he does, and his arms are what my dreams are made of, with thick, beefy muscles wrapped around muscles, and just...muscles. All the muscles. Seriously, bless this man and the time he spends on himself. I approve.

I finally move my gaze to his face, and I almost wish I hadn't. Because he shaved off that mustache days ago, and now he's got this hot scruff thing going on, and his eyes are dark as they stare right back at me. Hungry.

I swallow.

"Yoga?" he asks. And it's actually a question.

"Yes," I answer.

His eyes rake over my body, and I swear I physically heat under his gaze. If I had panties on, they would incinerate. This is not the same Will I knew in high school. It's not even the same Will of a few days ago.

"Also Pilates," I say, needing to normalize the situation before I launch myself at him.

"Right," he responds.

"What do you do?" I ask, then immediately regret it. He probably won't answer, and honestly, does it matter? Whatever it is, it takes effort and time and it produces this magnificent specimen in front of me.

He shrugs. "Weights. Run, but not distance. Stuff."

"Cool." I lick my lips, hoping to get some moisture back in my mouth from where his presence dried it up, and his eyes track the movement.

"Listen."

I straighten, my body immediately tuned to him.

He takes a step towards me.

I might stop breathing.

He steps closer.

I force myself to inhale. What is happening right now? I need to have a talk with my body. We can't act like this. This is inappropriate. He said no, and I haven't investigated how firm of a stance he's taking on that particular topic.

He stops inches from me, forcing me to look up at him. He smells unbelievable, like the forest after a rain with a little bit of man sweat running underneath it. I remind myself to breathe normally and meet his gaze. I haven't been this near him since we were teenagers, and I forgot...everything. His eyes, for one. He's looking at me like he could devour me.

"What's happening?" I whisper.

He scowls, and of course, instead of it scaring me, it just makes me think he's that much hotter.

"Seriously, Will," I manage to say. "Whatever you're—"

"Shut up."

My mouth snaps closed before I can even register what I've done. Again, I need to have a talk with my body. We do not thoughtlessly obey big, strong, fuck-hot men.

He reaches up and takes a coil of hair that's escaped my bun between his thumb and forefinger, pulling it taut and letting it spring back up.

Let the record show that I do not let people touch my hair. I especially don't let them do precisely what he just did, because my hair is not a toy.

Also let the record show that apparently I will allow this man to do whatever the hell he wants.

I lick my lips again—they're dry, okay?—and his eyes darken.

His chest heaves as he takes a deep breath, and fuck me if I don't synch my inhale right with him. My tits graze his chest, and I don't do a thing about it. We just keep breathing, staring at each other, and touching with every inhale.

Finally, he speaks. "You still want to sleep with me?"

"Hell yes." I'm answering him before he even finishes.

His lips hook up in an infinitesimal grin, and I feel like I just won the lottery. Then I realize what he said, and what *I* said.

"Wait. Really?"

"I have rules. Conditions," he says. His eyes travel to my tits, and the greedy things instantly peak beneath his gaze. Never mind that I'm wearing a sports bra.

"Of course you do."

"We do this once. Only once."

"O-kay," I say, drawing out the second syllable.

"And we're done."

"Right."

"I'm serious, Tori."

Oh, I can tell you're serious, big guy. "Got it."

He crowds me even closer, and I tilt my chin to maintain eye contact. The man has gorgeous eyes, and I swear they look the best when they're glaring at me. Which, of course, they're doing right now.

"We have sex once, we get it out of our system, we go back to normal."

I should get an Academy Award for maintaining my composure right now. Because if this man thinks I can go back to normal after sex with him, he's got another thing coming.

But sure. I nod. "Back to normal after one-time-only sex. Got it."

His eyes narrow. "Good."

We're silent again, only now I've got a big grin on my face because *I get to have sex with Will fucking Joseph*, and he's got a smile going on, too. That is, if a lip twitch counts, and on Will, it absolutely does.

"Fifteen minutes."

I blink. "Excuse me?"

He takes a step back. "Be in my room in fifteen minutes."

Oh shit. Oh. I did *not* see that coming. I open my mouth, but nothing comes out.

He swivels on his heel and stalks out, gifting me with a view of his ass and legs as he goes.

TORI

I TAKE THE world's fastest shower and send a prayer of thanks that I'd handled some, shall we say, *personal mainte-nance* two days ago.

Will Joseph.

I am about to sleep with Will Joseph.

I have no idea what changed his mind, and I don't care.

My heart pounds furiously as I dry off and rub in some lotion. There will be no ashy legs today, folks.

Briefly, I worry about what to wear, but realize it's going to be on the floor in a matter of minutes. So I throw on pajama shorts and a tank top, not bothering with a bra and again thanking the gods that my tits haven't yet completely lost their battle with gravity. It's inevitable, I'm thirty-seven, but today they're still holding strong.

I bounce down the stairs and check for any other guests as I go. None. I realize that I don't know where his room is, but it has to be downstairs, so I take a right around the banister and head to the back of the house.

There's a door at the end of a hallway that's ajar, and as I near it, the giddiness is replaced by a full-on attack of nerves, and I stop mid-stride.

What am I doing?

This is a bad idea.

What if I do this and it opens up all those old feelings? I shake it off. I can handle this. It's just sex. Okay, sure, I came home because I was ready to start living a life of consequence, and no-strings-attached sex is pretty antithetical to that. But it's Will Joseph. Who says no to sex with that man?

I move forward again, but the door swings open and I skid to another halt.

Because Will Joseph is filling the doorway and scowling at me. A white towel is doing its level best to hang onto his hips, his legs bulging beneath it, and I nearly sob at the sight of his chest. My mouth literally waters.

He moves backward and opens the door wide, one arm braced against the frame. "Get in here."

Yes, sir.

I practically skip towards him, the giddiness back, and barely resist the urge to grip his arm and swing on it as I go under it.

He shuts the door behind me and locks it.

"Aren't you worried about guests?" I don't know why I'm asking. I don't care.

He shakes his head, looking even more stern than usual, and my head empties.

"You are ridiculously hot when you do that," I say, deciding I may as well dive on into the deep end since we're here.

His scowl doesn't move. "Do what?"

I circle my fingers at his face. "That. The frowny thing. Hot."

He blinks, silent for a beat, then apparently decides to ignore the comment. "My condition."

"Your frowny face is a medical condition?"

"Tori."

I lift my arms, my hands in supplication as I giggle. "I know. One time only."

He steps towards me, and my legs clench. "And we never talk about it again. We finish, you leave, and it's over."

I swallow and nod, half grateful for the condition and half sad about it. "Just once."

He takes another step. "We're finishing what we started, and that's it. We're done."

I keep my face neutral, trying not to let the surprise show. Obviously I thought about him over the years, but only because I should never have let him get as close as he did. But *finishing what we started* could mean so many different things. Did he think about me, too? It doesn't matter.

He's so close now that I can feel the towel against my over-heated skin. "Agreed?"

I glance at his neck and see that his pulse is beating just as fast as mine. Glad I'm not the only one about to pass out. And even though I don't want to agree—I mean, the man is fine as hell and I'd like a lot more than one go at him—I consent. "Agreed."

Without another word, his hands are on my sides and he's lifting me up. I wrap my legs around him and grip his shoulders, instantly in heaven and already deeply regretting I didn't try for at least one repeat performance, because he's turned me and slammed my back against the wall. *Hell* yes.

I suck in a breath as he brings my lips to his, hungry and demanding. His tongue angrily plunders my mouth, and I groan as I take every bit of it. One of his hands pushes beneath my shirt and palms my breast, squeezing hard as a thumb swipes roughly over my nipple.

I gasp and buck my hips against his rock-hard stomach, knowing my sleeping shorts are flimsy enough that it's entirely possible he's already felt how wet I am.

He grunts, and when he speaks, his voice is flinty, commanding. "Tell me you like it."

"I like it," I respond, breathless.

He turns us and is at the bed in two strides. I let go and he tosses me like I weigh nothing, bouncing me onto the mattress. I scramble upright, leaning back on my arms and keeping my eyes on his.

"You'll do what I say."

I nod, refusing to break eye contact.

"Take off your shirt."

"Your towel comes off first," I shoot back.

"No," he growls.

I raise my eyebrow, ready to play. "Then my shirt stays on."

His chest heaves as he tilts his head to the side and considers me. "Take. It. Off."

"Make me."

His eyes flare as he moves with lightning speed, grabbing my feet and jerking me to the edge of the bed so fast that I fall onto my back. He spreads my legs and puts a knee between them, then leans over me, his arms bracketing me on either side. He's pissed, and I'm soaked. If he didn't feel it before, I guarantee he can feel the proof of it on his knee now.

"I swear, Tori, you will listen to me."

"Or what?" I gulp in a breath, feeling as though I've just sprinted a mile.

He doesn't hesitate, grabbing my shirt in his hands and ripping it down the front, exposing me to him.

The fabric tearing might be the sexiest thing I've ever heard. Or maybe it's the fact that he just *ripped my shirt off me.* I chuckle darkly. "Oh, this is going to be fun, big guy."

He clenches his jaw and straightens, then yanks my shorts down.

Released, and almost disappointed he didn't tear the shorts off, too, I scoot myself back up to the top of the bed, discarding my shredded shirt as I go and relishing the desire in his eyes as they follow me. I let my own gaze travel farther, taking in the smooth expanse of his chest, the way it tapers to abs so ripped they need their own zip code, down a dark line of hair aiming between the divots of his hips.

There I go, drooling again.

"Take off your towel." My voice is low, husky. As incentive, I pull my knees up to my chest, then run my hands from the tips of my toes up the front of my calves until I get to my knees. Slowly, I pull my knees apart, spreading myself bare for him.

His jaw slackens and his eyes go absolutely molten. "Tori." My name is a prayer.

I take a finger and dip it into my folds, then circle my clit, my stomach clenching at the growl that emanates from him. I repeat myself. "Towel. Off."

He unwraps it, and my fingers halt, because Christmas has come early.

He's huge. *Big boy, indeed.*

He smirks. "You'll take it."

"Without question."

Meanwhile: his legs. I have a new kink, and it's Will Joseph's legs.

"Don't move," he commands. He crawls onto the bed, a lock of dark hair framing a predatory expression as he comes toward me, growling, his shoulder muscles rippling with every motion he makes.

I remind myself to breathe as he dips his head to my pussy. He licks from bottom to top, but keeps going, trailing his tongue up my abdomen, to my belly, to between my breasts and up to my neck, then chin. As his tongue drops into my mouth and his lips cover my own, his hand clamps between my legs, gripping my pussy like it belongs to him.

The sensation is so good I nearly levitate. I moan into his mouth as the heel of his palm begins to circle on my clit, and finally I remember I have hands. I shove one into the back of his hair, grabbing onto the silky dark strands and pulling while my other grips his massive bicep and hangs on for dear life.

He pulls away and I nearly come at the look on his face. His eyes are hooded and only the navy blue ring of color remains. "Tell me you like it."

"I fucking love it, Will," I answer with a moan.

He slants his lips over mine again, covering my body with his, and the weight of him pressing down on me takes me closer to the edge. He pushes a thick finger into me, then a second, and I writhe against him, almost unable to process all the sensations. The rough edges of his unshaven mouth against mine; the weight of him tethering me to the earth; his fingers curling and pressing perfectly inside me and his thumb on my clit. But it's the way his other hand is softly cradling my head that's undoing me. The gentleness of it, the way he sweeps rogue curls away from my face as though they're precious.

Then he presses his palm hard against my clit again, and I explode.

"*Fuck*, Will!" The orgasm takes me so utterly and completely that the words tear out of my throat on a sob, as a tsunami of pleasure comes from nowhere and slams across my body in shuddering waves.

"Shh, there you go, come for me, Tori," he soothes, bringing me through it as I'm wracked with wave after wave, my core pulsing and squeezing as though it has never experienced anything better.

And it hasn't. *I* haven't.

I am wrecked.

He nuzzles my neck, kissing and whispering little praises to me, until finally I relax.

I open my eyes and meet his as he brings his fingers up and licks them clean, then pushes them into his mouth. He sucks, moving them in and out, and I watch, mesmerized.

"Will—" I whisper.

"No talking," he says, then pushes those same fingers into my mouth.

I take them, my body utterly pliant and completely taut all at the same time. I want to do whatever he desires, and watching his expression move from stern to turned on is all the encouragement I need. Reaching down, I take his cock into my hand for a more thorough inspection. He's shaved close, his balls totally bare, and I want them on my tongue. I pull them into my hands, tugging a little to see if he likes it.

His brow relaxes and he exhales, his fingers falling out of my mouth as he cedes just enough control to me. I take it, shifting us so he's on his back and I'm straddling him.

He's like a black-haired god of thunder, dark eyes boring into mine, and I swear I can *feel* the energy between us. It's palpable. But this is a one-time thing, so I force myself to focus on the here and now.

Running my hands over his shoulders and chest, I whisper, "God *damn* you're hot, Will."

He gifts me with the tiniest of smiles, his eyes almost appearing drowsy, but I see the control that simmers behind there. What I wouldn't give to see this man lose the tight rein he has on himself...but that won't happen.

I slide my pussy over the steel rod that is his cock, needing just a little relief, and it makes both of us groan. Leaning down, I palm his chin and push it up, exposing his neck. I lick the skin below his ear, tasting the salt of his sweat and breathing in the clean scent of him, then nip him with my teeth.

He jerks and moans, and I intensify the bite. He grabs my ass and grips it in answer. I'm not interested in leaving a mark on him, so after a moment I turn his neck and have my way with the other side, nipping his earlobe and scratching my hand down his chest. I move down his skin, kissing, licking, biting, and sucking as I go. His pecs are bigger than my head, and his abs are still ridged even as he lays supine beneath me.

Finally, I'm at his big, thick cock, and I look up to find him staring at me.

"You good?" I ask.

He nods, his expression studious.

"Tell me if you want something different," I say.

He nods again.

I push his legs farther apart and lean down to take his balls in my mouth and hum. He curses above me and I hum again, still sucking and licking him.

"Tori," he breathes.

"Still okay?" I ask, even though I know full well he is.

"Again," he says, his voice ragged. "Please."

And damn if that *please* doesn't make me clench my thighs. I give him what he wants, spending plenty of time there before finally licking up to the tip of his cock and swirling my tongue around the head, taking the precum into my mouth and delighting in the saltiness of it.

"You taste good, Will," I say, wrapping a hand around his base and squeezing hard.

He curses, his eyes flaring with desire.

I take him as far in as I can, hitting the back of my throat but not any farther. I've never been one to choke on a cock and even fuck-hot Will Joseph isn't going to change that.

He fists the curls at the base of my head and takes control of the rhythm, and I let him, sucking him hard and using my hands to squeeze his base, his balls. When he pulls me off, I nearly whine.

"Come for me," I say, then bend to him again.

"No," he growls. He flips us and is settled on top of me in two seconds flat, his expression hard. "You've had your fun. I'm not coming until I'm buried deep inside you, Tori. Deep. So fucking deep. Because that mouth of yours may not take all of me, but your pussy is going to beg for me. Do you understand?"

I nod.

"Say it."

A strangled sound escapes me. Overcome by the sheer size of him above me, and torn between the dueling primal needs I have to both submit to him and dominate him, I finally croak, "I understand."

He pulls my arms above me and grips them tightly in one hand. It hurts, but then his mouth, hot and greedy, is on my breast and I'm out of my mind with how good it feels. When he's had his way with one, he moves to the next, and then he lets go of my wrists to slide down my body. I spread my legs apart for him, but it's not enough, and his wide shoulders force me wider as his head descends.

He pushes a finger into me, and then another, then issues a command in a voice so deep I feel it in my bones. "You will come again for me."

I clench around his fingers as his mouth works my clit, the pressure of his tongue and teeth almost too much and not enough. I'm lost to everything but now, and nothing matters except the slick of his tongue, the thrust of his fingers, the scruff of his jaw, the intensity of it all, and then quickly, too quickly, I'm flying, yelling his name as I climax, soaring through explosions of bliss as they rip through me. It's nearly unbearable, and I don't know if the sounds that come out of me are sobs of pleasure or regret or something else entirely. All I know is that he's talking me through it again, murmuring praise against my pussy, but the blood pumping through my head is so loud I can't understand him.

Through a haze, I feel his fingers withdraw. I blink, then focus in on his large form as he shifts to grab a condom. He's quick, efficient in his movements, and he's back on top of me in seconds.

His eyes are gentle, all the lines around them smoothed, and I almost don't recognize the expression on his face. Then he says, "Are you ready for me, sweetheart?"

My breath whooshes out of me. *Sweetheart?* But I nod dumbly, words not an option, and in an instant the caring Will is gone, replaced once more by the dominant sex god I've found myself in bed with.

He pushes into me, and I take him, gasping at the feel of his cock.

"*Will*, holy—"

"I'm not all the way in, Tori."

Oh, *god*. He's going to rip me apart.

He pulls my knee up and cradles it against his side, then thrusts in again.

I moan as my body adjusts to him, taking every bit it can.

"Almost there."

"*Fuck*," I breathe.

"You'll take it. And once I'm done fucking this pussy, you'll never be the same."

I whimper and meet his eyes. The depths are unfathomable, filled with power and control, but not cruelty. No, they simply confirm his words are a promise.

He rams home, seating himself to the hilt as I arch my neck and moan, so incredibly full and absolutely convinced of what he said. Because he is right, I will never know this kind of pleasure, this kind of insanity, again.

"There you go," he says, his voice gentle as he praises me. "Tell me how it feels. Tell me how *I* feel." He moves steadily, slowly, fucking me like he's got all the time in the world.

"Incredible," I manage. "So good. Your cock, Will, *fuck*." More words, unintelligible, fall from my lips. Still he moves above me, his body so large that it's all my eyes can see, grinding into me with control and precision, as though he's known how to bring me to orgasm for years instead of minutes.

He's not even broken a sweat, and he's mesmerizing, all his muscles rippling as he takes me to the edge.

He releases my leg and I shift just enough to change the angle, and then I'm taking even more of him. His eyes roll shut and he curses, and for just a moment he loses his grip on that tightly held control. His entire face changes, lighting up and relaxing, smoothing out and reminding me of the gentle, quiet kid he was in high school. It's beautiful, burrowing itself deep inside me and locking itself away.

But I need more. Because he's right. I'm never going to be the same after this. So if this is all I'm ever going to get of this wonderful man, then I want everything. "Fuck me, Will," I grit out.

His eyes flash.

"*More*," I say.

His answer is to lean down and kiss me, angling my jaw with rough fingers, and I lose my breath. His skin is warm against mine, his entire body dwarfing me as he takes his fill of my mouth, and I grip his back, dig my nails into his flesh and rake them down. He breathes in sharply, liking the pain. I squeeze my inner walls around his cock, so full of him and yet still, I need more.

I put a hand to his chest and push him up, meeting his eyes. "Will. Give me everything. Stop treating me like you're going to break me. Make good on your promise."

It's all he needs. He rises onto his knees and pulls me into position, yanking my hips into the air and angling me how he wants me. "Find something to hang on to," he commands.

Twin sensations of panic and delight race through me as I grip the sheets, bracing myself.

And he explodes.

Over and over he pounds into me, his fingers digging into my hips so tightly I know they'll leave bruises, and it's glorious. He's ruining me, fucking me so hard and so deep, branding me with every thrust. His gaze spears me, absolutely unreadable as his jaw tightens.

"Yes, yes, *yes,*" I chant, no other words forming as an ocean of pleasure begins to draw tight. I've ripped the sheets off the mattress by now, and all I can do is take him. Take what he gives me. Take what he does to me.

He loses his rhythm, pistoning into my body, his expression ruinous. "Now, Tori."

"I'm...trying," I pant.

He growls, pulling out and flipping me over like I'm a rag doll, yanking my hips into the air and thrusting back into me from behind before I've had a chance to take a full breath.

"*Fuck!*" I yell, because he's hitting even deeper now, and it unlocks everything. A sensation I have never felt, deep and over-powering, tightens inside of me, growing taut and strained, a rubber band coiled past its limits.

Behind me, Will goes even faster. "*Now.*" He palms my hips, his fingers punishing.

I come, yelling into the now-bare mattress as Will roars through his own climax behind me, still pumping into me until he finally buries himself to the root, holding as my orgasm squeezes his cock, pulsing almost violently with wave after wave of rapture.

Finally, both our orgasms wane, and the only sound is our ragged breathing. A moment later, he pulls out and is off the bed to get rid of the condom in the ensuite bathroom. I collapse face first onto the bed, the quilt stitching of the mattress itchy against my cheek, the sheet itself bunched beneath my limp body.

He has absolutely and unequivocally ruined me.

Returning, Will allows himself to fall onto the bed beside me, the length of his body pressing against mine from shoulder to ankle. His large palm smacks onto my ass, squeezes, and stays there.

Our breathing evens out together. When at least five minutes have passed, I raise onto my elbow and rest my head in my hands to look at him. He turns his head to meet my gaze, and his expression is one I can't name. Maybe...contentment? Maybe this is just what Will looks like post-orgasm. His brow is smooth, the permanent brackets around his lips have disappeared. Something in my chest squeezes. He's *beautiful*.

And I am pissed. "What the fuck was that?"

WILL

I STARE AT her. She seems genuinely curious, so after a beat, I answer. "Sex."

She rolls her eyes and snorts. "That was *not* sex."

"Then what was it?"

"We tilted the earth off its axis, Will." She sounds angry about it.

I want to laugh at her and say it's what she deserves for dumping me twenty years ago for someone else. I want to gloat and tell her she's welcome. And I want to argue with her.

Instead, I shrug. "And?"

Her eyes widen and she sits up, crossing her legs as she does so. I suppress a groan at the sight of her pussy not even a foot from my face and drag my eyes up her body. She's a study in contradiction, with generous legs, hips, and ass leading to a trim, taut waist and belly that gives way to breasts hanging full and heavy in front of me. Her skin is soft, so fucking soft, a light brown that catches the light and sends it back out. Even now, her curls are tousled but they fall in soft coils down her back. And her eyes, a brown so deep that it's difficult to see where her irises stop and pupils begin. She's both soft and hard, light and dark. Impossible to predict. Like always.

She is everything I don't need.

"And?" she says. "*And?*"

I'm not having this conversation unclothed. I sit up and swing my leg over the bed, then grab some boxer briefs out of the dresser and pull them on. When I turn back to her, she's clamping her mouth shut and swallowing at the sight of me.

Good.

I lean against the dresser and fold my arms across my chest. "What do you want me to say?"

Her eyes flash. "I don't know. But that—" she gestures at the mattress—"was *not* sex."

"You've already said that," I point out.

The truth is, I'm just as unhinged as she is. I'd gone somewhere and felt things that I'd never experienced before, and I need time to process it. The woman brought out emotions in me that no one else ever had. If anyone should be pissed in this situation, it's me. I was doing just fine. *She's* the one who'd waltzed back into town. *She's* the one who propositioned me. *She* is entirely responsible for the outcome.

She scoots off the mattress, and I finally see the mess we've made. The pillows, comforter and flat sheet are on the floor, and the fitted sheet is hanging by a corner, the rest of the fabric twisted into a bunched-up heap at the bottom of the bed.

Tori stalks towards me, her finger jabbing the air. "You made me almost cry, you asshole. And if I'm not mistaken, I think you almost did, too!"

I clench my jaw. "We're not talking about this."

"But—"

"*No!*" I nearly shout, and she stumbles back, her eyes wide. Exhaling, I soften my tone. "No. It was sex, Tori. That's all it was. I'm glad you enjoyed it, but that's all it was. That's all it was supposed to be. And now we're finished."

Because she needs to be out of the way—far, far out of the way, not distracting me—while I look for the woman I'll spend the rest of my life with. Whoever the fuck that is.

Her eyes tear up, but there's no mistaking that they're tears of anger. She rakes her gaze down and up my body, and when she deigns to meet my eyes once more, the warmth is completely gone. Her face shutters, and she nods once. "Yeah. We're finished."

And because I'm an asshole, I leave, walking into the bathroom and shutting the door. I turn the shower on and stare at myself in the mirror, and only then do I see what she's done to me.

Bite marks are dotted around my collar bone and upper chest. Deep red marks trail down my side, and when I look at my back, it's streaked with more of them, some so deep that pinpricks of blood dance along the surface.

Fuck.

She knew exactly what I wanted, and she'd given it to me. She'd let me take her how I wanted her, but she knew I wanted her to take control as well. Not a lot—I never, ever give up control—but she understood how much I was willing to give, and she went right to that line.

I shake my head. It had to be a one-time thing. I can't be pulled into her orbit again, where my every thought is about her. What she's doing, how her day is going, what it'd feel like to bury my cock in her any time I want.

I step into the shower and hiss as the too-hot water stings my back. But I stand there and take it, because I deserve any pain I get.

When I'm finished, I dress and head to the kitchen. I need to bake. It's the only thing that will let my mind empty, and after that, I'll make my list of how to go about getting a wife.

No.

Yes. Yes, because I need someone. One who isn't the woman

upstairs. It can't be. She'll just hurt me again, and between her and my mom, I've had enough of the women in my life being careless with my heart.

Scanning the contents of the pantry, I decide on blueberry scones. They'll go well with the lemon curd I made yesterday.

I throw the butter into the freezer while I whisk together the flour, sugar, baking powder, baking soda, and salt. Then I pull the butter out and mix it with some yogurt, cream, egg, vanilla, and blueberries in a different bowl. I fold it all together, gently kneading it by hand until it's in a ball. The trick is not to over-work the dough, and as much as I'd enjoy mindlessly kneading it until both the dough and I are a gooey mess, that won't make for good scones.

I put the dough on the flour-dusted counter, pat it into a circle, and cut into wedges. After that, it's onto a baking sheet and into the oven. I clean up the kitchen while they bake, and by the time the scones are coming out, I'm a little calmer, but not much.

Especially when I see Tori go past the door, slowing her steps to investigate who's baking in the kitchen. The look on her face as her eyes meet mine is almost enough to make it all better, because she's shocked. Guess none of the town gossips bothered to tell her that I bake.

She moves on and a moment later I hear the door shut, and I'm by myself in the house. I take a deep breath, and as I exhale, I try to empty my mind.

It doesn't work.

Because even though I've showered and baked, I can't get the scent of her out of my nose, the same warm blend of browned butter with brown sugar and shea butter as in high school. The moment my nose met her skin, all the memories came flooding back in vivid detail. The times we'd gone out, the emotion the two of us seemed to pull out of the other, the light in her gorgeous brown eyes when I took her to get Blizzards at Dairy

Queen after one of my football games. No one else looked at me the way she did, not before or since. I would have done anything for her.

Shoving off the counter, I shake it off. There's no point in dwelling in the past, especially mine.

WILL

"EARTH TO WILL. Come in, Will." Price's hands wave in front of me.

I scowl at him.

He beams. "There's my grumpy guy. We're trying to figure out some things, so if you could pay attention, that'd be super."

"Figure what out?" We're sitting around the table at the fire station and he shouldn't even be here. "Don't we have guests to tend to?"

He waves my concern away. "All but one checked out this morning. No new ones today. Two rooms booked starting tomorrow. And—" he holds a finger out to keep me from saying anything—"the laundry is getting done."

"Good," I grumble. "And no fabric softener on the towels."

"I know, Will," he says. "The whole damn table knows."

"It reduces the absorbency."

The entire crew chants it with me. Bastards.

Chief laughs, right along with Buck, Zach, Mike, Aaron, and Price. "We thank you for your laundry tips, Will. Can we get back to it?"

Price takes that as his cue and stands to distribute the pages he has in his hand. "We're back in the black, thanks to the calendars. But we still have a ways to go. I'm starting a TikTok page for us and have some ideas to go viral, which honestly won't be that hard. I mean, look at us." He grins and pats my shoulder as he lays the last sheet of paper in front of me. "Hulk, I've got some *great* concepts for you."

"No." I don't have to think twice. No way am I doing any stupid dances or whatever the hell happens on that app. All of it is stupid. "And stop calling me Hulk."

"Better than 'Not Hulk,'" Aaron says, pointing to himself.

Price shrugs. "How's Tori doing?"

I glare at him as Chief sits up straight.

"Tori?" he says. "Tori Welch?"

"No," I say.

"Yes," my idiot brothers respond.

Chief's eyes light up. "I heard she was back."

"Better than back, Chief. She's staying at the inn," Aaron says.

"Two down, one to go," Chief says, rubbing his hands.

"No," I repeat, knowing exactly where this is going. "You weren't responsible for Aaron and Devon getting together."

"That was Samson," Price pipes up, referring to Devon's dog.

"And you weren't responsible for Price and Jodi," I finish.

"Oh, I don't know," Aaron says unhelpfully. "It *was* his idea for Jodi to stay at the inn."

I stand up. I don't want Chief's attentions on me and Tori. For one, we will never happen. For two, if he had any clue about how the past two weeks had gone, he'd be planning a damn wedding. Never mind that they'd consisted of me trying to avoid her, to no fucking avail. She's everywhere I turn, conducting free yoga and Pilates classes in the living room for fellow guests, her long, muscular legs wrapped in one set of bright leggings after another, or over at Daily Dose, chatting with some or all of Ceci, Devon, and Jodi.

The worst part is that she's all sunshine and smiles until her gaze falls on me, and then it's icy with a heated undercurrent. As though she's pissed at me, but still wants to tear me apart in bed.

Which is exactly how I feel.

I need her to leave.

"Are we done here?" I ask. "My shift was over at six and I need to get to the inn."

Price and Chief exchange a meaningful look, but I don't care enough to parse it.

"Just tell me if I need to do something," I say.

The table is quiet as I leave, but the conversation starts back up as soon as I round the corner.

The tension has almost left my shoulders as I approach the back door of the inn. Stepping into what's now a large laundry room, I inhale the scent of detergent, bleach, and softener deeply, glad to be home. This is where I belong these days, not at the station. Problem is, they still need me, and I don't know how to tell Chief I want out. Price taking the Assistant Chief position was the best thing to happen to me in years. Granted, the salary drop didn't help with my savings plan, but I simply started spending less. Not like I go anywhere or do anything. Everything I need is in this house.

Except for the tidy matter of finding someone to do this with.

I can't make the damn list. Every time I try, my brain lists off everything that makes up Tori Welch, and I can't shut it off.

After swapping the laundry and folding the towels, I load them into the basket and walk to the front. And that's when I hear the very woman who won't get out of my head.

"Okay, one last exhale, and fully relax. Let your mind empty.

Relax your feet, your ankles, your knees and hips. Let your hands and fingers relax, and your wrists, your arms, your neck. Let your jaw go slack, and just breathe."

Her voice roots me to the spot, and my body desperately wants to obey her words. *Relax. Let go. Just breathe.* Ridiculous. Who has time for that? Gritting my teeth, I tighten my grip on the basket and round the stairs.

Her head whips toward me, and we lock eyes.

She's flushed, with more of her luscious skin on display than usual and her hair pulled into a loose bun at the nape of her neck. Her shiny lips flatten right along with her expression as she stares at me.

Then I remember what Price said. We didn't have any guests other than her. Which means…what is she doing? Giving free classes in our inn? What if someone gets hurt and sues us? The woman is a walking liability as it is; I can't imagine what'll happen if this keeps up. I glance at the floor, and the fact that it's only Ceci, Jodi, and Devon in various states of relaxation does nothing to make me feel better.

I narrow my eyes at Tori, and she returns the glare. *"Later,"* I mouth.

She rolls her eyes and flicks her fingers, dismissing me. I clench my jaw and pound up the steps, knowing they'll hear it and not giving a shit.

I shove the towels in the linen closet on the second floor and re-fold the fitted sheets that Price had done a shit job at, forcing them into perfect rectangles despite wanting to use them as rope to take Tori to task. The things I want to do to her…

I shake my head. No.

I put everything away and pound back down the stairs just in time to see the door close behind Devon.

Tori turns to me with a furious expression. "What the hell, Will?"

"No more of that in this house." I turn away from her and stalk to the laundry room.

"Oh, screw you," she shoots back. "It's not hurting anything. No one is *here*."

"I said *no*," I say, putting the basket on the dryer and turning around again.

She's right there, inches from me.

"Move," I growl.

She cocks her hip and folds her arms across her chest, pushing her breasts even more into the air than they already are in a barely there sports bra. "Or what?"

"Do not fucking tempt me," I say.

Her brown eyes flash, and I read equal parts anger and hunger in them. "And what if I want to?"

I'm on her in a millisecond, moving on furious instinct and flipping her over my shoulder, ready to find many creative ways to punish her.

She squeals in outrage, pounding my back and kicking, but she's not trying very hard.

"Give *in*," I say, palming her ass and heading to the front door to lock it. I have no intention of anyone coming inside with the things I'm about to do to her.

"Never." She growls it.

I scoff. "You want this as much as I do, sweetheart. Ow, *fuck!*" I roar as she bites the fleshy skin right below my shoulder.

Turning towards my room, I rear my hand back and spank her. The sound of my palm hitting her spandex-clad ass is sharp and satisfying in the crisp air.

"What the *hell*, Will?" she shrieks and wiggles.

I chuckle darkly and continue down the hall. "It's cute how you think I'm letting you down."

In my bedroom, I kick the door shut and throw her onto the

bed, watching the way her tits bounce as her butt hits the mattress. "Stay," I command her with a pointed finger.

"Oh, fuck you," she seethes, then starts to get up.

I'm over her instantly, standing between her legs and forcing her to lever her body all the way down as I fist my hands on either side of her. She glares up at me, her chest heaving and eyes feverish, spots of color high on her cheeks. But she's not truly angry. No. She's just as turned on as me.

"Will—" she starts.

"Shut. Up," I say, keeping my voice low. "For one minute in your life, just keep your mouth shut."

She clenches her jaw, and I can't imagine what it's taking her to be quiet. So I decide to reward her for it.

Slowly, I move both her arms above her and hold them in my grip. Then I take my finger and run it right up the valley between her legs. She inhales sharply, her eyes darting between mine, and there's no mistaking the way her hips slant up. I smirk and remove my hand, delighting in her narrowed scowl and furious exhale.

"You want this as much as I do," she says, her voice like honey.

I release her wrists from my grip and lie my ass off as I straighten. "I don't."

Tori rises to a seated position and glances pointedly at my half-hard dick before meeting my eyes. "Liar."

"No more free lessons in the house." It's all I can think to say. I shouldn't have brought her in here, and I need to get us back on track.

She rolls her eyes and stands up, and because I don't move, she's inches from me.

I grit my teeth, forcing myself to breathe shallowly.

"Listen," she says. "It's almost Christmas. Why don't we both give ourselves a little gift?" She raises her eyebrows.

It takes everything in me to stand my ground. I won't cede

control. Not to her. Never to her. She's already broken me once; I won't let it happen again.

She licks her lips, her pink tongue darting out, and I nearly groan at the thought of her taking my cock into her hot little mouth.

Chuckling, she says, "Exactly," as if she could read my thoughts. "Come on, big guy. Let's have a new set of rules and regulations."

I don't say anything, but I tense as her finger comes up to trace my collar bone.

Her voice is velvet at midnight when she speaks. "I know you don't like me, Will, and that's okay," she purrs.

Her statement is not true at all. I like her plenty. Which is part of the fucking problem.

"I'm not really all that sure I like you," she continues.

And that, right there—*that* is very much the problem. Partly because I think she's lying.

"But the sex we had was incredible, and I don't know about you, but I could use more of that in my life. So here's my proposition."

The fact that I stop breathing pisses me off. The fact that she can feel my heart rate kick up because she's still right there, still tracing my skin, makes me even more angry. But she waits, silent, her finger moving methodically across my chest, winding its way down to my abdomen, as I remind myself to inhale and exhale, the movement no longer instinctual.

"Sex."

She grins. "Sex." As her finger continues to trail around my torso, she continues. "Forget that I've propositioned you twice at this point. Forget our history. Forget everything but the way you felt buried deep inside of me, and agree to this."

I don't know if I can do that. I'm impressed she can, and that's great for her, but she's already taken up residence in my head and my house. What if I do this and she shacks up in my heart?

But being able to touch her again. Feel her again. I'd jerked off more times in the shower to thoughts of her than I could count, both before *and* after we'd had sex. Now, with her standing an inch from me, smelling so incredible, wanting it just as bad as me, I'm having a hard time remembering why I'd said we needed to be a one-time thing.

"Fine," I say.

Her smile turns feline. "Good boy."

I dip my head to take her lush mouth, but she ducks away and steps to the side. I resist the urge to stomp my feet like a toddler, but I can't stop the groan of frustration that leaves me.

Her hips sway as she walks to the door, fully confident that I'll drink every inch of her in. And I do, committing the image of her wrapped in red yoga shorts and top to memory. Her soft skin practically begs to be caught between my teeth like a siren song, and I clench my fists with the effort to stay where I am. I have no doubt that if I wanted, I could take her right this instant.

With her hand on the doorknob, Tori looks at me over her shoulder, her eyes sparkling with mischief. "See you later, big guy."

Without her scent in my nose, a tiny bit of reason returns. "Wait."

She does, looking at me expectantly.

"Rules." *Rules, rules, rules,* my mind chants.

"You have them. I know." She twists the lock open.

"*Wait.* Dammit, woman, just wait," I growl.

Of course, she opens the door by an inch. Testing me.

But I'm too busy trying to lay out guidelines in my head. Some kind of roadmap on how this is actually going to work.

"Look, Will, the rules are simple: we have sex when we want

to have sex. We tell no one. End of story." Her tone is easy, straightforward. "No games."

"We need an end date."

Her eyebrows shoot up. "Why?"

"Because—" *Because I can't let this go too far. Because I might fall for you again. Because I need some fucking control here.* "One month."

The look she gives me is enough to send blood racing to my cock. She waves a hand down her body. "You really think you can have me all the ways you want to have me in just one month?"

I blink.

"Three months," she says. "Since you're set on a timeline."

Fuck my life. I nod, swallowing to clear the tightness in my throat and hoping it does the same for the tightness in my jeans. It doesn't. "Three months. March 20."

She hums, rakes her eyes over me one last time, and leaves, shutting the door behind her.

I drop onto the bed, finally able to breathe normally.

I have no idea what I've just gotten myself into.

Tori

I HAVE NO idea what I've just gotten myself into.

Proposing to Will that we be...god. Fuck buddies? Frenemies with benefits? I honestly don't know what I was thinking. It was just that he looked so *angry*, and it was delicious. And when he threw me over his shoulder? Angels sung in heaven. I know I'm in danger of letting my heart get involved, but seeing as how I managed to keep it safe last time—barely, but still—I can do it again.

Because really, it's just physical. I spent the rest of yesterday hiding in my bedroom, willing every part of me to stay put and not go down and ravage the man. I needed to spend some quality time with his thighs, for one thing. But I held myself together, just barely.

This morning, I put myself through the most rigorous Pilates workout I possibly could with the few props I had, and once I'd wrung myself out, I still couldn't guarantee I'd be able to contain myself if I laid eyes on him, guests or no guests. Thankfully, a text from Jodi popped up, inviting me to the coffee shop for a meet-up with the girls. So I showered, threw on some comfy leggings and sweatshirt and made my way to the Daily Dose.

The shop is cozy and welcoming as I walk in, the bell dinging merrily above me. Darius catches my eye and smiles, waving me up.

"Hey Tori, what's it gonna be today?"

"Something that screams holiday," I say.

He considers. "Peppermint mocha?"

"Ooh, yes," I answer. As he turns to make it, my phone dings with a new text, this one from Conner giving me shit for leaving Atlanta and demanding I return. And I realize I haven't followed through on my promise to Darius, which I need to fix immediately. After a couple of back and forth texts with Conner, I fix my prettiest stare at Darius.

"So, Darius."

He looks over at me, still working on my drink. "So, Tori."

"Ready to talk about my guy Conner?"

"We still doing this? Because you left me hanging after bringing it up two weeks ago."

"I know. I'm sorry. But he's interested."

He huffs. "Also white."

"Child. You're a gay black man in Talladega, Alabama, and you're hating on his skin color?"

He grins at me sheepishly. "Okay, true."

"That's what I thought. You scared?"

He sighs. "Maybe."

"Well, don't be."

"Where'd you say he lives?" He hands over my drink.

"Atlanta."

"Sounds expensive."

"He is." I love bantering with Darius. He's fun.

Darius grins. "I can't afford expensive."

I grin right back, preparing to play one of my better cards. "That's where the fact that he's rich helps."

Darius's eyebrows shoot up. "I'm listening."

Got ya. Time to reel him in. "He's a great guy. Super nice, very funny, and definitely ready for someone like you."

"Someone like me?" he repeats. "Fabulously poor?"

"No. Fabulous, yes, but also creative, smart, and kind. I've known him a long time and I wouldn't mention him if I didn't think you two would hit it off."

He considers me. "What's he do?"

"He's a dentist."

Darius gives me a look. "He better look good, because I'm not trying to have you set me up with the nerdiest, whitest gay boy in Atlanta. I know they grow 'em just as hot as summer over there."

In response, I open my phone and show him a picture.

Darius's jaw drops. "Holy..."

I giggle. Conner is tall, dark, and handsome in a Henry Cavill kind of way, and regularly fights off all manner of men and women, regardless of their age. "Is that a yes?"

"That is a hell yes, and that is a we're fighting because you've been holding out on me yes," he answers.

"Perfect," I say, putting my phone away and making a mental note to text Conner later.

Devon, Ceci, and her twins arrive. After hugs and orders, Devon and Ceci join me with their coffees at one of the tables off to the back. Luke and Eva tuck into coloring books at an adjoining table.

"Do they listen to whatever y'all talk about?" I ask Ceci, jerking my chin at the kids.

She shrugs. "It's like when they listen to music on the radio. They hear the lyrics and sing them loud as hell, but don't really understand the meaning."

"Good. Because if I don't tell you all what I've been up to, I might die," I say.

Devon's blue eyes sparkle. "This sounds intriguing."

Before I can say anything, Ceci narrows her gaze and she tilts her head. "You had sex with Will."

I balk. "How the hell...?"

Devon bounces in her chair. "Oh my gosh, really?"

Jodi appears and deposits two hot chocolates with generous amounts of whipped cream at the adjoining table for Luke and Eva and sits beside me. "No way. You slept with Mr. Scary?"

I blink. "Wait. Mr. *Scary?*"

Ceci snaps her fingers. "Focus. Did you or did you not bang him?"

I tilt my lips up. "More like *he* banged *me*, but yeah."

She holds her hand up for a high five and I give it, unable to control my laughter. "Thank god," she says. "He needed a good roll in the hay."

"Maybe he won't be as growly the next time he comes in here," Jodi says.

Devon snorts. "Please. That man is the embodiment of Stern Brunch Daddy and no amount of sex will change that."

I laugh even harder. "You're right, because it gets better."

"Ooh, were there ropes involved?" Ceci asks. "He looks like he'd enjoy a good spanking."

Jodi reddens and Devon gasps, but I wink at Ceci. "I like how you think, but no ropes." Then I take another sip of my peppermint mocha and tell them the whole story, recounting how I'd initially propositioned him, then how he'd forbade me to give any more classes in the house and thrown me over his shoulder, and how I once again made a sex deal with him. I absolutely do not tell them my worry about feelings getting involved.

"So to be clear," Devon says, "You straight-up told Will you wanted to have sex, and he said no, but then said yes, so you did. And then, he tells you no more lessons in the house, and in response, you propositioned him for *more* sex...for three months."

"And he agreed," Jodi says.

I nod. "That about sums it up."

Ceci cackles. "This is so much better than the real reason we got together today."

"Absolutely," Devon agrees. "My wedding plans can wait."

I swivel my head between all of them. "We're here to talk wedding plans? I thought we were just…here."

"Well, we are, but we also have to plan my wedding before Aaron gets tired of me dragging my feet and whisks me away to Vegas," Devon says.

"Chief probably has a license—just get him to do it at the firehouse," I say.

Each of them comically stops as one, as though we're playing Farmer and Statue and I've just turned around to catch them. "What? Did I say something wrong?"

"I. *Knew.* I. Liked. You!" Ceci hits my arm with every word. "Brilliant, this one."

Jodi's eyes are as wide as her red-lipped smile, and Devon's thinking. After a moment, Devon nods. "Yes."

"Yes?" Jodi says hopefully. "Really? Yes?"

"Yes." This time, the *yes* is emphatic.

We all squeal—I can't help it, these three are infectious—and Ceci grabs the notebook from in front of Devon and tosses it on the ground. "Done. Let's get back to the task at hand. Will." She turns to me, her eyes bright. "Please, *please* tell me he's as growly in bed as he is out of it."

"You're bossy," I say.

"Uh-huh," Eva says from the next table.

I laugh as Ceci looks at her affectionately.

Devon grins mischievously. "All I have to say is, welcome to the club."

"Devon!" Jodi says. "Be nice."

"What?" Devon says, winking. "It's a *great* club. You and I both know that the Joseph brothers are where it's at."

"Agree to disagree," Ceci says. "Because Rick—"

"Don't you dare," Devon says.

The table wobbles as Devon swats at Ceci. "You are a violent bunch of women," I joke. Then I smirk. "And yes. He is absolutely as growly in bed as he is out of it."

Ceci claps her hands once and points at Devon and Jodi. "I *knew* it! Just like—"

"I swear on all that is holy, if you say my brother's name I will dump this coffee on your head," Devon says to her. Turning to me, she says, "Rick is nothing like Will, but Ceci loves to mess with me."

Ceci waves her off. "I'm gonna bet he's a lot like Will where it counts, but we'll move on."

"I remember Rick," I say. "Did he ever grow more than the chin stubble he rocked in high school?"

Ceci nods knowingly. "He grew a lot more than that."

"*Shut up,*" Devon groans.

"Oh my gosh," Jodi says, her eyes wide, "maybe the four of us will all be sisters-in-law!"

I rear back. "Slow down, sister. What Will and I have is an arrangement. That's it." I ignore the memory of Will above me, checking to make sure I was okay before he ravaged my body with the passion of a thousand fiery suns.

The three of them look at me for a beat, then share a look among themselves, and start laughing. And it's not a funny *ha-ha* laugh, it's more like they've fallen into hysterics.

"What?" I ask. "What did I say? Why are you laughing?" But even as I say it, I can't help the way a smile tugs at the corner of my lips. Because even though they're clearly laughing *at me*, I can't shake the feeling of being home. As if this is where I'm supposed to be.

Devon breathes out another laugh and wipes the tears from her eyes with a napkin, flinching as she does. "Jodi, I thought you were going to get new napkins. These are terrible."

Jodi laughs harder. "I *know*! But now I kind of love them.

They make me remember things," she finishes, her voice growing soft.

Devon shoves her playfully. "That man has got you so turned upside down you don't know which way is up."

Jodi's smile brightens even more. "He really does."

"And Tori," Devon says, turning to me and patting my hand like I'm a naïve child, "if you say you and Will just have an arrangement, then okay, sweetie. We believe you." But she snort-laughs as she says that last part, and they all collapse into laughter again.

I roll my eyes. "I do, and we do. That's all it is. Can we talk about something else now?" I beg. "Like where I'm going to give y'all yoga lessons? Because I don't have a spot since Will said I can't do them at the inn anymore."

"Upstairs," Jodi says. "Now that I'm all moved in across the street from the inn, you could do it there."

My heart *leaps*. I lean forward, gripping the bottom of my seat out of fear I'll float away in happiness. "Really?"

"Sure," she answers.

"What about—" I'm almost scared to ask, but I do it anyway. "What about semi-permanently?"

"Ooh, like a real studio?" Devon says. "That would be awesome!"

Jodi purses her lips. "Why semi-permanent and not just all the permanent?"

"Because I—" I stop. *Jump. Jump. JUMP.* Everything in me is screaming it. "You know what? Permanent. Fuck it."

Matching smiles of delight spread over all three of their faces.

"Seriously?" Jodi says.

"Permanent like you're going to stay for good?" Devon says.

"Says the woman who swore *she* wasn't staying for good," Ceci mumbles. "Ow!" she says, rubbing her arm from where Devon hit her.

"Honestly, you three," I say. "Tell you what. Let's just say I'd be willing to sign a year-long lease. What do you say?" I ask, looking at Jodi.

After a moment, she says, "I don't see why not."

Ceci and Devon grab onto each other as though they're about to lose their minds, wearing positively unhinged looks on their faces as they practically vibrate.

But honestly, my own face probably matches theirs as what we're agreeing to sinks in. "You're serious?"

"Yeah," Jodi says, her own grin slightly maniacal. "Why not? We'll need to work out a bunch of stuff, but absolutely."

We all squeal again—I have a feeling I'll be doing a lot more of that—and I blink away the tears that threaten and swallow the lump in my throat. "You have no idea how much this means to me."

She smiles and raises her coffee mug to me. "The look on your face tells me everything."

"Aww, I love this," Devon says. "Look how happy you are!"

"You sure it's not just because she's been getting slung over Will's shoulder?" Ceci asks.

"Shut up, Ceci," we all say.

WILL

I AM NOT a fan of Christmas.

Too many people forced to be together who would much rather not be. Forced cheer is not anything I'm interested in participating in.

Of course, my brothers don't agree with me. And it's not that surprising—they don't remember the way our parents fought, and I'm glad for it. Doesn't matter that Price is only two years younger than me; those two years made all the difference in what he remembers. Aaron was totally oblivious, and I worked hard to keep it that way until very recently. He didn't learn about everything until a couple of years ago, when he told us he thought he was the reason Mom had left.

Idiot. Of course he wasn't the reason.

I was.

It's the part that no one but Mom and I know, and I plan on keeping it that way.

Shit. I look down at the gooey mess in the stand mixer. I let the paddle work the dough too long. I curse again and toss the batch into the trash, washing my hands and preparing to do it once more.

"Broseph!" Price bounds into the kitchen, the very picture of an unaffected Joseph brother.

Must be nice.

I grunt, not in the mood for a conversation. I'm determined to make this croquembouche for Christmas if it's the last damn thing I do.

Price eyes the spread of ingredients and my expression. "Whatever it is, it's going to be unbelievably yummy. Wanna know how I know?" he asks, his eyebrows waggling.

"Shouldn't you be at the station?" I ask.

"Because of how mad you look," he answers, ignoring me. "Anytime you're this pissed off about pastry, it means the end result is going to be," he kisses his fingers and winks at me, "chef's kiss."

"No one actually *says* chef's kiss," I say. "It's implied when you kiss your fingers, you idiot."

"Yeah, but if I did it the right way, I wouldn't rile you up, and where's the fun in that?"

I grit my teeth and turn away from him.

"Anyway, I'm not at the station because Mom told me she'd be here by now," he continues. "And, I wanted to check on our guest. Are you the only one here?"

"What do you think?"

"I think you're really into your feelings right now," he says. "Do you need a hug? I think you need a hug."

"I will fucking punch you."

He ignores me and wraps his arms around me, his front to my back, and squeezes. "So good. *So good.* Feel the love," he says. Then he licks my ear.

"What the *fuck*, Price?" I swat him and try not to laugh. "You dick."

He laughs. "Smile, asshole, or I'll lick your other ear."

I grin, swatting him away as he comes at me again. "Stop it."

"Yes!" he says, raising his arms Rocky Balboa-style. "A smile! Victory!"

I scowl at him, and it only makes him laugh harder.

"Hello?" A timid voice reaches us from the front.

I stiffen, and even Price seems to reset. Mom.

"Hello?" The voice grows closer, and after a moment, she appears in the kitchen's doorway, a small smile on her face.

"Mom!" Price's voice is warm as he greets her, meeting her and wrapping her in his arms.

"Hi, my beautiful boy," Mom says.

Price releases her and she turns to me.

I jerk into motion, meeting her halfway and leaning down to hug her. I'm always struck by how small she is. Fragile. Even though she seemed none of those things when we were growing up. "Hi, Mom."

"Hey, Will," she says, her grip so strong that it almost takes me by surprise. She has a tone of voice for each of us. For Aaron, it's still a little hesitant, like she's afraid he'll reject her. For Price, it's warm and generous. Then there's the one she uses for me. The one that reeks of secret betrayal.

I release her and take a step back, assessing her. Too many years of treating her body like hell took their toll on her, so she appears older than her sixty years, but she looks good. Healthy. Her blue eyes are clear, her skin bright.

"How was your drive up?" Price asks.

"Easy," comes the answer, her gaze still on me. "How are you, Will?"

I wonder if she can see the torture that Tori has been putting me through, not to mention the growing desire to stop working at the station. Doubtful. So I shrug, not interested in talking to her about anything even remotely personal in my life. "Fine."

She hums thoughtfully. I turn away, focusing once more on the croquembouche recipe on my phone.

Price, always the better host, keeps up a litany of chatter as he gets the two of them sparkling waters from the fridge and pops the cans, telling her about his new place across the street. My ears perk up when he asks how she's been doing.

"Really well," she answers, her voice sincere. "I've got a new job as a house cleaner down on 30A," she says, referencing a section of beach on the Alabama coast that's always packed with tourists, no matter the season. "Not as boring as working in a hotel, and the owners are really great. You boys should come down. I could—"

"Can't," I interrupt her.

Price's response comes quick. "Maybe *you* can't, Mr. I Work So Much and I'm Very Important, but that doesn't mean Aaron and I couldn't make time to get away."

Mom's laugh is subdued, and I feel like an asshole.

Standard.

"Sorry," I say, turning around. "We're booked up with hardly any breaks for the next six months. That's what I should have said."

Her expression clears. "Oh, that's great to hear. So you're doing well with this? It's a gorgeous house."

I offer a tight smile. "We are. Thank you."

"Come on," Price says, standing. "I'll give you a tour and we'll pick your room for the next few nights."

"I'm not imposing by being here, right?" Mom asks, looking once more at me. "If you're booked up..."

"You're not imposing, Mom," Price says gently, glancing over at me and narrowing his eyes.

"We only have one guest right now," I add, then shrug at him when Mom looks away. "So it's fine."

Price rolls his eyes at me behind her back. "And you're never an imposition. You're our mother. We'll always have a place for you to stay."

He starts to guide her away when Tori appears in the kitchen, still in her red puffer coat and unwrapping a scarf from her neck. She smiles brightly at Price and Mom. "Hi!" she enthuses. "Did I just hear you're their mom?"

Every instinct I have tells me to shut this interaction down, because nothing good can come from it. I take a step forward before I can stop myself, and it's enough to draw Tori's attention for a moment. The look she gives me is quick, but heated, and now the only instinct I have is to throw her over my shoulder once more and have my way with her in the bedroom.

"Yes," Mom is saying. "I'm Barbara Joseph."

"I'm Tori Welch," comes Tori's response. "It's so nice to meet you. You're in town for the holidays?"

"Yes. Just a few days," Mom says.

They talk for another few moments, enough that I can look at Tori without interruption. She makes my chest ache. She's *luminous*, drawing Price and Mom into her orbit like moths to a flame, and a weird sense of jealousy comes over me. Since she came back, she's not looked at me like she's looking at them, so open and warm. The looks she gives me are more guarded, more careful.

Except for when I was fucking her.

I shake my head to clear the memory, but all the movement serves to do is draw Tori's eyes to me once more.

"I need to speak with Will for a moment. Please excuse me," Tori says, and begins making her way across the kitchen.

Price and Mom go upstairs as Tori nears and I stand straighter, clenching my jaw to force the memory of her body stretched out beneath me out of my head.

"Hey," Tori says, breaching my personal space and leaving only an inch between us.

She smells incredible, and I shut my eyes to steady myself. When I open them, she's watching me, a careful expression on her face, like she's trying to decipher my mood and adjust her approach accordingly. It's the same look almost everyone gives me, and I've welcomed it over the years. But on Tori? I hate it. I thought at the very least she wasn't wary of me. But maybe I was wrong. "Hi," I manage.

"Your mom seems nice," she says. "Sweet."

I'm hauling her to me and kissing her before I realize what I'm doing, tasting the gloss on her lips and shoving my hands under her jacket to grip her hips. Clearly she's on board, because her lips part to allow me additional access, and I take it, all the blood in my head racing to my dick as my tongue meets hers. Dimly I'm aware that kissing her in the wide open of the kitchen isn't a good idea, and in fact, I'm pretty sure this thing between us needs to stay *only* between us, but all the logic flees as my hands find the silky skin of her waist.

She rips her mouth away from me with a gasp, her eyes blazing, her mouth even more lush and ripe than usual. "Jesus, Will."

"Just Will is fine."

She huffs a laugh. "Did you just make a joke?"

I allow a tiny smile to cross my face, and she blooms.

"Oh my god, you *did*. Okay, Just Will. I see you." She lowers her voice and takes a step back, putting enough space between us that I can't touch her.

I growl.

She smirks. "You don't like that, do you?"

Not in the fucking slightest. But with the distance comes clarity, and I definitely should not have kissed her. It's been days since we came to our agreement and I'm on eggshells. Which is stupid, but I can't manage to make it stop. My head and heart are a tangled mess, and I know it's my fault, but my dick is absolutely certain that an arrangement was made. Am I supposed to instigate? Is she? Did she change her mind? What if I imagined how good we were in bed and it's all a joke?

I hate this. I don't even recognize myself. In an effort to reclaim some part of me, I straighten and say, "Sorry. That shouldn't have happened. The rule was we'd keep this to ourselves."

A look of disappointment shimmers across her face. "I have a question." She takes my silence for what it is and continues. "How, exactly, are we supposed to, um…" she trails off and looks away from me. Then she seems to gather herself and pins me with her deep brown eyes. "How should I let you know when I want you to fuck me?"

My dick twitches as though it's been summoned, so I close my eyes to steady myself. I take my own moment, and when I open my eyes, she's staring at me with an amused expression. "Do you think this is funny?" I snarl.

Her lips tip up. "A little, yeah."

I should never have agreed to this. It was a bad idea.

"Send you a text? Pass you a note? Carrier pigeon?" she prompts, her smile growing wider with every suggestion.

I can't fucking *think* around her. My head is muddled, all I can smell is the warm spice of her skin and all I can taste is the strawberry of her lip gloss.

"Smoke signals? C'mon, Will, give me something."

I glare at her. "I don't know, Tori!"

She bites back a laugh. "God, you are fun."

"You're infuriating."

"Yeah," she says softly, her gaze tracking the length of my body and back up. "So are you." She backs up, making her way to the kitchen door. "Tonight, Will."

WILL

AARON AND DEVON show up to take Mom to dinner several hours later. I'm on high alert, still unsure how Aaron and Mom are really doing. But Devon's warmth, like Tori's, goes a long way towards easing any tension there might have been in the room.

"I'm not the greatest cook," Devon is saying, "and I didn't want Aaron to be focused on cooking when he should be visiting with you, so we're actually going to pick some pizza up from Moody's."

Mom's eyes widen. "I haven't had that pizza in so long," she says with a sigh.

"Is that okay?" Devon asks.

"Oh, it's wonderful," Mom says, reaching across the kitchen table to pat Devon's hand.

Devon and Aaron both visibly relax, and I focus once more on the recipe book I'm flipping through as I lean against the island.

"Should I bring you some back?" Mom asks me.

I try to keep the frown off my face, but I doubt it shows. "I don't eat that stuff," I say.

Aaron snorts a laugh. "His body is a temple, Mom. He may bake and cook like a normal person, but that doesn't mean he actually eats it."

"Ah," Mom says.

Devon stands up and gathers the mugs of tea from the table and takes them to the sink.

"Leave them," I say.

She snickers. "Happy to," she says, then gives me a side hug.

I raise an eyebrow at her. "What."

She just smiles. "Oh, nothing."

"You look like you swallowed a secret. I don't like it."

Her smile broadens. "Okay, first of all, the teacher in me loves the way you put that. Very poetic."

I grunt.

"Secondly, what I do or don't know is none of your business." Her eyes shine as she goes on her tiptoes and pulls me down to plant a smack on my cheek. "The place looks great, Will."

Her words have the intended effect, and I relax. "Thanks."

In moments, she's got Aaron and Mom out of the house, and I finish making notes on the recipe I'm considering for the green bean casserole for Christmas dinner.

My stomach chooses that moment to growl, so I make myself a quick meal of salmon, quinoa, and veggies. I clean up the kitchen and head to my bedroom, stepping into the ensuite bath to take a quick shower. I come out and nearly skid to a halt.

"Hi, Will."

"Hi," I manage to get out.

Tori is kneeling in the center of the bed, looking every part the naughty Christmas gift she very much is. She's wearing red silk lingerie, her breasts swelling behind white fuzzy trim, and a Santa hat is perched on her head. The light brown of her luscious skin pops against the red of the teddy and the navy blue of the duvet. Her eyes roam over me, widening appreciatively as she clocks the obvious effect she's having on me beneath my towel.

"Glad to see me?" she asks, her glossy lips curving up.

I push my hair off my forehead, trying to get my body to move. But I'm too focused on what she's holding. "What is that," I demand.

She holds up the length of red silk. "This?"

I nod.

"Well, I decided we have more rules," she says, moving off the bed to come and stand in front of me. She smells of spice and shea butter, and it's a struggle to keep my eyes open as I breathe her in. She lets the silk unfold to the floor, and it looks like it might belong to a robe.

"The rules are," she continues, "whoever wants the sex, is the one who controls it."

I swallow. "No."

She laughs softly, lifting the length of silk and draping it slowly around my neck, the movement itself a promise of pleasure to come. "See, here's the thing, Will," she says, her voice low and velvety. "I think you spend your entire life in control. And you're not going to let go completely, I know that." Her hands grip the silk and gently pull, bending me to her. When my lips are an inch from hers, our eyes still caught together, she speaks again. "But tonight, you're going to let me have you how I want you."

I hear the slightest tremor in her voice, and it's enough to let me know that she's out on a ledge. That she isn't nearly as cavalier about this as she wants me to think she is. And thank god, because I'm right there with her. Not that I can tell her that. Whatever this is, it's fragile. And as much as I want to smash through it, retreat from this and ask her to leave, I can't. Something in her eyes, the infinite depth of them, compels me.

And at the same time, there's no way I can let her in.

So as I tuck my heart safely away, I smirk at the gorgeous and dangerous woman in front of me. "We'll see about that."

Her eyes flash, and I pick her up and toss her on the bed. She lands with a surprised gasp. "Will!"

I let my towel drop. "Tori."

Her gaze falls instantly to my dick. "Dammit," she sighs. "Cover that up. I can't think when you're naked."

A laugh comes out of me, and it surprises both of us. "Don't you want me naked?" I ask.

Her lips part and she blinks at me. "Okay, whatever is happening right now, I want you to stop it."

I tilt my head. "What's happening?"

She points at my face. "That. You're—you're *smiling*. Stop it. Stop it right now."

She looks so distressed, so genuinely put out, that I start laughing. And I keep laughing as I crawl onto the bed and over her, crowding her against the headboard and threading my hand into the coils at the nape of her neck. I'm still chuckling even as I incline my head to hers, capturing her lips. She tastes like strawberry lip balm.

"What—Will—stop. *Stop.*"

Immediately I pull away and raise both hands in the air.

She heaves a breath and seems to pull herself together, her eyes searching my face. "Are you okay?"

"Yes," I say. "Are you?"

"Did you hit your head in there?" She nods toward the bathroom.

I grin. "No."

Her eyes widen once more. "There it is *again*. Stop it!"

I smile. "Stop what?"

She points a finger at me and scowls. "That. You can't do that. Oh my god. You have dimples, Will. *Dimples*. On both sides of your grumpy-ass face. Do you have any idea what that does to a person?"

"Of course I have dimples. I've always had them. You saw them in high school."

She rolls her eyes. "No, I didn't."

"Yes, you did."

"No, I didn't, because I promise you, I would have remembered. And it's not fair of you to, to *wield* them all willy-nilly like that."

I narrow my eyes at her. "Did you just say 'willy-nilly'?"

She shoves at my chest and grumbles. "Can we start over? How about you go back into the bathroom and we do this again?"

"How about you tell me what you planned to do with this?" I lift the length of silk from where it rests against my clavicle and wiggle it.

She heaves a breath, drawing my attention to her breasts. "I wasn't sure. I just grabbed it and figured I'd let the moment take me wherever it took me. I didn't intend for you to smile and throw me off my game."

"Well," I say, looking her over. For as shallow as she acts like this is, there's more than she's letting on. Or maybe I'm delusional, and I need to guard myself. "It's mine now." Releasing the silk, I take a finger and trace the white trim lining her breasts, watching as they swell with every breath she takes.

I keep tracing her skin, my fingers floating down one arm and back up, then over her chest and down the other arm. She's quiet, but I can see the way her pulse is racing in her throat. She's so beautiful, it hurts. Physically hurts.

I meet her gaze. "Do you trust me?"

She nods.

I lower my voice and growl the next part, because it's what she expects, and it's what she wants. And I can't stop wanting to give her everything she desires. "One word from you and I stop. Understand?"

Her eyes flare with heat as she nods.

I put my hand around her neck, feeling her pulse kick up even more. "I need you to say it." I tighten my hand and feel her swallow.

"I understand."

I loosen my hold and tip her chin up to claim her mouth. She arches into me, giving as good as she's getting, and I pull the hat off her head. "Don't ever wear that again," I growl, then bite her neck, groaning at the taste of her skin.

"Oh my god," she gasps, her arms flying up around me.

But I pull back, breaking her hold and pulling her wrists into one hand while I yank the silk from around my neck. I raise her hands and bind them.

"That's tight," she whispers.

I look down at her. "I know."

A wicked grin steals across her face.

"Don't move," I say.

"Or what?" she prompts.

I should have known she'd be playful, even now. I don't answer, getting off the bed and rounding to the foot of it. She tracks me, remarkably staying still. I grab her feet and yank her towards me. She doesn't fight me, her arms bound tightly above her head, her legs spread in front of me.

I kneel before her, happy to see that the little outfit she's worn for me is a two-piece. I yank the bottoms off, not bothering to be gentle. This woman drives me absolutely crazy, and gentle has no place here. Without preamble, I bury my tongue between her legs, and she shouts.

Fuck, she tastes so good. I groan, unable to control myself, and wrap my arms tight around her thighs to keep her in place.

"Oh my god, Will," she moans. "What are you—*fuck*." She unleashes a series of unintelligible groans.

I could live right here, between her beautiful legs, listening to her sounds, feeling her tense and writhe beneath me. Bringing her to orgasm over and over. She's already there now, yelling and cursing the binds around her wrists, bucking as I suck her clit and grip her thighs. She stiffens as I take her over the edge, then a sound of utter pleasure wrenches out of her, and I commit it to memory immediately. I gentle my mouth on her to bring her down, my ego and dick swelling as I listen to her come back to me.

"How the fuck can you do that?" she murmurs incredulously. "It's not—*how*? I can't—but I did..." she trails off, half-laughing.

I don't answer. Instead, I stand up and take her in, bound and sprawled before me, her gorgeous tits hidden behind the bra, her face blissed out, her eyes glassy. A beautiful mess. "There's a lot more where that came from, Tori."

"My wrists," she whines.

I shake my head. She's not serious, so no. "Not yet."

Before she can say anything else, I flip her over and push her farther onto the bed.

She yelps, whipping her head to the side to see me. "What are you doing?"

I grunt. It's the only acknowledgment she'll get that I heard her.

I let my eyes feast on her. She flexes her hands above the red of the silk, and her dark brown hair halos out from her flushed face. The back of the silk corset is almost all red, save for some white piping, and the entire thing is pulled together by the tiniest red zipper imaginable. The corset stops at the natural curve of her waist, which fans out into an ass so perfectly lush and bitable that I have to fist my hand to keep from doing just that.

As I watch, she wiggles her ass just a little, clenching her thighs and whimpering.

"Will..." she says, the sound of my name pure sex out of her mouth.

In answer, I trail my fingers up and down the backs of her legs, watching the goosebumps erupt in my path. I spread her legs and kneel on the bed between them, catching the scent of her arousal as I do. I can't stop the groan that comes out of me, and she writhes in response.

"You're killing me," she whispers.

She has no idea. I lean over her, putting my mouth next to her ear and breathing, letting the air hit the delicate skin.

She shivers.

"Tell me what you want, Tori. If you're a good girl, I might give it to you."

She laughs out a moan. "Fuck, Will."

I lick the shell of her ear. "That's not an answer."

Her voice is low, needy. "I want you to fuck me, Will. That's what this is, right?"

A spike of icy heat spears into me at the words. But she's right. That's what this is. Nothing more. It's why I needed her hands bound; they felt too much last time.

I rise up and focus once more on her ass, grabbing it and kneading it, watching the way her hips roll in response. And because I can't help myself, I lean down and bite it, letting my teeth sink into the tender flesh and feeling my dick throb with want.

Above me, Tori issues another moan.

I push a finger into her without warning, unable to hold off any longer. She shouts as her walls clamp around my finger, and I push another into her.

She sobs in pleasure above me, and I pump my dick with my free hand a few times to ease the pressure.

"You like that, don't you?" I ask, letting her set the rhythm and movement against my fingers. She's pure velvet around them, hot and wet. "But you want my cock. I know you do. You have to earn my cock, Tori. Come on my fingers first."

With my other hand, I spread her ass and position my thumb against her tight hole. She tenses, so I push my fingers into her pussy even farther.

"Fuck," she draws out, swirling her hips. "Fuck, Will, *please*."

"Please what?" I demand, pushing the tip of my thumb into the puckered entrance.

"*Please* let me come, god, please Will, please please," she chants, taking my thumb without another word as I continue to pump my fingers into her pussy.

I smirk. "There you go. Take it. You're tight, baby."

"*Fuck*." She shudders as an orgasm wrenches through her. She arches up, unable to control her body as she yells. I watch her, taking in her parted mouth, the way her eyes are squeezed shut, how the tips of her knuckles are nearly white with the effort of squeezing her hands.

When she collapses, boneless onto the bed, I pull my hands away and lean over her, taking the corset's zipper between my teeth and pulling it down.

She shivers beneath the touch, and exhales as it comes all the way undone. Indentations from the corset go down her back, and I clench my jaw at how sexy it is. Leaning down, I lick the lines, tasting her skin and commanding myself to stay in control. But the noises she's making, little mewling sounds of praise, are about to make me explode.

I launch off her and flip her over. The corset is loose around her, but can't come off with her wrists bound.

"Take it *off*," she commands, her voice deep.

"Only one way it comes off, baby," I answer.

"Then do it." Her eyes are molten.

I don't hesitate, tearing the straps away in two satisfying rips of fabric.

"You are so fucking *hot*, Will, holy shit," she breathes.

I meet her gaze. And before I know what's happening, the words are out. "You ruin me, Tori."

Her eyes fly wide and her mouth opens, but I crash my lips onto hers before she can speak, plunging my tongue against hers with a promise of what's to come. She slams her arms down on my back and threads her legs around mine, pulling me as tight to her as she possibly can, as if she understands that I need the pressure.

What I need is pain, but she can't know that. It's bad enough that I can't control my emotions with her, but if she gave me what I needed, too?

I wrench my mouth off hers. "Don't say a word," I warn. "You talk, you make a noise, you don't get to come again."

She nods, a flicker of excited fear evident in her eyes.

I fight a satisfied smile, instead pulling her hands back over her head and commanding, "These stay up here." Then I descend on her breasts, taking one into my mouth as she arches into me with a gasp.

They are the most perfect breasts I have ever had the pleasure of touching. Full and luscious, filling my palms and so sensitive. I've known that Tori has been the bar that every other woman has been measured against, but it's only now, with her nipple pebbling in my mouth and her body moving beneath mine, desperate for my cock, that I realize how wide the chasm has been. It's infuriating.

I pull off her and grab a condom from the bedside drawer, enjoying the way her dark eyes flash with desire as she watches me. She bites her lip, watching me without any sense of embarrassment, and I want to fucking *preen* beneath her gaze. All of this—all of *me*—is for her. It always has been, and I can't let her know that. Not when all she'll do is hurt me again.

So I position myself between her legs and thrust in. Hard.

Her mouth opens in a silent scream, and I groan. "Fuck, Tori," I grit out.

She raises her legs, opening as wide as she can for me as I pull back and slam into her again. A squeak comes out of her and I glare.

"*No*," I command. "Not a fucking *sound* out of you or I stop."

She squeezes her eyes shut and grits her teeth.

"Good girl," I say, pounding into her. There's nothing gentle about what I'm doing. Something in me needs to punish her, make her feel the agony she puts me through, and how the hell me fucking her is going to do that, I don't know.

I reposition myself, reaching up to wrap my hand around the silk that binds her hands, and let loose once more.

Tori's eyes catch mine, and I can't look away. There's a whole world inside of her, and for one brief second, she lets me see it. I want it so badly, *need* to curl up inside of it and let her soothe me, that it pisses me off.

"Fuck!" I yell, pulling out of her and flipping her over again. I can't look at her. Can't have her see what she's doing to me.

I push into her again, feeling how close I am. She is so tight, so incredibly warm and lush against my cock, taking absolutely everything I'm giving her without question, obeying me with ease, and she is going to be my undoing.

I lose the rhythm, going onto my knees and grabbing her hips to pull her with me. My fingers dig into her skin and I zero in on the red silk on her hands as they move up and down the mattress. So close. Heat builds in the base of my spine and with two more thrusts, I'm almost there. So I let her have hers, too.

"*Now*, Tori. Make as much noise as you want."

Instantly she moans. "*Holy fuck, Will*," she growls, unleashing a torrent of sounds and grunts and outright screaming as I begin to come.

"More, more, more, more," she demands, and I give it to her, thrusting with every word that issues from her. The walls of her pussy clamp down and I shout, then groan as they begin to pulse against my cock with her orgasm, milking my own climax and drawing it out.

Finally we quiet, the only sounds the two of us catching our breath. After a moment, I pull out of her. She collapses onto the mattress and I go to the bathroom to dispose of the condom.

Tori's eyes eat me up as I walk back to stand next to the bed, and she pulls herself up to sitting. Scooting to the edge so her feet hit the floor, she gives me a satisfied smile and holds her arms out. "Off, please."

I untie the silk and unwrap her wrists. As expected, they're a little red and bear the markings of the hold, and it's sexy as hell. I trace the indentations with my thumbs, commanding myself to pull it together, then meet her eyes.

"That was…something," she says softly, pulling away from me and rubbing her wrists. Her eyes flick down and back up, and when they meet mine again, they glint mischievously up at me. "You're a fucking beast, you know that?"

I shrug and back away, turning to grab some boxers out of the dresser just so I have something to do. *Beast* isn't the word I'd use. *Possessed*, maybe. *Obsessed*, definitely. But this has to remain as sex only. Any more than that and she could shred me.

"Will?" Her voice is small and searching, a far cry from the woman beneath me a few minutes ago.

I put on a mask of indifference as I face her.

It must work, because her face shutters as she says, "Never mind." She tips up her chin and rises as regally as if she were a queen, gliding to where a red silk robe is puddled on the floor. Somehow I'd missed seeing it. She picks it up and puts it on, then plucks the tie off the ground and threads it through the robe to knot it at her waist. Her breasts hang heavy and low behind the silk, and I want to bury my head between them.

I watch as she grabs the ruined corset and discarded panties, not trusting myself to say anything. So I stay quiet as she walks to the door and leaves.

TORI

MOM SMILES AS she wraps me in a hug, pulling me tight against her. "Merry Christmas, baby girl."

I squeeze hard, reveling in the way the embrace grounds me. Same as it always has, really. No matter how my days went growing up, I knew as long as I could get a hug from my mom, that everything would eventually turn out okay.

Come to think of it, the only time it hasn't worked has been since I've returned. I need more hugs.

"Merry Christmas, Mom," I say.

We release each other and I shrug out of my coat, and Mom finally gets a look at me.

"Victoria! Did you leave the house in your pajamas?"

The grin that spreads over my face is huge as I wave down at my red and green checked flannel pajama set and Ugg slippers. "Obviously!" I step around her and head to the kitchen, still talking. "Listen, it's your fault. If you'd just let me stay here like a nice mother, then I wouldn't be forced to leave the house like this." Never mind that 'like this' actually included a bra and panties and some clothes in the bag I'd brought. And makeup and hair product to put on later.

But not shoes. I draw the line at getting fully dressed on Christmas morning, so the Ugg slippers are my last line of defense.

The sound of holiday music drifts toward me and I inhale deeply. "You already working on the pancakes?"

She winks at me. "Look at how I'm dressed. What do you think?"

I take her in. She's still in her pajamas, too. "Yes, but barely. Lead the way."

Stanley is in the kitchen, and I almost draw up short. He'd been so quiet that I had no idea he was here, but there he is, sitting at the island like he belongs here, his bald head shining in the light.

"Hi, Stanley," I say, pushing a smile onto my face. I'd assumed he wouldn't be here first thing, and now I'm realizing I really need to rethink, well, everything.

He gives me a warm smile behind glasses and a silver goatee shot through with streaks of gray. "Merry Christmas, Tori."

"Merry Christmas," I respond, and realize that Mom really *hasn't* started the pancakes yet. Or bacon. Or eggs. I pour myself some coffee, careful not to bang the pot, and lean against the counter.

Mom looks so happy. Like, ridiculously happy. And that makes *me* ridiculously happy. "So," I say, opening the fridge and pulling out ingredients, "What'd you get me for Christmas?"

Stanley's kids and grandkids have come and gone, naps have been taken, dinner has been prepared and eaten, presents have been exchanged, and it's only seven o'clock. And as I sit in the living room and take in the tiny fake tree and tidy piles of unwrapped gifts, I practically itch to leave. What I need is a snowball fight, something that just *screams* holiday shenanigans, but Alabama isn't giving me snow at Christmas. It's not even close to a winter wonderland out there. So I decide it's time to go home and hole up in my room with a bottle of wine and my Kindle.

Before I can think too hard about the fact that I just referred to the inn as *home*, Mom walks me to the door and shakes her head at me. "Can't believe you kept those on all day."

I grin down at my flannel. "Eh, just never felt I needed to change."

She chuckles. "Don't ever change, baby girl," she says fondly.

"Pretty sure I'm as settled in my ways as I can possibly get," I joke.

Her expression gets serious. "You figured out your next steps yet?"

I nod. "I told you, I'm going to open a Pilates and yoga studio over Daily Dose."

"You're really doing it?"

I pat her arm. "I'll be fine, Mom." I always am. Sure, my life until coming home was pretty shallow and meaningless, but I made money and that counts, right?

Right. If I tell myself that enough, I might actually start to believe it.

Outside, the air is crisp and clear. Lights are on in nearly every house up and down the street, and I imagine all of them are filled with big, loud, messy families. My heart twinges, and for just a moment, I let myself wallow in it.

This is not where I thought my life would be at thirty-seven. I assumed that at some point I'd get married, maybe have a kid or two. Then again, in order for that to happen, I would have had to stop and actually be open to something like that along the way. My standard love 'em and leave 'em approach is definitely not going to get me on the husband and kid track.

But that ship has sailed. Probably. The kid ship, anyway. Not sure I ever actually *wanted* kids, honestly. They're great and all, but seeing as how the longest I've ever kept anything alive is Sir Plantsalot, my peace lily plant of five years who even now is probably hanging onto life by a thread in my room at the B&B, I don't see how I would have thrived at keeping an actual tiny human alive.

Anyway, it's not worth worrying about now. And I know that occasional hot sex with Will is not a step in the right direction, but I couldn't keep myself from him if I tried. My stomach flips at the thought of Will, and I want it to stop. But it's been doing that a lot, and the sensation is both heady and nauseating.

I hop into my car and drive to Daily Dose. Pulling up, I throw the engine into park and jump out, taking in the twinkle of the darkened shop's colorful Christmas lights along the windows. Then I look up at the top floor.

Mine, I think giddily. *All mine.* The feeling that flows through me is one I've never quite experienced: elation and terror and gratitude all mixing together in a heady combination that has me flushing beneath my coat. I'm really doing it. Really starting to do something that doesn't have anything to do with drugs or entitled doctors or smarmy businessmen. Something that can help heal just by listening to the body. Something *meaningful.*

"What are you doing here?"

I yelp and turn, my hands up in a pathetic attempt at self-defense, and come face to face with Will.

My stomach does more than just a flip this time. It free falls. Because there he is, Will freaking Joseph, all done up in what's probably a starched navy Talladega Fire Department t-shirt and pressed navy pants with the crispiest of crisp fold lines going down the front of them. His eyes are dark as he scans me up and down as though he suspects me of killing puppies, and when he meets my eyes, his flare almost imperceptibly.

I like him.

That's what this stupid stomach thing is. I *like* him. Shit. So I ignore what is, coming from Will, a blatant display of leering, and launch a scowl his way. "Do you make it a habit of scaring women in the dark, Mr. Scary?" I ask, crossing my arms.

His face smooths in surprise. "What did you just call me?"

I step back, still unreasonably pissed that he'd appeared out of nowhere and brought a really horrible realization with him.

"Tori." His tone is gruff, commanding, and my belly tightens. I want to hear that voice close to my ear, with him behind me slamming into me while he pulls my hair.

Yes. Sex. That's all this is—I just need to get banged. Desperately latching onto that thought with both hands, I use my best seductive voice and say, "Yes?"

"What did you just call me?"

His anger is like a cool, comfortable balm, and I welcome it like an old friend. I arch an eyebrow. "What does it matter? And anyway, why are you out here? Shouldn't you be down the block?" I jerk my chin towards the fire station at the end of the street.

He clenches his fists, then releases them. Instantly I think of *Pride & Prejudice* and the infamous Mr. Darcy hand-flex, and it does things to my lady parts. "I asked you first," he says.

I sputter out a laugh. "What are you, ten?"

He doesn't answer, continuing to stare at me as if I owe him an answer. *Well, guess what, Mr. Scary? I don't owe you crap.*

"You called me Mr. Scary." There's no question in there, just statement. Standard.

"To be fair, I'm not the one who made it up. And I'm willing to bet you've known about the nickname anyway. The way you stomp and scowl, you've probably been scaring the residents of Talladega for decades, Will. Which brings us back to my original question: why are you lurking around here?"

He crosses his arms and stiffens his spine. "I needed some air."

"Well, fancy that. Me, too," I shoot back.

"Shouldn't you be celebrating?" He says the last word like it's dirty.

"Shouldn't *you*?" I ask.

His face is bathed in the Christmas lights, making it easy to see the way his scruffy jaw ticks. "Do you always answer questions with questions?"

The warmth that's flowing through my body has everything to do with how he's looking at me. "Do you have any idea how sexy you are when you're irritated?"

I didn't think it was possible, but his scowl deepens. The throbbing between my legs intensifies.

He's about to say something, but his phone explodes into life, sending the unmistakable refrains from the *Macarena* song soaring into the air.

I laugh as he jerks in surprise, pulling his cell from his front pocket and glaring at it. His irritation cements as he reads the screen and mutters, "Fucking Price." He holds a finger up to me in a *stay right there* gesture, and answers the call. "What."

The night is quiet enough that I can hear Price's response. "Tell me you loved hearing the sweet sounds of Macarena when I called."

"No," Will growls.

Price laughs. "You've been off shift for an hour. Come home, you big Grinch. It's Christmas."

My heart squishes in a very inconvenient way. Why hasn't he gone home to his family?

"Soon," Will answers.

"We're waiting on you to open presents. And that croken-whatever thing looks good as hell but Mom won't let us touch it till you're here."

"Croquembouche. It's French, you dumbass."

My mouth waters at the mention of the delicious tower of puff pastry goodness. I'd seen it this morning on my way out, and assumed it'd be decimated by now. Apparently not.

"You're very fancy, making your fancy French pastry," Price says. "So come home and we'll eat it and tell you how much we love it, and by extension, you."

Will grunts and ends the call, then shifts his attention back to me.

"Seems you're wanted at home," I say, gesturing at the phone.

"You're coming with me."

I bristle. "You can't tell me what to do."

"You live there, Tori."

"So?"

"I swear you argue just to argue," he says, shaking his head.

I might. I look away, trying to shove down the very inconvenient feelings I'm still having. Messy, complicated, heart-squishing feelings that have no place in whatever it is that Will and I have.

He sighs. "You'll show up eventually. Come home."

My gaze snaps to his face at the word, and I see the surprise that flickers across his stony expression. Why do I want that word to mean something that it can't possibly mean? I need it to stop. And yet, I don't want it to. I was the one who had that same thought mere minutes ago, and here he is, using it.

But he can't mean it. He can't want me the way I want him.

I feel sick. I can't stand here and have a revelation right in front of him. I can't look at him, all handsome and growly in the Christmas lights in front of my Pilates studio, and think about my future. And want him in it so desperately that it makes me almost cry.

Panicked, I put on the sexiest sex-kitten smile I can muster and purr, "You just want me curled up in your bed, don't you?"

Another flex of his jaw. "Let's go." He turns without waiting to see if I'll follow, and it's the most bitter relief I have ever felt.

I don't go with him. I have my own damn car.

WILL

I CAN'T BELIEVE she didn't come with me. Her tires are practically bald and it could be icy in spots, but no, little Miss I'll Do What I Want can't possibly do anything that's *safe* and *logical*. She's messy. Messy with her life, messy in her room, messy with her words…messy.

I grip the steering wheel so tight it protests under my hands. She didn't even bother to immediately get in her car so I could at least follow her home.

I'm getting her tires changed.

How can I be expected to focus when she's around? Standing outside her car—which was wide open, by the way, *anyone* could have gotten inside while she wasn't looking—staring up at the top floor of Jodi's coffee shop like it held the answers to the universe. I don't know why she was there. What I do know is that I fully planned on going home, but I wanted to make one last check on the ridiculous Santa blow-up that Chief insisted be put outside the station, even though it constantly fell over and caused a fire hazard *in front of the fire station*, and there she was.

Obviously I had to check on her. Maybe she'd hurt herself.

Maybe one of her bald tires had gotten a flat. Honestly, what was she doing there?

It didn't matter. She didn't care enough to share, so I shouldn't care about…any of it.

I pull into my parking spot at home when my watch pulses against my wrist. *Elevated heart rate*, it warns.

Yeah, no shit. Because a certain woman won't do what's best for herself.

Cursing, I head inside, but stop before I walk in and make myself take a deep breath. I need to be calm. Focused. Mom's here, and that means I need to be careful. I need to remember that everyone will watch me to see how I act, and I have to act like it's fine.

She really did seem like she was doing well. She'd not asked for money in a year, and that had to be good. Her sponsor hadn't called me in longer than that. But what was a year to an addict?

I square my shoulders and walk in.

Laughter rings out from the front parlor and the scents of a rich, not even close to healthy, Christmas dinner swirl around me. I'd planned on cooking, but ended up covering for another guy. My stomach growls.

"Will, is that you?" Devon calls seconds before she appears. She smiles and gives me a hug, wrapping her arms around my middle and squeezing tight.

I pat her back.

She releases me, all cheery and happy and probably a little tipsy. Aaron better be stone-cold sober if they plan on driving home tonight. "Merry Christmas!" she gushes. "Come on, I bet you're hungry." She threads her arm through mine and I let her lead me to the kitchen.

I close my eyes at the mess, already calculating how long it'll take me to clean this up. The counters are dirty, and the top of the oven is horrendous. I can't see inside the sink yet, but I'm willing to bet it's got unrinsed plates and silverware in it.

Mom comes in and heads straight for the refrigerator. I tense. What is she doing?

"It's been hours since we ate," she says, smiling tentatively at me over her shoulder. "So we put everything away. The boys wouldn't let any of us tidy up," she continues as she sets container after container on the island.

I nod, commanding my stomach to unclench. What did I think she was going to do—down a bottle of wine in front of me like she did when I was a kid?

Price, Aaron, and Jodi come in next, followed by Rick and Ceci.

Rick leans to shake my hand and we do our usual nod. He's the only one who understands my desire to say as little as possible. We've been friends for what feels like forever.

"Twins and my dad are still in the living room," Ceci says. "Figured we should have an adult watching them, seeing as how they busted out the finger paints."

Rick holds up a hand at the look of horror on my face. "She's kidding. Ceese, c'mon," he chides.

She grins at me. "But it's so much fun."

"Everyone certainly thinks so," I grumble.

"Hey, where's Tori?" Jodi asks.

I stare at her, not even remotely knowing how to start answering that question.

"Okay, Hangry Man," Price says, apparently clocking my expression and wanting to diffuse it.

There's nothing to diffuse. I'm fine.

"I think we need to get some delicious food in that tummy of yours, diet be damned," Price continues, and in moments, they've all worked like an overgrown army of ants to produce a plate filled with ham, turkey, green bean casserole, stuffing, mashed potatoes and gravy, sweet potato pie, and a heaping serving of cranberry sauce on the side. I'm hustled to the table, which is also an unmitigated disaster of epic proportions, and they all sit.

"I don't need company," I say, eyeing the candles in the centerpiece. They shouldn't have still been lit while no one was in here to keep an eye on it, especially with kids in the house. I glare at Price. Who knows better.

He tosses a shit-eating grin back, same as he always does, even though he knows exactly what I'm irritated about. "Merry Christmas, asshole," he says.

"Price!" Mom admonishes.

I look at all of them as they laugh, cutting a piece of ham and eating it. They all look back at me expectantly, like they're waiting for something. "What?" I finally ask.

"I think Price is really just waiting on you to finish dinner so he can have some croquembouche," Jodi says with a soft smile.

I study her. Something's different. Or maybe she's finally not scared of me every time I look at her. She's the one who dubbed me Mr. Scary, after all. I know enough to know that. "Fine with me if you dive in now."

Price is halfway across the kitchen before I've finished my sentence. He's got the tower of puff pastry in his hands, walking triumphantly back to the table, when my neck prickles with awareness.

Tori's home.

"Hi everyone!" comes her sunny voice, acting as if we didn't just have a discussion outside the coffee shop that ended in a stalemate.

Jodi, Ceci and Devon are up and hugging her, Price, Rick and Aaron nod a hello, and even Mom is smiling as if she doesn't have a care in the world. All for one chaotic person. I sure as hell didn't get that kind of welcome. Not that I expected to.

"Ooh, are you about to have the croquembouche?" she asks, not once glancing in my direction. Me, the one who made said croquembouche.

The chatter continues as the women get Tori set up with a glass of wine, and I can't help but check to see how Mom handles that. But the look on Mom's face doesn't change; she looks just as charmed by Tori as the rest of the table, my brothers included. Even Rick's normally stoic expression has softened, and somehow, that makes it all worse.

Finally, I've finished my dinner and everyone else is back at the table, with Tori and her shea-butter and spice scent sitting right beside me.

She smells so good. I hate every moment of this.

"How does this work?" Price asks, hovering above the croquembouche.

"Did anyone take a picture?" Devon asks. "It's beautiful."

My chest puffs out a bit at the statement, because it is. Prettiest thing I've made, in its own way. It's a cone-shaped tower made up of small, one-inch round cream puff pastries. They're a gorgeous golden brown, because I ruined several batches before I got them just right. Delicate strips of caramel are swirled all around the tower to hold it all together. "I did," I answer. Not that I'll do anything with it. But at least I have proof I made it.

Looking at Price, I say, "You just grab the first one and go from there. The caramel will break and allow you to grab a piece of the pastry."

Surprising no one, Price grabs several from the top at once, and pops one in his mouth. His eyes widen. "Broseph. This is amazing."

The right side of my mouth curls up in a smile, making Price beam in return.

Price doles out the pastry to the table, which erupts as each person tries one. Clearly, it's a hit.

But the only person's reaction I care about is Tori, and I hate myself for it. I try to pretend that I'm not watching her, but when it's obvious I can't get away with it, I give in and watch as she lifts one to her mouth. Her short nails are a Santa red, catching the light as her dark pink lips close around the pastry. Her eyes close in pleasure and her lips tilt up in a delighted smile as she moans, and all I can think of is how she's made that same sound in my ear, writhing beneath me.

I grit my jaw and swallow, and as I quickly glance around to make certain no one is paying attention to me, my gaze snags on Aaron. He lifts an eyebrow meaningfully, and I give a subtle shake of my head.

He smirks, and I fist my hand under the table.

"Wow, this is really good, Will." Tori turns her attention to me for the first time since getting here, and I'm helpless against it. Her dark brown eyes look at me with no hint of the ire that flashed in them earlier, and it makes me almost weak with relief. Which is stupid. What she does or doesn't feel isn't my concern, no matter how much I might want it to be.

"Thanks," I manage to say gruffly.

Devon snickers, and I scowl at her. She winks at me and takes a sip of her wine.

I don't like the way she's looking at me. Or Aaron. If they know something, they need to keep the hell quiet about it.

"Aren't you going to try one?" Tori asks, her expression somewhere between mischief and innocence.

"I had one as I made them."

She holds a pastry out. "That was yesterday."

"They taste the same."

"Maybe. Maybe not. Come on," she prompts.

"I think the woman wants you to eat it," Aaron chimes in, putting just enough emphasis on the 'eat it' part that I know, I fucking *know*, he knows about us. And no one was supposed to.

Holding Tori's gaze, I grab the puff out of her soft fingers and toss it in my mouth. The cream is light and airy, the ratio of it in exact proportion to the pastry itself. It's perfect. Of course it is. I wouldn't have allowed it to be served otherwise.

"Well?" Tori asks, not looking away. Her eyes are luminous.

I shrug. "It's good."

The table laughs, and Mom says, "Of course it's good. If it's not perfection, Will doesn't like it."

My eyes fly to hers, instantly trying to parse the meaning of her words. But she's looking at me fondly as she says it, no hint of anger or disappointment. Or betrayal.

"Maybe we should call you Mr. Perfect, then," Devon teases, and I tense.

"Oh, I'm sure just Will is plenty," Tori says, smiling broadly at me. It seems like it's her version of a peace offering, but I'm not sure, and I don't know how to respond. So I do what I always do and stay quiet.

Price laughs and doles out another round of the pastry, and as soon as I think it's socially polite to do so, I scoot back from the table and say, "Kitchen needs cleaning."

"Not yet," Aaron says. "Presents first."

"Then you can clean the kitchen as much as your little obsessive heart desires," Price quips.

I sigh. There's no point in arguing with them. "Fine."

Everyone gets up from the table, leaving the table as it is. My hands itch to clear it. At the very least, can't we at least grab the plates and napkins? And maybe wipe it down?

Tori's hand lightly touches my arm, and I nearly jump out of my skin. "I'll get the plates," she says quietly.

I stare at her. "You don't have to do that."

She gives me a look of understanding. The same kind she gave me in high school. "I know."

I won't let her do that for me. I let her back then, and look how that turned out. So I shake my head. "No. I'll do it in a little while. You're a guest."

Her eyes dim a little at the word, and I turn away from her before I get caught up in something I can't be.

I settle in the living room with the rest of my family, still seeing places I could have made the decorations look a little better, a little straighter or cheerier somehow. But overall I'm happy with it. There's a ten-foot pre-lit Christmas tree that's giving off a soft multi-colored glow, with a giant red velvet bow sitting on top and ribbons of red velvet running down the tree. Red and silver ornaments dot the tree. The fireplace and mantle are also decorated with real pine boughs, and little scenes depicting holiday traditions around the world are placed throughout the bottom level of the house. Soft sounds of holiday music come from the nearly unseen speakers beneath the television.

Mom bends to the tree to get the presents, but Aaron stops her with a light hand on her arm and a smile. They exchange words I can't hear, but it's obvious the two of them are getting along better than ever. Price has always been easy with Mom, but that's his nature. He loves easily and is easily loved. Nights like this, when I can see how the family I wanted so desperately to be happy is *actually* happy, make it worth what I did before.

I was the one who made Mom leave. It's our dirty little secret, and one we never talk about. I was sixteen years old, and I'd had it. I was tired of listening to her fight with Dad, tired of finding bottles of vodka squirreled away in places that Aaron or Price could find, tired of her being drunk or sad all the time. I absolutely blamed her for it, too. I didn't understand that she had depression and was an alcoholic. I certainly didn't understand that those weren't things she could control; that they were each their own horrible disease, so I kicked her out. Dad never knew that I was the one who told her to leave. He thought it was Mom's idea. And later, when Price found out, Mom and Dad acted like I had nothing to do with it. When Aaron and Mom had their meeting at the Daily Dose, I thought for sure she'd give my brothers the whole truth, but she didn't call me out.

"Catch!"

I jerk my head up in time to see a wrapped bundle fly through the air at my face. I grab it, scowling at Price.

He smiles and turns back to the tree to help Aaron, and I realize with a start that Tori isn't in here. I jerk to standing, the present falling to the floor, and leave to find her.

Of course she's in the kitchen, doing exactly what I told her not to do. "Tori."

She looks over her shoulder from where she stands at the sink. "Will."

I'm at her side in an instant, crowding into her space to reach around her and slam the faucet handle down. I can't stop the hand that goes to her waist any more than I can stop the sun from rising, and when I hear the soft inhale she makes in response, the one that tells me she's just as affected by it as me, I want to growl like a fucking caveman. *Mine.*

She's not mine.

But because I'm an asshole who doesn't know what's good for him, I let my nose drop into her hair, inhaling the scent of her and letting myself have one second of not being in my head.

She pushes me back. "What are you doing?" she hisses.

"I told you to leave all this." My voice is scratchy.

"I don't give a shit," she sasses back. "I don't have anything else to do and—"

"You belong in the living room," I say.

She stops, surprise flickering across her face. "What?"

"We're all in there. You should be, too."

Her eyes soften. "Will."

I pull my hand off her waist and force myself back. "Come on."

She searches my face, looking for who knows what, but whatever she sees must convince her. That, or she's finally tired of arguing with me for one damn night. She dries her hands and gestures. "You first."

"No."

She smirks. "Always have to be in control," she mutters, making certain to slide her body against mine as she walks to the living room.

I watch her ass all the way there.

I don't miss how Mom's eyes light up when Tori enters the room, and dogs everywhere can hear the squeals of delight that Devon, Jodi and Ceci make. I sit in the lounge chair while they pull her onto the giant couch between them, shoving Price and Aaron to the edges enough that Aaron gives up and sits on the smaller loveseat with Mom, while Price just snuggles that much closer to Jodi. Rick and Ceci's dad are on the other couch and the twins are tearing into their remaining presents in the center of the room, ignoring everyone.

"Open your presents, asshole," Price says to me.

He knows I hate this shit. It's exactly why he does it. But I also know that the entire room is on his side, and I don't feel like having them all gang up on me any more than they already do. I grab the first present, from Mom. I can't stop the way I inspect it, looking for any signs that she's fallen off the wagon. I don't know what I expect to find. The paper is thin and cheap, and there's no bow or even a tag; she's written my name on it in black marker. My throat tightens at the sight of her handwriting, and I will it to go away. I bet I was ten the last time I got a wrapped present from her.

I open it. It's a plain, light-blue t-shirt, but it's the softest material I think I've ever felt, and when I check the size tag, I'm surprised to see that it might actually fit me.

"I know it's not much, but it'll be great with your eyes," Mom says, a self-conscious smile on her face.

I swallow the emotion stuck in my throat. "Thank you," I say, hoping that the gruffness isn't misunderstood for anger like it usually is.

Her smile broadens. "You're welcome."

The silence that had seemed to descend lifts, and the attention finally drifts away from me.

Except for Tori. I glance at her, unable to keep my eyes off her for more than ten seconds, and she's looking at me with an expression I haven't seen since high school. It's gentle and warm.

And I don't need any of it.

TORI

I LOVE NEW Year's Eve. The glitz and glam of it if I'm going out, or the terrible cheesiness of it if I stay home and flip through the various celebrations on the television. Tonight, it's a combination of both, because it's a girls-only gathering at Jodi's house across the street since all the brothers are on duty and Ceci's husband, Rick, is watching the twins. And if across the street isn't a wonderful location, then I don't know what is. So even though I'm sorely tempted to keep on my leggings and sweatshirt, I'm putting on a cute silver crop top to go with my red satin high-waisted pants. And fuzzy socks in Uggs, because hey, it really is just the girls at Jodi's house.

Satisfied with my makeup and hair, I head downstairs to the kitchen, saying hello to one of the other guests rummaging around the snack basket on the table. She smiles back.

"Where do you keep the good stuff?" the woman asks.

I snicker. "I think that depends on your definition of the good stuff," I say. "What are you after?"

"Chocolate," comes the answer. "Candy bars, M&M's, that sort of thing. I'm sure you know where they're squirreled away."

My heart thuds at the unintended inference. Because I should have found a place of my own at this point, but if I did that, then I wouldn't have regular access to the kind of soul-altering sex I'd had with Will last night. And can't bring myself to willingly step away. This dance he and I are doing is one of willful ignorance.

Ha. Will. Full.

I was *certainly* full of Will last night. The way he'd thrust into me from behind, hips swirling as he'd fisted my hair and whispered how my pussy was the sweetest thing he'd ever had…like I'm not going to keep staying here.

The man's cock is worth every penny.

I don't even blush as I head to the pantry to find "the good stuff" for her. Will hates the sweets—no way will he put them in his incredible body—but Price keeps it fully stocked and I've been known to ransack the pantry every now and then. Turning back, I dump some goodies into the basket.

"Thanks," she says, grabbing a pack of regular M&M's and a trail mix. "You live here, right?"

"In Talladega? Yes."

"No, here. The inn. The way you and Mr. Joseph look at each other is enough to set some place on fire," she jokes.

I try to keep the look of shock off my face, but there's a reason I've always lost at poker. "I'm just a guest."

Just a guest. God knows the man likes to remind me regularly.

Maybe I should get him to say that while he fucks me.

The woman chuckles and grins at me knowingly. "If you say so. Thanks for this," she says, lifting the candy in a salute before turning away. "Happy new year!"

"Happy new year," I call back, then set about grabbing what I'd come in here for in the first place: a charcuterie board to end all charcuterie boards. I may not be the best cook, but I can appetizer my way into heaven. And if you give me some cured meats and delicious dairy products, then step aside, because I'm about to make everyone's dreams come true.

I pull the board out, happy to see that my note on the plastic wrap about not touching it or suffering the wrath of the woman on the second floor managed to work. Then I grab the chilled bottles of wine and champagne, throw them in my tote, and make my way across the street.

I have to laugh as I step outside. The two houses' exteriors are both done up in lights, but it's obvious which brother was in charge of the B&B versus the house across the street. The inn's lights are a crisp white, and I bet if I looked I'd find that they were hung perfectly, not even a millimeter's difference in height around the porch and frame of the house. The porch itself is beautifully decorated for daytime, with boughs of pine and red velvet ribbon draped across the railing and a ribbon-trimmed wreath for every window. It's the picture of classic simplicity.

Price's house, on the other hand, looks like an entire company of elves came by and threw up on it. Multi-colored lights trim the house, but they missed a section that even I can see. Plastic candy canes line the entire outside of the yard and walkway leading to the front porch, and I've been around the brothers enough times now that I'm willing to bet Price deliberately made the line of candy canes uneven just to make Will see red a little every time he glanced across the street. Then there's the blow-ups. Five of them dot the lawn, depicting carolers, elves, trees, and whatever else Price could lay his hands on. And up on the roof, slanted just so, is a Santa and reindeer set. The whole thing is incredibly cheery and a little chaotic, and I absolutely love it.

I ring the doorbell and it's mere seconds before Jodi is throwing it open and pulling me in. "Get in here! Oh my gosh, you didn't wear a jacket?" Her blue eyes go wide as she looks at me.

I shrug. "I walked across the street. No big deal." I hold up the board. "I brought cured meats!"

She smiles broadly. "Perfect! Come on in."

The house is cozy, though a little sparsely decorated. Which makes sense, given that they only moved in at the beginning of December. All the more reason why the outside decorations crack me up. "Did Price go crazy on the yard just to piss Will off? I'm dying to know."

The question comes out right as we walk into the kitchen, so I direct it to all of them.

Devon starts laughing immediately. "That's exactly what I asked her!" she says. "You look amazing, by the way."

Ceci grins into her wine.

"He absolutely did," Jodi says, rolling her eyes. "Rather than do anything productive inside the house, he insisted on buying up every random thing he could get his hands on and throwing it outside. Looks like a bunch of drunk elves did it."

I snort. "Precisely. Charcuterie board?" I lift it in question.

I'm met with an enthusiastic cheer, and in no time at all we're digging in and chatting away. It's the first time I've really gotten to hang out with them outside of the coffee shop, and the only difference is that Jodi isn't behind the counter, and we're all drinking alcohol instead of coffee. Turns out, Ceci gets even more inappropriate when she's got some wine in her.

"How many ways have you two fucked?" she demands.

Jodi sputters into her wine glass. "Jesus, Ceci. Do you *ever* have a filter?"

Ceci levels Jodi with a look. "I've been married for years and have five-year-old twins. While I'm happy to tell you that Rick and I have perfected the art of the two-minute shirt-optional simultaneous orgasm in the laundry room, I'd also like to hear what it's like to have hours of uninterrupted time to have your body worshiped. And since you two won't tell me nearly enough, I'm going to ask our girl Hurricane here."

"Hey, I resemble that remark," I smirk.

Ceci toasts me with her wine. "See? She gets it."

"In that case, it's time to start talking," Devon says.

I peer closer at Devon. Her hair is in glossy blonde waves to her shoulder and held back on the side by sparkly barrettes. But it's the mark on her neck that's drawn my attention. My lips curl into a smile as I say, "Seems I'm not the only one who has some talking to do, Miss Thing." I point at her neck.

She blushes as Ceci's eyebrows raise and Jodi acts like she's not interested, when it's clear she absolutely is. "I *told* him you all would notice."

"Hard to miss when you pull your hair back," I say pointedly.

Devon giggles. "Yeah, fine. We went on a hike without the dogs and I..." She trails off, but Jodi picks up.

"She gets hot on hikes," Jodi says.

"*Very* hot," Ceci laughs. "At this point, the word 'hike' will get either of them going."

I grin. "So where's the best *hike* around here?" I ask, leering at Devon.

"Noccalula Falls," she answers without hesitation.

"Where the Native American princess threw herself off the cliff rather than be forced to marry the white guy?" I say incredulously.

"I mean, yes, but that's not really what I'm thinking about when we're there," Devon says.

I snort. "Go on."

"There's a spot behind the waterfall, and it's kind of hidden."

"And you can get all freaky back there?" I finish.

She gives me a mischievous grin. "Yep."

"Okay, enough about Devon and the baby Joseph brother. I need to know about Mr. Scary Stern Daddy. Are those muscles for show, or is he putting them to use?"

"Definitely to use," I answer. "No hikes at this point, and

we're limited to the bedroom since there are other people there, but that man throws me around like I'm a rag doll."

They all stay quiet.

"Oh. You want more?" I ask.

"You're the one with the whole 'friends with benefits' thing happening so yes, we want details of the benefits," Ceci says. "Unless there's more to it than just benefits?"

I freeze, but before she can jump on my obvious stalling, Jodi says, "I can't decide if it's weird to hear about my boyfriend's brother or not."

The three of them have a side tangent about the concept while I stew. I want more than just friends, and at the same time, it's terrifying. I can't open myself up like that. For god's sake, I alternate between wanting him buried so deep inside me I can't remember my name, and wanting to throttle him for being so closed-off and cold. That can't be love, right?

Outside the bedroom, I can feel him watching every move I make. And I fucking *preen* under it like a damn cat, tiptoeing along a windowsill and twitching her tail in triumph at the dog on the other side of the glass that can't get to her. It's never stopped since that very first day, when I wanted to rub myself against him and leave my scent on his beautifully massive body.

But when we're in the bedroom? Forget about it. He's an entirely different person, vast and wide, an ocean of intensity that I want to dive into and explore. I'm desperate to know every part of him, to explore the deepest parts of him and return victorious. And isn't that some shit. I am all up in my feelings about him, and they keep growing, and it's not okay. I don't want to feel something so deep.

"Hello?" Jodi waves her pale hand in front of my face. "Did we lose you?"

"I'm here," I say weakly.

Ceci's lips curl up. "She's about to admit to what I told her would happen."

I shove a cube of pepper jack cheese in my mouth, needing the soft bite of spice to focus me. I level my best Will Joseph glare at her. "Shut up. I am not."

Ceci starts laughing. "She likes him."

Jodi claps. "This is amazing!"

I point at Jodi. "No. This isn't amazing. This is terrible. We're not even *friends* with benefits. We just have benefits." I sit up straight. "Nope. I have my resolution for the new year. New Year, New Tori, and it's that I will not catch feelings for that man."

"Too late," Ceci says, and pops a grape between her teeth.

She's right, but I'm going to fight this. "Shut your mouth."

Devon snickers and Jodi looks ecstatic.

"Admit it," Ceci presses.

"Can we talk about something else? Please?" I beg.

"Ooh!" Jodi says. "I heard that Larry was going to be able to finish getting the studio ready this week, right?"

Now *that* was something to be excited about. I lift my wine glass in a toast to the subject change. "Yes! We've got almost everything ready. The Pilates equipment arrived but it's gotta be set up. Everything's painted and things are nearly finished," I gush.

The night moves on, and soon enough, we're watching the ball drop in New York, then it's midnight here, and then it's two hours later and we're dancing to country music, which is terrible, but everyone got their thirty minutes and this is Ceci's... and we know that no one argues with Ceci. Even though her music choice is terrible.

I giggle and fall onto the couch, exhausted, happy, still a little drunk but heading towards sobriety. The other three keep dancing, and I can feel their contentment. Their lives are all on track, despite having gone off the rails in one way or another, and I'm envious. I want what they have, want to feel that kind of safety. But maybe that's just not for me. Maybe I'm not built for safety; just the very chaos that everyone sees.

The song ends and I stand, ready to head home. I share hugs with all of them, shove my feet back into my Uggs, and step into the night.

I cross the street but stop on the sidewalk on the other side, looking up and taking in the stars in the cloudless sky. A half-moon sits prettily over to the side, and the Orion constellation shines bright above me, arcing towards the right of the night sky. I breathe, inhaling the serenity that the constellation always provides. I can't explain it, only that there's something about looking up at it. Maybe it's because Orion is the only constellation I know. Or maybe it's because he's there every fall and winter, no matter what. He's consistent, and I'm very much not.

Maybe that's what my resolution needs to be. To be less chaotic. Not that I even know what that would entail. But I can try.

I shiver, the lack of jacket finally getting to me in the thirty-degree night, and head to the door. I'm quiet as I let myself in, the only sound the snick of the door closing behind me. I take another deep breath, new Tori in, old Tori out. New year, new beginnings, all that stuff.

I round the corner and jump at least five feet in the air.

Because Will is sitting on the stairs in the dark.

"Seriously?" I hiss, my hand on my frantic heart. "You look like a deranged Grinch!"

He says nothing, his muscled arms resting on bent knees, his hands clasped lightly, his eyes devouring me. There's just enough light from the night lights strategically placed throughout the downstairs and upstairs that he's lit up like an avenging angel of darkness, his dark locks falling into his eyes as they scan each part of me, and the heat of want settles low in my belly at the sight of him. I command my body to get ahold of itself.

He finally meets my gaze. "Yes. Seriously." He sounds tired.

Every instinct I have is screaming to go to him, to run my fingers through his silky hair, to smooth the line that's almost permanently etched between his brows and only goes away when we're alone in his bedroom. But I stand firm. Because if my resolution is to be less chaotic, then it means I need to lock down my dumb heart.

It pisses me off. I broke up with him in high school to avoid it, and since then, no man has ever been worth the trouble. Ever. But then I come home and there he is again. Will fucking Joseph, King of Grumpy Glares, ready to flay my heart open with one well-placed growl.

But tonight, he's not glaring. No, he's looking at me like I'm the one he's come to Earth for. And since I don't know what to say next, I take a page out of his book and stay silent.

"You didn't wear a coat," he says.

"No, I didn't."

"It's cold."

"It was across the street. Pretty sure I can handle it."

He jerks his chin down, a quick nod, and stands so quickly I nearly jump again. He fists his hands and relaxes them, and the heat in my belly goes lower, settling into a deep ache between my legs. Him and his fucking fists are going to ruin me. He's standing there, feet planted wide, something like anguish on his face as he looks at me, and all I can do is stare up at him and fight the urge to drop to my knees and ask him to let me worship him. Because apparently I need to add "masochistic" to my list of qualities to work on.

He starts down the stairs. "Just needed to make sure you got home okay," he grumbles, angling his body to step around me as his feet hit the bottom floor.

I catch the scent of something sharp and biting. Fire. A gasp comes out of me, unbidden, and I grab his biceps. Trying hard to ignore its bulk under my palm, I say, "But are *you* okay?"

His eyes glint, and he turns away. "I'm fine."

Goddammit. "Will." I don't let go of him, and I feel how he stiffens.

"What."

I sigh. "Turn around. Look at me."

He exhales loudly, as if he, too, is just as annoyed with this situation as I am. But he turns, and my hand, the betrayer that it is, loosens but stays in place so that now it's on his ribcage, and it won't move, completely ignoring the part of me that tells it to.

"Talk to me," I command.

His eyes flash in the dim light. "You don't want to talk, Tori," he sneers, and the implication that I only want sex from him is clear.

I jerk my hand away, my heart fracturing at his words. "Fuck you, Will." I step away, infuriated with him and the tightness in my throat. I'm an idiot.

"Tori. Wait."

I don't, bounding up the steps.

"Victoria. Please."

The words stop me in my tracks. He's never said either of them.

I turn.

He stares up at me, the very picture of misery. "I'm...sorry," he bites out.

I want to laugh. It's clear he's not said those words in quite some time.

A muscle ticks in his jaw. "It's been a long night, and it's reminded me that, *fuck*, I don't—I don't want to do it anymore."

I slowly walk back down the stairs, suspecting I know what he means. If anyone knows what it's like to hit a wall like this, it's me. But I don't think he's ever allowed himself to say it out loud. "Don't want to..."

"Be a firefighter." He meets my gaze, and I read entire galaxies of hurt and frustration.

There's so much he's not saying. So much he's not going to say. Not to me, anyway, and certainly not tonight.

He drops his head, his hands on his hips, and if I didn't know better I'd think he was going to cry. "So I just needed to be sure you were okay," he says, still looking at the floor.

I shouldn't want to fix him. Hell, I *can't* fix him. But that knowledge doesn't stop me as I close in on him and wrap my arms around his waist to tuck myself against his chest. He stiffens.

"You don't want this," he says.

"Don't tell me what I want and don't want," I retort softly. Because I want him. So much it steals my breath.

He squeezes his eyes shut, his whole body taut, his hands still fisted on his hips, and I can't handle it. I cup his jaw. "What do you need, Will?"

His eyes open and spear into me. He's wide open, giving me access to everything he's feeling, and my entire body erupts in goosebumps in response.

Say something, I urge silently. I hold my breath and wait.

"I need it to stop," he says gruffly. "Just for tonight. Please. Get me out of my head."

Relieved, I exhale. "Anytime, Will. I'll give you whatever you need any—"

His mouth crashes onto mine in a bruising kiss and stops my words. I feel him pour into me, and I take it. I take all of it, opening myself up, and I'm certain I'll drown in it. In him. But I want to. I've never wanted anything more, and as I kiss him, I hope he can feel what I don't know how to put into words.

He hauls me up and I wrap my legs around his waist. He turns us to his bedroom, and once we're there, he keeps me held in one arm but uses his other hand to fist my hair and yank it to the side, exposing my neck for him. He descends, biting so hard I jerk, my hips rolling, my center shamelessly pressing against his belt buckle.

He lifts his mouth to my ear. "This isn't going to be gentle."

I chuckle darkly. "When is it ever, big guy?"

And as he strips me, the emotion pouring off him, I try really fucking hard to keep my heart in check.

I fail.

Spectacularly.

WILL

I'M IN LINE with Aaron at Daily Dose when a tiny finger taps me on the butt. I turn, and it's Eva, one of Rick and Ceci's twins.

"My mom says you should buy us hot chocolate," Eva says. "To help keep away the chill from all the ice outside."

"There's no ice yet," I say, but the little girl just stares up at me.

Aaron snorts in amusement, and I look over to where Eva came from. Sure enough, there's Ceci and Devon, along with the other twin Luke. Tori's not with them, so I assume she's upstairs teaching a class in the studio. Maybe Pilates people aren't scared away by the threat of ice. The studio's been open for a week, and I can't help the way my gaze sweeps toward the stairs that lead toward it. When I glance back at the table, Ceci smirks knowingly at me.

I nod at Eva. "Sure thing."

She smiles and palms a lock of white-blond hair out of her eyes. "Thanks, Mister Will."

"She wasn't fazed in the least by your face," Aaron says, chuckling.

"She's known me her whole life," I counter. "And have you seen her dad? Rick isn't winning any congeniality awards."

Aaron raises his eyebrows and chuckles in response. "Wow, Will, you're downright chatty this morning."

"Fuck off," I mutter, and we step up to order.

Darius gives me his usual once-over, which I'm so used to at this point that I think I might be more worried if he *didn't* do it. "Hey, Will," he says with a smile. "Your usual?"

"Add two of the hot chocolates for Luke and Eva," I say. Then I smile at him, just to mess with him.

Sure enough, his eyes widen and he nearly stutters the total at me. I keep my face impassive, but inwardly I laugh. Darius is a good guy.

"Hang on," Aaron says. "He's paying for me and we're getting the station a dozen muffins and some lemon squares."

I look at Aaron. "No, I'm not."

"Yes, you are. You lost the bet."

I grunt. "I didn't agree to that bet." More like I'd not been paying attention when Chief was blathering because my head was filled with Tori and thoughts of what I'd do to her the next time I got her in bed, and before I knew what was happening, I was agreeing to the wager and then promptly losing it.

He grins. "Too bad. Chief says you're paying, then you're paying."

I hand my card to Darius and mutter, "Fucking ridiculous."

Aaron laughs even louder. "More like perfect. The bet was for you to go a whole day without growling or grunting, and you did it five minutes later."

I stay silent, taking my card and black coffee from Darius without comment.

Jodi hands the pastry box to Aaron and I pivot to leave, but she calls me back. "Take these to Eva and Luke?"

I exhale a sigh for patience, then deliver the tiny cups of sugar topped with more sugar to the twins.

"Thanks, Mister Will!" they say in unison, their legs swinging as they wiggle on the seats.

I grunt.

"Thanks, Will," Ceci says.

Aaron joins me at the table and leans down to kiss Devon. I avert my eyes, not interested in seeing it and also not pleased with the twinge it produces in my chest. Whatever this is with Tori, it's getting worse, and I need it to end. It *has* to end. I can't let myself fall the way I'm falling. I've avoided her all week, figuring the distance will stop my feelings cold. All it's done is make me grouchy and more on edge than usual.

"How's business at the inn?" Ceci asks.

"Fine."

She grins. "Tori still there?"

I stare at her. She knows Tori is still there. She's only asking because she caught me looking at the stairs, and *dammit* I just did it again.

Ceci's grin broadens. "Thought so."

"I'm leaving," I tell Aaron, and make my way back to the station, my feet crunching on the giant rocks of salt strewn along the sidewalk. I doubt the storm system is going to be as bad as the weather guy made it sound, but I made sure Chief had our crew salt down all the sidewalks within a three-block radius of the station just in case. Ice isn't anything to play around with. The city doesn't have a salt truck, so unless they asked a bigger city like Birmingham to come down here, then we're up a creek. Then again, the race track might have some.

I shake my head. Now that I'm no longer the assistant fire chief, those details aren't my job to worry over. And I never wanted that gig anyway, so thank god my brother took it.

Back at the station, Chief gloats over the pastry like he just won an Olympic sport. "Ah, victory," he says, snagging a lemon square and eating half of it in one bite. Powdered sugar covers his mustache as he says, "Did you see Tori while you were there?"

"Does it matter?"

His eyes gleam with satisfaction. "Just curious. Maybe we should see if she'll give the station Pilates lessons."

I nearly spit out the coffee I'd taken a drink of. "Wh—Chief, why on earth would we ask her something like that?"

He shrugs. "I just think we need to be more involved in our community."

That's a load of bullshit. What he *really* thinks is that he's looking for a way to get under my skin. It takes everything in me not to tell him I quit. But it's not time. I need to be certain the inn is able to sustain me and Price. Another year, maybe two. The hospitality business is fickle, and I want plenty of cushion for us. Besides, what if someone hurts themselves on the property and sues us? Or the inn needs major repairs? I have to keep working as a firefighter.

I swallow to clear the tightness in my throat. All this thinking puts me back three weeks ago to New Year's Eve. Fuck. That night...I'd been such a wreck. The whole day had been one call after another. People in small towns doing stupid shit because there wasn't anything else to do but be stupid. Not one but two accidents during broad daylight thanks to drunk drivers, a small fire in a back yard full of old cars because kids were playing with fireworks, and then a call to help an old man who'd fallen at his house and no one was around to help him. That one was like staring at Coach all over again, and it was terrifying. That couldn't be me. But at the rate I was going, it was going to be. No one wanted to be with a controlling, mean-looking asshole who'd literally scared kids before, and not on purpose.

Then I'd gotten home to a house that felt so fucking empty. Never mind that there were guests sleeping upstairs—it was that Tori wasn't there. And I knew it because I could feel that she wasn't there. And what the hell was that about? We had sex. That was it.

That was what she'd asked for and it was what I'd been dumb enough to agree to, because I couldn't help myself. But of course, it was more than sex. She pulled every emotion out of me, wrung me dry and put me back together. Because apparently I needed to not only see the train that was falling in love with Tori, I needed to lash myself to the tracks in front of it and let it decimate me. So I'd sat there, waiting, and when she'd come home, she fucking broke me.

Chief is still talking. "How long is Tori staying at the inn?"

I shrug. I can't answer, because if I do, the words out of my mouth will be something idiotic, like *I want her to stay forever and be more than my fuck buddy*, and I sure as hell won't be doing that. It's bad enough I let the thought in my head.

Within the hour, the rain starts coming down in a slushy mix of ice and water. And in two more, the roads are coated with a sheet of ice. I've already heard from Aaron that the coffee shop is closed, which means Tori's studio had to have closed as well. Meaning she's home, safe. I hope. Outside, the world looks beautiful, but treacherous. Right about now is when people start to act really stupid, and I can't think about that. If I do, I'll spiral.

The lights flicker, then go out, and five seconds later the power flares back to life.

"That was a long one," Chief says.

It was. The station rarely loses power, and when it does, it's quick. Like hospitals, fire stations are simply places that can't lose power.

But it's not the station I'm worried about. It's the inn. We have generators so I'm sure it'll be okay, but I pull my phone out to call Price anyway.

"Yes, the power is out over here and yes, I've already started the protocol," Price says when he answers.

I relax by the tiniest amount. "Good." Of course we have a protocol. We're two firefighters who own an inn.

"Looks like it's the whole block, from what I can see," he continues. "How is it over there?"

Chief is already on the phone, probably getting a status update from the chief of police.

"Station's back on, but hard to tell just yet," I say.

Within five minutes, we have full details. Massive outages across the city caused by the ice already, which means it's going to be a long few days. I've already worked an extra day to cover for another firefighter, and I'm bone-tired at the prospect. All I really want is to be in the inn, where it's quieter than this, and where I can bake in peace.

Another hour later, we've double-checked the automatic snow chains on the apparatus and I'm breathing a millimeter easier when I get a call from Price.

"Is the generator out?" I ask.

"Where's Chief?" he returns.

I put the phone on speaker because I'm at the kitchen table with Chief, Aaron, Buck, and Zach. "Okay, go," I say. "You're on speaker."

"The inn is now completely booked and the local hotels are also full," Price starts. "How are the calls?"

"None so far," Chief answers. "But it's only a matter of time."

I tense. We weren't ready for this. Then again, it's the south, so we're pretty much never ready for an ice storm. Besides the power loss, the problems are car wrecks and falling trees. Neither are great.

"Police chief and the mayor are already vying for who gets credit and who gets blame, so we'll handle the actual emergencies while those two act like idiots," Chief continues.

"I'd like to come on in and swap out," Price says. "And before you ask, big brother, I've already put the snow chains on my truck."

Aaron smirks at me. I don't care; let them make fun of me as much as they want, as long as they're safe.

"He's the assistant chief," Buck says. "Probably should be here. No offense, Will." He throws the last line to me like an afterthought.

"Come on in," Chief says. "But I need Will here until you're here."

"Be there in ten," Price says. "Tori's helping over here and said she could handle it."

My spine straightens. Tori has no business doing that; if anyone, I'd send Jodi over there. My thoughts whirl. She'll have everyone doing yoga, or she'll have a giant game of hide and seek going. Or something else ridiculous and headache-inducing. Or she'll break a bone. Or someone else will. How old is that one couple? *Shit.*

"One other thing," he says. "We had to rent out Tori's room."

"Explain."

"She's a softie, Will. Had a family come in and saw their faces when I told them we already had run out of space in the living room—"

"What? Stop," I demand. "What do you mean, run out of space in the living room?"

Price exhales. "It's bad, man. We've got people piled on top of people over here. And since Tori knew she could stay at her mom's, she just offered up her room."

I don't have to look to know that Chief has a giant grin on his face. Because there is no way in hell I'm letting Tori drive in this weather, and he knows it. I don't know how he knows it, but he does.

"Has Tori gotten new tires yet?" Chief asks. "Can't have her on those tires in the ice."

I fight a groan. Chief's meddling ways are getting worse. "I told her to do it two days ago. I made her an appointment at

Johnson's." I don't tell them the way her eyes flashed as she said, *"You're not the boss of me, Will."* And I sure as hell don't tell them what I did to her as punishment after she said that.

But Price disconnects before I can say anything.

A few minutes later, Aaron tips his chin towards the kitchen, so I follow him. "You good?" he asks once we're in there.

I raise an eyebrow. Since when does my baby brother ask me if I'm okay? "Are you running a fever?"

He scoffs, dismissing my clear avoidance tactic. "You looked a little pale in there."

I force my death grip off the counter so he can't see the white knuckles. He's way more observant than he was as a kid. I miss the days when he was oblivious. "I'm fine."

He stares at me. I cross my arms and get comfortable against the counter, staring right back. I can play this a hell of a lot longer than he can.

"Dammit, Will, what the hell's going on?" he asks.

I don't bother fighting my smirk. "Knew you couldn't handle it."

"Seriously," he presses. "You've been weird lately. Even more quiet than normal." He steps closer and lowers his voice. "What's with you and Tori?"

My jaw tightens. "It's none of your business," I bite out.

"Bullshit. You're my brother, and you're my business. I'm way past being blocked out of your life, Will." His eyes are dark.

"Hey, it's my favorite brothers!" Price calls as he walks in and tosses his keys to me, knowing without us even having to talk about it that I'll use his truck since it's already chained up. Then he skids to a halt, his work boots squeaking on the linoleum floor. With his gaze swiveling between the two of us, he says, "What's going on in here? Tension is not good for the souls, bros."

"I need to go," I say, pushing off the counter and making to go around Aaron.

"What you *need* to do is get your head out of your ass and start talking," Aaron says.

I whirl on him. "I have spent my entire life taking care of you. *Both* of you. Not once have you bothered to ask me about shit. And suddenly you want in, and you're pissed when I don't immediately roll over and show you my belly? Fuck off." I shoulder-check him as I push past.

Outside, I stomp to Price's truck and get in, slamming the door and punching on the ignition. Gripping the wheel, I try to breathe. What the hell is wrong with me? Since when do I let Aaron get under my skin like that?

I shake my head. I'm fine. Everything will be fine. I just need to get to the inn and then I'll relax.

WILL

DRIVING ON AN icy road does not help me relax. But Price's truck is huge and heavy and it's got chains on it, so I manage to get home in under fifteen minutes. My heart is in my damn throat by the time I throw the door open. I'm prepared for absolute chaos, with the kitchen under siege and the television turned up too loud, possibly even kids running around like gremlins.

But it's relatively quiet when I come in. The place is filled with people, that much is obvious, but there's no group yoga happening. No hide and seek. Just people. Way more than is probably safe if there were to be a fire, but if Assistant Fire Chief Price didn't worry about it, then I don't need to worry about it.

A voice laughs hysterically inside my head at the thought that I'll stop worrying. I shake it off and nod at the couples in the living room as I walk in to check on the fireplace. It's a gas set-up, one that I'd all but insisted we get put in, and right now I'm extremely grateful for it. The generator will hold up, of that I have no doubt, but the back-up heat source allows me to breathe a little easier.

"Hey, Will," Mr. Thompson nods at me as I kneel to inspect the fireplace. I glance at the couch and see him and his wife, both in their sixties, cuddled up beside each other. He's got a phone in his hand and Mrs. Thompson is working on a book of Sudoku puzzles.

I nod at them as I straighten. They both know I'm not one for conversation. Hell, the entire town knows it.

"We're real grateful for you and your brother letting us stay here," he continues.

"Oh, you're the other owner?" a voice comes from behind.

I turn, and there's a woman with a baby on her hip. She smiles up at me while the baby grabs for a chunk of her hair. Nodding again, I say, "I am. Will Joseph."

"I'm Noreen Harris, and this is Angel. My husband is out of town and he was beside himself at this ice. I've told him we're good, but he made me swear to tell you thank you. Jerry?"

Recognition hits. Of course. Jerry Harris was on the football team with me and was a walk-on at Auburn for the offensive line. Now that I look closer at the baby, his chubby cheeks and bright smile are nearly identical to his dad's.

"Tell him I said hello," I say. "Happy to have you here."

Our neighbor Miss Betty is next. "Will," she says, taking my arm and leading me off to the side, "I know you're probably madder than a hornet having all of us here and not paying, but I just have to say how grateful I am that you and Price were kind enough to open up the place."

I tense at the *not paying* part, but can't be mad about it. Price's bleeding heart probably gave in the moment the first bit of ice fell from the sky. So I manage a "not a problem" to Miss Betty.

The back of my neck prickles with awareness. When I look, Tori is standing at the threshold between the foyer and living room, her dark eyes fixed on me. I read her like a book, seeing a galaxy of emotions run across her face before she finally seems to settle on a tight smile.

I make my way to her and slow just enough to touch her hip and guide her to the bottom of the stairs a few feet away. She follows.

"Thank you," I say, getting the words out before she can launch into whatever she plans on launching into. "For this."

She blinks rapidly, clearly surprised. Then she smiles, her lush lips wide, and it nearly knocks me on my ass with how beautiful she is. "You're welcome."

I fight the urge to gather her into my arms and bury my nose in her hair. "It's just—you're a guest and you shouldn't have had to watch over the house," I continue. The second the word 'guest' leaves my mouth, the smile disappears, and I want to throttle myself. *Good job, asshole. Hope you enjoyed those two seconds of her thinking you might actually be a decent human being.*

"Right," she says, the shine gone from her voice. "Just wanted to tell you that all the banana bread you made got eaten. That was a big hit with everyone. And Price stocked up on some dinner basics before the storm hit, so you should have plenty to work with on feeding everyone. So I'm going to go—"

"No." The word shoots out.

Her eyes flash and she crosses her arms, ready for battle. "No?"

"No," I repeat. I step closer, feeling the crackling energy roll off her and welcoming it like the comfort it is. "Because you didn't listen to me when I told you to get new tires, did you?"

She opens her mouth.

"And because you didn't listen to me *then*, you're sure as hell going to listen to me *now*," I finish, my voice low.

"You can't—"

"Oh sweetheart," I say, letting a grin settle on my face, "I can, and I will. Because your crappy little car's got no chance on the ice. So I'll let you go across the street to Jodi's, but I'll be damned if you're going to drive."

"You'll *let* me?" she seethes. "Since when do you think you get to *let* me do anything?"

"Because it's not safe, Tori, and I'm not joking. So go to Jodi's. I know Price has a generator over there." Boom. Check.

Her cheeks flush with red, and the thrill of the win sends sparks through me. "She's out of room," she says, and my satisfaction takes a turn. "Ceci and her family, including her dad, are already there."

I grit my teeth, because I already know what's coming. My goal of staying physically away from her in the hopes I can stop falling for her is in the toilet.

She cocks her head and a mischievous smile grows. "Looks like you're stuck with me, Mr. Scary." She closes the distance and pokes my chest with each word that follows. "In. Your. Bed."

Check*mate*.

Feeding thirty people isn't hard, but it isn't easy, either. I boil an army's worth of pasta and make three pots of sauce and seven loaves of garlic bread, completely by myself in the kitchen because I waved off the multiple offers of help. I need the focus. Because I'm going to have to share a bed with Tori, and I'm pissed. Or maybe it's not even that I'm pissed, but instead I'm... highly irritated? Angry. Terrified. Frustrated.

Fine. I'm pissed.

But the way she'd looked as that flush had crept down her cheeks and onto her neck, disappearing behind the high-necked shirt she wore...I wanted to know how far down it'd gone. Then I wanted to lick every bit of that heated flesh, and help myself to the rest of her body while I was at it.

And there will be absolutely none of that happening. Thinking I could handle three months of no-strings-attached sex with Tori Welch was the stupidest thing I have ever done. All I can do at this point is hope a row of pillows down the middle of the bed can save me.

I roll my shoulders and will the tension to leave my body, but I know it's here to stay. I've been coiled like a goddamn spring ever since Tori rolled back into my life nearly two months ago, and no amount of stretching is going to change that. I pull out the paper plates, cups, and plastic ware that Price got from his emergency run to the store this morning, and let the ground floor know that dinner is ready. Then I make my way up to the second and third floors, knocking on doors and to alert them as well. It's early, only five-thirty, but I need them all to eat so I can clean.

It's loud and crowded when I come back downstairs. Two kids dart in front of me, chasing each other, and I bark, "No running!"

They skid to a stop, eyes wide, and the younger one's eyes immediately fill with tears. A woman I don't know appears, grabbing both of them by the hands and looking at me with a familiar expression of fear. "Sorry," she says, then turns to the kids and leads them away.

"Was that really necessary?" Tori asks from behind me, her voice low and chiding.

I turn and stare down at her, clenching my jaw. She doesn't understand. What if they tripped and fell? Kids do that shit all the time. And I can't risk them getting seriously hurt right now. This isn't the time. My phone's pinged multiple times with all the alerts the station is getting, so I know what's happening out there. It's not good. We're in a bubble here, and I need it to stay that way. A nice, safe bubble, free of broken bones and gashes.

But I don't say any of that. I never do.

Tori watches me, not speaking. Then she nods, seeming to

have come to some conclusion that's probably wrong, and moves past me.

Hours later, the guests have eaten, the kitchen is clean, the generators are still running safely, and I just need everyone to go to their damn rooms and get quiet. To my surprise, Tori appears beside me with blankets in her hands.

"What are you doing?" I grumble.

"I'm handing out the spare blankets, Will," she snarks. "Get your head out of your ass and help."

I blink. She's right. Wordlessly, I turn and take the stairs to the linen closet on the second floor, and in no time we've handed out all the blankets and pillows to be had. Tori dims the living room lights and bids everyone a good night, then turns and raises her eyebrows at me.

"See? Not that hard," she says under her breath.

I clear my throat as I watch her go, then follow a few steps behind, fully resigned to my fate.

The woman has already pulled off her shirt as I open the door and step into the bedroom. My body constricts at the sight of her bare back, and all I can manage is a strangled, "What are you doing?" as all thought empties out of my head.

She turns, and I swear I should get a fucking reward for not immediately looking at her incredibly gorgeous breasts. But I'm a gentleman, dammit, and I manage to keep my eyes on her face.

Barely.

She lifts an eyebrow. "Changing into my pajamas. What does it look like I'm doing, Will?"

I close my eyes and swallow. "Please put your shirt on."

"It's nothing you haven't seen before, big guy," she taunts. "Besides, I didn't say this was a look-but-don't-touch situation."

I fist my hands and breathe deeply, still keeping my eyes shut and hoping to hell she's dressed by the time I open them. "We can't do that tonight."

"Why not?" She cups my cheek.

I flinch at the unexpected touch, my eyes wrenching open and moving immediately to her chest.

She's still undressed.

In fact, she's even *more* undressed than before. Because now, all she's wearing is a tiny black thong that curves indecently over her hips.

"Christ alfuckingmighty, Tori," I grit out, unable to stop my hands from gripping her hips and yanking her towards me.

She grins, the cat who caught the canary. "Much better," she purrs.

I glare down at her and increase the pressure in my hands. "How is this better?"

Her smile widens at the touch. She likes it, I know she does, and yet I keep thinking that the threat of punishment will be enough to keep her in line.

I can't seem to get it through my thick fucking skull that Tori will see the line and then do a damn *leap* over it, and that no matter what I do, she still wants more. Needs more. Craves more.

So, fine. If she wants it, she can have it. God help me.

Tori

IT HAS BEEN the longest week of my life. Ever since New Year's Eve, Will and I have been insatiable, having untold amounts of acrobatic-like sex on every damn surface in this bedroom and adjoining bathroom every day that he isn't at the station. We're clearly avoiding talking about our feelings, and the sex, in turn, has been insane and glorious. You'd think I would be sated.

You would be wrong.

Because a week ago, he went to the station for two days, and when he came back, something had changed. He hasn't touched me. In fact, he's flat-out avoided me. But now, we're in the same room, forced into the same bed, and so help me I'm getting to the bottom of this.

Because I could not be more pissed off at him.

I also could not be more turned on by him.

I don't know which way to go or what to do, but I need a reaction from him. Hence, the naked thing.

Glaring, he reaches up and grabs the curls at the base of my neck, pulling hard and quick.

I gasp in surprise in one second, but curve my lips in pleasure the next.

"I told you *no*," he growls, "and yet you insist on pushing me." He keeps pulling my hair, lifting me so that I have to stand on my tiptoes, and runs a finger down my chin and between my breasts. He moves it lower and lower, until he's right at the line of my panties.

"*Please*," I whimper, still tipped up, my arms hanging limp by my sides. I'm desperate to touch him, but I want to let him have the control he so desperately needs.

"Please what?" His voice is low, menacing. Hot.

Heaving a shaky breath, I say, "You haven't touched me in a week. Please *anything*, Will."

His beautiful silver eyes glint in the light as they rove my body, heating my skin as effortlessly as if his hands were doing the touching. His thick brows are pinched and he's not shaved in days, giving him an even more sinister look. A muscle ticks in his jaw.

"You want this as much as I do," I say. "So take me. Punish me. Do whatever it is you need to do as long as you fucking touch me, Will. Do I need to beg? Because I'll fucking beg." I'm close to begging for more than his touch, if I'm being honest.

His mouth crashes onto mine and his grip on my nape releases, but it's immediately replaced by his other hand circling the front of my neck. I wrap my arms around his waist and push into his hand, knowing he wants to do it and desperate to let him.

A grumble releases from his throat as his fingers tighten around my neck, and the excitement shoots through my veins.

"Skin," I manage through the kiss he's not letting up on. "Need your skin."

He pulls away from me and reaches behind his neck to rip his shirt off in one smooth movement, revealing the wide expanse of neck and shoulders and torso that I literally dream about. Smooth, unmarked flesh that I've had my greedy little mouth all over.

I swallow and hurry to shimmy out of my panties. In the next moment, he's unbuckling his belt and yanking it off one-handed, then toeing off his shoes and undoing his pants. He pushes those and his underwear down, then stands before me, his hard cock bobbing proudly, his body held in taut control by thick muscular legs I'll never get over.

"Fuck yes," I whisper.

He's on me in less than a second, turning me and walking me to the wall, pressing me against it while his body pushes against mine. He grabs my left arm and flattens it against the plaster, then yanks my right one behind my back, hard, while biting my shoulder. The pleasure mixes with the pain and my eyes flutter.

"You will not say another fucking word, Victoria," he growls against my neck.

I suck in a breath.

"And you will not make a sound," he continues, his breath hot in my ear. His cock presses against my ass, velvet and steel, and need shoots through me. "One word, one sound, and I stop."

"Will, you know there are people about to get it on all over this house," I say, my voice husky.

He smacks my ass. "My rules, Tori. I fuck you my way, or not at all."

I shut my mouth.

He chuckles. "I finally found what works to get you to obey me. And my command starts now—so no back talk."

I grit my teeth. He's a bastard, but fuck me if I don't lo—

No. No way was I about to think that.

He chuckles. "Glad to know that this is what it takes to get you to listen to me." He smacks the other side of my ass next, then soothes it with his hand. "Spread your legs for me, Tori."

I obey, my chest heaving, as he releases my arms and sinks to his knees. In seconds, his hot mouth is between my legs, and I clench my fists against the wall as spikes of pleasure spear through me. His hands grip my ass and he licks up, closer to a different hole.

"You're going to take me right here, sweetheart," he rumbles, and I feel his finger press against it. "And you're going to like it."

Hell yes I am.

I've been waiting for him to do more ever since that first night, but because I can't say anything, all I do is wiggle my hips and arch my back, telling him silently that I'm into it.

Without another word, he pushes two thick fingers into my pussy, his tongue stroking my clit. *So fucking good.* I take a deep inhale and bend my knees as my walls clamp around them, wanting so much more. Wanting him inside me, filling me, stretching me.

He withdraws his fingers, sliding one to my other hole and pressing against it, his tongue still working me. I press back, and his finger goes in. Pleasure shoots through me.

He groans softly against my folds. "Can't wait to feel you around my cock, Tori."

He surges to his feet, his eyes dark with desire as he turns me around and pulls me to him. "Need you," he whispers, his arms tightening as he squeezes me in a hug so fierce I lose my breath. He lowers his hands to my waist. "Jump," he commands, and I do, my legs circling his thick waist as his hands grip my ass to hold me in place.

He walks us to the bedside table and leans down to grab a condom, then holds it up to my mouth. "Teeth."

I bare them, and he sticks the foil between them for me to hold while he rips the package. With that done, he walks us to the chair in the corner of the room and sits down, me going onto my knees while he puts the condom on behind me.

His mouth fastens onto one of my breasts, and my hands fly to his head, pressing him against me and threading into his hair to grip and hold him in place.

I lower my hips and grind against the length of his cock, pleasure radiating out from my clit and his mouth against my nipple, and I want him inside me so badly it almost hurts. My breath comes out in stuttered pants, and he looks up at me as he pops off my breast.

"Do you want my cock, Tori?" he asks, his voice low and dark in the chill of the room.

I nod. "Y—"

His hand flies up to my mouth and presses against it as he tsks. "No noise, remember?"

I swallow the moan and nod, trembling with anticipation.

He pulls his hand away and pinches my nipple, and I clench my teeth, still staring at him. Still waiting for what comes next.

"You want me to fill you up and fuck you?" His hand slides against my chest and up to my throat, resting there. "I'm going to make you feel so fucking good, Tori. And you aren't going to make a goddamn sound while I do it." His eyes darken even more, the pupils luminous in the dim light. "And I love the sounds you make, the way you talk when you're about to come. But tonight?" His fingers encircle my throat. "Not a word. Not a groan. Not a fucking thing. All I want to hear out of you is your breath and the noises your pussy makes as I fuck you. Do you understand?"

I nod, my pulse skyrocketing.

"Up on those knees, gorgeous," he murmurs.

I move quickly.

"Now, you're going to lower yourself onto my cock, but only as much as I let you." He notches himself against my entrance.

I begin to move, but the moment his head breaches me, he stops.

"That's enough," he says, one hand still lightly circled

around my neck. He moves the other to my clit, brushing it with his thumb and then bringing it to his mouth to lick. He grunts as his eyes close, and when they open again, he says, "A little more."

I lower again, but he stops me quickly. He shifts, pulling a breast into his mouth and sucking while holding onto the other with his hand. My pussy clenches at the feel of his tongue swirling and teasing my nipple, and he chuckles darkly.

"You want more, don't you?" He increases the pressure of his mouth and hands, and all I can do is swirl my hips in response.

"Be still," he orders, his teeth on my nipple as he speaks.

Fuck. I stop moving, but if I die, it's all his fault.

"Good girl. As a reward, you can lower a little more."

I move slowly, and he lets me go farther, maybe a third of the way down before stopping me.

"You're going to come *before* my cock is completely inside you, Tori. If you don't come, you don't get my cock."

My legs are burning with the effort of holding upright, but I can't say anything. All I can do is smirk at him, so I do.

His eyes flash. "This is no game, Tori."

I raise my eyebrows. *Isn't it?*

He squeezes my throat a little more, his eyes hungry as they rove over my breasts and stomach. I lean towards him, testing, and his hand smacks my ass, his lip curling up the tiniest bit. I inhale at the smack but don't retreat, and he says, "You like being punished, don't you?"

I want to nod, but can't. So I hope my expression does it.

And it must, because his face goes absolutely feral. He raises a thumb to my mouth, and his voice is even lower as he says, "Suck."

I open and he pushes in, his thumb calloused and not even close to gentle. I do as he asks, sucking and licking his thumb like my life depends on it, because at this point, it feels like it does. My inner walls pulse, making his dick twitch inside me, and I close my eyes.

"Watch."

He pulls his thumb out and hovers it over my clit. "Give me your tits, Tori."

Gratefully, I lean toward his mouth. He tilts his head, but stops a millimeter away. His eyes flick up to mine, half hidden by a rogue lock of hair that's fallen onto his forehead. On most people, it would be cute. But on Will—on beautifully big, thick, mountain of a man Will—it's positively wicked. My breath catches at the sight. What would it be like to have this man for the rest of my life?

"When I touch you, you have exactly two minutes to come for me. You do not move. You do not make a sound. And you better fucking come. Do you understand?"

My entire body is shaking and my breathing is erratic. I'm pretty certain I won't need the full two minutes. Not with as tightly wound as he's got me.

He squeezes my neck. "Do. You. Understand?"

I take a deep inhale, as much as I can, and dare the tiniest nod on the planet.

"Good girl."

He's going to pay for this. I don't know how, but I can't wait to make him pay.

He attacks, his thumb pressing down onto my clit as his mouth wraps around my nipple, and explosions of pleasure streak through me.

Fuck. Fuck this man and his magic tongue and thumb and absolutely fuck his dick. I clench my fists, feeling the crescents of my nails dig into my palm as I fight the instinct to bear down on him. I'm desperate. His mouth, god *damn* his mouth, hot and wet and absolutely everything I have ever needed in a man and of course, of fucking *course* it's Will Joseph.

His thumb circles and presses against my clit, and I can feel myself racing to the edge. I breathe faster, unable to do anything but that, clenching my teeth and pressing my eyes shut.

He squeezes my neck harder, nearly cutting off my air, and—oh god. Oh—

I shatter, my entire body convulsing as it takes everything to stay quiet. He releases my neck and I gulp for air, meeting his eyes and shuddering all over again at the expression I see there. Possession, obsession even, something dark and light all entwined together.

Before I finish coming, he grabs my hips and slams them down, impaling me on his cock. Holy shit, holy *shit* it's never—fuck me he has *never*—it's like his already sizable dick has doubled in length and width, because he's thrusting into me and moving me on top of him and I can feel him in my fucking throat.

"Fuck, Tori," he grunts. "Look at you. Look at you being so good, so quiet. Your reward is this cock. Do you like it?"

I nod vehemently, my breaths coming out with every push of him into me.

"Stay quiet and you'll get more rewards. You'll get my mouth on that pussy."

My blood is on fire. I dig into his shoulders, my entire world centered only on him and the way he feels, the way he looks at me. He's so *big*, everywhere, and it's so fucking glorious that I want to pray and sob and shout. I lean forward, changing the angle and allowing him to go even deeper. I grab onto the back of his head, bringing his mouth to mine and sealing our lips together.

He kisses me the same way he's fucking me: with desperation. As though he needs me to survive. God knows I need him that way. And then he wrenches his lips off and presses his forehead to mine. He wraps his arms tightly around me, locking me into place before he unleashes, pounding into me and careening the both of us to the edge. Our eyes are fixed on each other, and he whispers his next command. "Come for me, Victoria. Now."

It's the *Victoria* that does it. He grabs my hair and yanks, exposing my throat as he sinks his teeth into my flesh, the intensity of his teeth and the pleasure of the orgasm sending me soaring. He groans against my skin, his arms holding me close as he licks and soothes the bite as we both come down. Finally he stills, his breathing just as hard as mine.

I'm about to say it, tell him I love him, but then he speaks, and his voice is steel.

"Get on the bed."

WILL

SHE'S UP AND off me in an instant, taking the few steps to the bed and climbing on.

"Stay there," I direct, then head to the bathroom to dispose of the condom. I nearly stumble when I come back in, because how is she mine?

She's not. She doesn't want you, and she will break you.

I swat that line of thinking away and take a moment to appreciate the woman in front of me. Her skin is bright against the white of the sheets, her cheeks and chest flushed a deep rose from exertion and the two orgasms I've given her. Her hair is a dark brown halo of coils, perfectly mussed from my hands, and as my gaze falls to her face, she licks her lips.

I would do anything for her.

It's terrifying.

I close the distance to the bed and step back into the comfort of control. "Spread for me. Let me see that pretty pussy."

She reclines onto her elbows and opens her knees, showing me the world.

I force myself to breathe normally. The room is cool and quiet, and I can hear the hum of the generators behind the house. I crawl onto the mattress and lean down, putting my mouth close to her pussy. I could live here, giving her pleasure. Looking up, I meet her heated gaze.

"You ready for your reward, Tori?"

She sucks in a breath and nods.

Keeping my eyes on hers, I swirl my tongue once around her clit, then pull away.

She doesn't make a sound, just grips the sheets on either side of her.

And then I feast, diving once more into her sweet center as though I'll own it for the rest of my life. She writhes around me and I let her, and after a moment I push a finger into her. She grabs the top of my hair and pulls, trying to hold me in place. I swat her hand away, then turn back to making her come. I need her utterly relaxed for what comes next.

It doesn't take long before her breaths are coming faster, and I feel her legs tense. I tap her legs in a silent command, and she grips my head with her thighs. I push another finger in, then another, sucking on her clit the way I know she likes, and in seconds she's squeezing her thighs against me so hard I can't move, her pussy pulsing against my fingers as she comes for a third time.

After a moment, her legs relax and I pull my fingers out, listening to her breathing. It's heavy, but sated. I lean over her to reach into the bedside table again, grabbing another condom and the bottle of lube. Her eyes track me, but she stays silent. I trace her body, feeling the way goosebumps rise as I circle her gorgeous tits, down the soft of her belly, and down to her thighs and back up. After a few minutes of caressing her curves, I put the condom on.

"Turn over," I say. "And put those pillows under your hips."

Her eyes flare with excitement and she obeys, her hips pulsing slowly against the pillows. Every move she makes tells me she's ready to come again, and I'm happy to get her there. I push a finger into her pussy, biting back a groan as I lean over her, my mouth near her ear.

"You're so wet for me, Tori. Such a good pussy. Almost don't need any lube, do you?"

She shakes her head, her breath coming in soft pants.

I scrape my teeth over her shoulder, nipping it as I move away and grab the lube. She raises her hips and spreads her knees, giving me access to that tight little hole. My cock jumps, eager as ever to get any piece of her, but she's not ready for that yet.

"You gonna let me have your ass, gorgeous?" I murmur.

In response, she raises her hips even more. I squeeze the lube onto her, then bite one of her cheeks. I slide one hand to her clit, circling and pleasuring her, then knead her ass with my other, sliding my fingers through the lube and pressing a finger into her.

She exhales, and pushes against me, taking more of my finger, already primed for more. I work her slowly, widening her, watching the backs of her muscled legs quiver.

When she's ready, I pull my fingers out and notch my cock in place. "Get ready for me, Tori."

Before she can react, I push in, nearly blacking out at how tight she is around me. "*Fuck*," I bite out. I let out another curse, grunting as I pull out and thrust farther in this time.

A low sound escapes her, and I can't be bothered to punish her for it. I'm too far gone.

"Baby, fuck, look at you," I say, my voice thick. "Look at how you take my cock so well. Such a good girl, listening to me. For the first time ever," I push in all the way on that last word, and blink away the stars that threaten. Holy *shit* this woman. The way her hips swivel, the sheen of sweat between her shoulder blades. "Maybe this is what you need when you run that smart mouth of yours. Taking it so good. You like this, don't you?"

She moans, and even though it's a soft moan and it means

she likes it, I smack her ass.

"No noise," I remind her.

She slams her hips back against me in response, and I chuckle. "So feisty. I'm taking you to the fucking edge, sweetheart, but if another noise comes out of you, I'll stop fucking you. You won't. Come. Again." I pound into her with every word, but she meets me just as hard.

I'm about to blow. It's a miracle I've made it this long. I reach around to her clit, pressing hard, then pinching. She bucks, every part of her tensing, and it's all I need. I explode, doing my damndest to stay quiet as I come, knowing I probably sound like a strangled bear. The darkness takes me for a second, a wave of ecstasy unlike anything I've ever known crashing over me.

After a moment, I come back to myself, pulling out and stumbling to the bathroom to dispose of the condom. In a daze, I make my way to the bed, falling onto my back, my arms splayed wide.

Instantly, she's straddling me, grabbing my jaw with her hand and jerking my attention to her. I feel her pussy, soft and wet, against my groin, and my cock jerks in response. Probably wanting mercy, but I swear to god if this woman wants to go another round, I will pull myself together through sheer will alone.

She stares at me, silently, her eyes practically on fire, and I can feel the frenetic energy radiating from her. I'm about to tell her she can speak, but her grip intensifies, and the pain feels so *good* that I almost wonder if something's wrong with me. Then her mouth descends, and the instant her lush lips meet mine, she owns me. She pours herself into the kiss, pushing everything she's feeling into it, and what I feel from her is everything. Fucking *everything*. It's euphoric, it's wanton, it's angelic and wicked, it's so intense that I feel her in every single part of me. She's kissing me like it's the only thing she can do, and the next thing I know, she's pulled me up to sitting, her legs wrapped around my waist, holding onto me so tightly that her muscles are shaking.

My cock has sprung to life between us, and she grips it in her hand, pressing it against her clit as she rides the growing length of it.

"This is *my* fucking cock, Will," she growls.

"It must be," I say, unable to stop the way my mouth hooks up. "Because no other way would I be this hard so soon otherwise."

"I want you bare," she says. "Will you do that for me?"

I gape at the question. "I've never—" I start.

"Me neither," she says, her eyes searching mine. "But I need this. I need you. And I think you need me, too. Aren't you tired of pretending?"

The air whooshes out of my lungs and I go rigid. She's not saying what I think she's saying. She can't be.

"I'm clean," she says, either not noticing my panic or choosing to ignore it. "Bonus of working in pharmaceutical sales: lots of testing. And clearly you're the only man I've touched since I got here. Come on, Will," she says, leaning close and nipping at my lower lip. "Don't you want to feel what it's like to come inside my hot little cunt? Because I want to know. I want to feel your dick inside of me, and I want to feel your cum drip out of me."

I groan and squeeze my eyes shut. How did we go from me telling her to keep her mouth shut to me about to worship at her feet?

Because I would do anything—*anything*—to see that.

"Will."

I snap my eyes open.

She rises up, hovering right over me. "Put your big fucking dick inside me, baby, and make me see stars again. Own me. Please."

I surge into her, all logic lost, and nearly shout at the feel. So warm and tight.

"Fuck yes," she whispers, settling onto me and rocking her hips. "You feel so good. So big and thick, you're so perfect for me. I'm so full. I can't wait to feel your cum inside me, Will."

I shudder as her fingernails dig into my shoulders, tiny pricks of pain that manage to ground me even as she takes me into outer space. I drop my head against her shoulder as I push into her wet heat, my arms banded around her.

"Look at me," she says.

I raise back up, and she captures my chin again with her hand. Still taking me to church with her pussy, she says, "You didn't answer me earlier. I'm tired of pretending. Fucking done with it."

I thrust into her, desperate to shut her up.

Her eyes roll back into her head as she releases a guttural moan. "God, yes." Then she focuses those espresso-colored eyes back on me and squeezes my cock with her inner muscles. I nearly choke on my tongue. "I love it when you're scared, Will. You fuck me so good when you're scared." Her expression is knowing, and I want to fuck it off her face.

So I do. I lift her off me, flip us over and bend her in half, her knees beside her ears, and I pound into her. "You want to be owned?" I growl, nearly wild at this point. "I already own you, Victoria. You were mine the first time I fucking *kissed* you."

"Just like I owned you, asshole," she shoots back. "Twenty years of this shit." She slaps a hand over my mouth. "Now make me come."

I want to roar, to rage at her, to tell her she's wrong. Instead, I pull one of her fingers between my teeth and bite it.

Her eyes flash and she yanks at the back of my hair with her other hand, forcing me to release her finger. God only knows where the strength comes from, but her legs push at my chest, unfolding her and lifting me up and back.

I pull out of her, and she smirks. "That's *definitely* not going to make me come."

I go onto my back and yank her on top of me. "You want the control so bad, then fucking take it," I seethe.

She laughs, then lowers herself onto me. "Oh, baby," she says, leaning over and putting one of her tits in my face, "I've been there all night."

I groan, giving in. I take her nipple into my mouth and suck as she hisses in pleasure and rocks back and forth on me.

"There we go," she says. "That's what I need. Right there, Will," she praises, cradling my head against her as I work her nipple. "God, right there. See? We can do this. We're so fucking good at this."

I reach my hand between us to get at her clit, knowing that's the magic button, and she moans as I swirl a finger over it.

"Tell me we're done pretending, Will." She sits upright, a goddess over her domain, her lush body commanding mine.

I can feel the orgasm building as my lower back tightens. Even my feet are tingling, and all I can concentrate on is the way she feels around me, warm and soft and so fucking amazing and everything, literally everything I have ever wanted. It's her. It's always been her. No one else has ever come close.

"Tell me," she urges. "Give it to me. Give in. Come on, Will. I have you. You have me, I'm already yours. *Fuck*, you feel so good, oh my god." She tilts her head back, breaking eye contact, her inner walls beginning to flutter around my cock as her orgasm starts.

"Victoria," I breathe, my voice choked.

She snaps her gaze back to mine, eyes wild with lust and something far more dangerous that I refuse to name. "Will. *Please.*"

"I'm yours," I say.

And then we explode.

TORI

THE FIRST THING I think when I wake up is how hot I am, followed by how sore I am. As the memories of last night crash into me, I realize I'm draped over Will's chest, his arm locking me against his side. There's no getting out of his embrace. Not if I don't want to wake him up.

Commanding myself to breathe normally, I take in his chiseled features as he sleeps. There's no tension between his thick brows, and his deep-set eyes aren't pinched in worry over one thing or another. His jaw is covered in thick scruff, almost a full beard at this point since he clearly hasn't shaved in days. Dude could go all mountain man on us if he wanted.

But back to his face. It's peaceful, beautiful and strong. What will it look like when he wakes up and remembers what he admitted last night? Will he regret it? Deny it?

My chest squeezes at the thought of him acting as though it didn't happen. But it did. Boy, did it ever.

The way he controlled me, and I controlled him, never in my life had it felt so...peaceful. Which doesn't make any sense, and yet it makes all the sense in the world. I gave in, and the relief was so palpable, so intense, that my near-admission clawed at me to get out. There was no way I could keep it inside anymore. It didn't matter that I was terrified. It had gotten to the point where it was more terrifying to keep it inside.

So I'd admitted it. Came as close to telling him I loved him as I could. Because I have no idea if this is love. This is...well, if I thought I was chaotic before, then this is a whole other level of chaos. Whatever it is, I want more of it. I want it to consume me just as much as it consumed me last night. I want Will consumed, too. I just don't know if he'll admit it or not.

I've gone entirely stiff with worry. I take a deep breath in, hold it, and exhale, doing it all as quietly as possible to keep from waking Will up.

Speaking of stiff...I smirk.

Yes.

Yes, that's *exactly* what I want to do.

Moving slowly, I reach up with my free hand and move Will's hand up and off me, resting it gently on the mattress. Then I slide down his body, taking the sheets with me and revealing his torso as I go. God, he's beautiful. And his dick in the morning is nothing short of miraculous, tantalizingly thick just like the rest of him. I scrape my nails lightly over his inner thigh to bring him to consciousness, and hear him inhale deeply as he begins to wake.

When he speaks, his voice is rough and low. "Tori, what are you—*fuck*," he breathes out.

Because I've already wrapped my mouth around him, the velvety warmth of his cock instantly hardening even more as I take him to the back of my throat. I work him slowly, taking my time, worshipping his cock with my hand and tongue and tasting the saltiness of his pre-cum.

His hand threads loosely into my hair. "Let me see, sweetheart." The request is just that, a request, delivered in the gentlest tone I have ever heard from him.

I shift so that he can see me, pulling my mouth to the very

tip of his head and circling my tongue around it. I give him the show he wants, hollowing my cheeks out as I move back down his length, taking him to the back of my throat and up again. He curses softly, his hips gently moving with my mouth.

"I need you," he says, his voice decadent and lush. "Sit on my cock. I want to feel you."

I move my mouth off him, pressing a kiss to the glorious divot on his pelvis, then his stomach, and chest, until finally I'm straddling him and meeting his gaze for the first time this morning.

His eyes are luminous and soft, his hands resting on my waist as I notch him at my entrance. His lips tip up in the tiniest of smiles, and my heart squeezes. He says nothing, but I read a world of feeling in his eyes, the color a deep gray in the bright morning light.

I can't stop the small moan that escapes me as I sink onto him, or the flood of emotion that tightens my chest. But I don't look away from him. I can't. "You feel—"

"Fucking perfect," he finishes, thrusting into me. "You're perfect. This is—" He doesn't finish, just stares at me.

"I know." Because I do know. Whatever this is, whatever we created last night, it's blooming this morning. I shiver, goose-bumps exploding across my skin as he rolls his hips.

He moves his hand to where we're joined, pressing a thumb to my clit and sending a riot of delicious tension streaking through me.

I bite my lip, whimpering. I'm so full, but it's not just his cock that fills me. It's him. His expression. The absolute love I feel pouring out of him and straight into me.

"I'm not going to last," he says.

Me, neither. He'll destroy me, drown me, and it'll be the sweetest death anyone has ever experienced.

His voice is rough and thick. "You feel too good. God, baby, your pussy. You've ruined me. So tight and hot and wet. *Fuck.*"

He keeps talking, his hands digging into my hips as he takes over the rhythm, praising me with every thrust.

My inner walls tighten as a heavy, luscious weight settles into my core. "Now, Will," I manage to say. And as the weight lifts and I begin to come, the waves of ecstasy are so intense that tears spring to my eyes.

Will climaxes with me, his head tilting back as he cedes his grip on control for one precious moment, his face a mask of unrelenting pleasure. His cock pulses inside me, spilling his release.

Finally, he relaxes, and his eyes immediately find mine again. "Kiss me," he says.

There's something in his voice, so vulnerable and raw that the tears of my climax turn into something else entirely. I lean down, cupping his face to press my lips to his, feeling his arms band around me and tighten, holding me not just to him but tethering me to the earth.

He shatters me with his kiss, breaking me apart and sending me into the stratosphere. But the gravity of him, the solid surety and strength of him—it stitches me back together, piece by piece. I fall, letting go of every last shred of sanity and logic I ever possessed, and hand it right over to him.

"Will," I breathe.

"Not yet," he begs. "Don't say it. Not yet."

I rest my forehead to his, basking in the warmth of him, letting everything we aren't saying rest over us like a winter blanket, and nod. I want to argue with him, to let the words come and dare him to not say it back, but the tears are tinged with fear, too. What if all of this comes crashing down? What if I take this step, and it all blows up in my face?

But I'm so tired of being scared. I want to change. I want this to be worth something. Want *me* to be worth something. So I whisper, "I won't say it, but you know."

"I know." He swallows, and his jaw ticks against my palm. "Me, too."

I smile softly and kiss him again.

WILL

WE MAKE QUICK work of a shower, despite every part of me that wants to pin Tori against the tile and have my way with her. She's an evil temptress about it, too, because she knows I want to, and she knows I'm almost as desperate to get out of the bedroom and see what kind of chaos the inn's guests have wrought.

Never mind that it's only six thirty and I haven't heard a peep outside the door.

"Hey." Her voice is gentle as she gets my attention.

I straighten from tying my laces and look at her. Has she been talking? I have no idea. Because I've been way inside my head for the past few minutes, getting dressed and generally trying to pull myself together to face a ton of people.

I'm not even remotely close to processing what happened with us last night and this morning. I just know that I want it, and that I'm tired of acting like I don't want it. Want her. And somehow, she wants me back. I can't quite believe it.

"Out there. Do we...?"

I raise an eyebrow. "Do we...what?" Because even though I

didn't want her to say what I thought she was going to say in the bed, I *do* want her to say this.

She huffs and stomps her foot, sweetly exasperated. "Are we together, Will? I know I probably sound like a stage-three clinger right now, but I don't do good with the gray. I need black and white."

Nearing her, I grab her hands and look into her deep caramel eyes. "I actually would have thought you carried a bucket of gray paint everywhere you go." She swats at me and I catch her hand, holding it against my chest. "Yes."

Her whole body relaxes. "Yes?"

I nod. "If you'll have me."

"I want you, Will. So much." Her voice is soft.

My chest feels like it's going to explode, and I take another deep breath to keep myself under control. She wants me. *She wants me.* Maybe if I repeat it enough times, I'll believe it.

"Can I touch you? Out there?"

"There are children in this house, Tori," I say.

Her eyes widen. "Did you just make another joke, Will Joseph? Oh my god, you did. Have aliens abducted you?" She touches my forehead. "Is that why you've got this almost-beard thing happening? Because it's not really you and the aliens got everything right but you have some kind of beak or scaley thing happening on your jaw and—"

I shut her up with a kiss. Once again, she melts against me, her soft curves molding perfectly against my body, soothing the jagged edges. When I lift my mouth from hers, I say, "Aliens have not abducted me. I don't shave when I'm on shift; it's tradition. And things have been a little hectic since I got home."

"And touching?" she prods.

I swear, it's like she knows every part of me already. But she doesn't. And she's still going to run screaming when all my ugly parts are bared for her to see, but I'll deal with that soon enough. For now, I'll take every second this amazing woman chooses to grace me with her presence. "I don't—" I search for the words. "I'm not good at this."

Her lips tilt up and she pulls me down for another kiss. "It's okay, Will."

But I see the way her eyes are just a little dimmer. I know she doesn't like it. I exhale. "I'm not Price. Hell, I'm not even Aaron."

She studies me. "I never said you were."

"I don't have the fancy words to explain it. I just—no."

She nods. "Okay. I understand."

She doesn't, it's obvious, and it's also obvious I haven't explained myself. But I can't even explain it myself. For fuck's sake. I'm messing this up before it even starts.

I turn to go, needing to breathe air that she isn't in. I need time.

"See you out there," she says.

I grunt. It's the best I can do.

The house is quiet, and just as chilly as the bedroom, if not a little more. I start a pot of coffee and check the generators, then return to the kitchen to start work on breakfast. There are a lot of people to feed, and even though I need to go for quantity over quality, I can't help but want whatever I make to be the best thing they've tasted. I have a huge bag of potatoes and plenty of onions, so a hash is definitely going to happen. And lots of flour and eggs, so maybe some pancakes for the kids. I check the fridge for other items, decide on a path forward, and get to it.

A few minutes later, Tori appears. My breath catches and my body warms at the sight of her, as though I didn't just spend the night with her and see her a mere ten minutes ago. But damn, she's gorgeous, those dark pink lips widening into a glossy smile as she strides towards me on legs I'd give just about anything to have wrapped around my head and hips twenty-four seven.

She rises onto her tiptoes and kisses my cheek, and I inhale her scent. How can she still smell so much like *her* when I know she used my body wash? She meets my eyes as she lowers. "You just look so perfect in here, and no one's in here yet. I had to kiss you," she says, her smile soft and knowing.

I feel every part of me soften.

"And now, coffee," she says, letting her arm curve around my waist and trail off as she walks away from me.

It's not long before people begin to wake, and slowly the kitchen becomes a hive of activity. I work without interruption, and it's not until I look up and around do I see it's because Tori has been running interference for me. But it's not just that, I realize with a start. She's actually been *controlling* the chaos instead of causing it. Everyone has coffee or water or juice, and there's a stack of plates and silverware waiting for the first round of food to be ready. The house is warmer, and I'm willing to bet it's because she got someone to ramp the fireplace back up now that everyone's awake.

I finish the massive skillet of scrambled eggs and search for Tori. She appears, practically from nowhere, and has a line of kids with her. "What do you think, kids?" she asks then. "Did Mr. Will cook enough for you?"

They all nod and cheer, and Tori looks at me with a grin. "I'm going to get them fed. Good?"

In response, I open the oven and pull out a baking sheet that's piled with pancakes, and get more cheers.

Eventually, everyone is fed and I get help from Tori, Miss Betty, and a few others to clean up and set the kitchen back to rights. They don't do it to my liking, of course, so I have to go behind them to really get it finished, but I got enough glares from Tori to realize I needed to shut up and take the help. Chief calls, and it's a decent bet that most of the city won't get power for another day. The only good thing is that there haven't been any major calls to the station, and I'm grateful to hear it.

"How's Tori?" he asks.

"Drop it," I warn.

He chuckles. "Seems to me the two of you would be just about perfect. And wouldn't that be something? All the Joseph brothers, matched by me."

"You're delusional, Chief."

"Your dad would have loved to see it, Will," he goes on. "He was such a softie."

I tense. Dad was so blinded by love he couldn't see the disaster that was playing out in front of him, and it was up to me to keep the house running. So 'softie' isn't the word I'd use. Weak. Spineless. Unwilling to do what needed to be done. Those are better words.

Wisely, Chief doesn't say anything else, so I wrap it up. "I need to go," I say, then disconnect.

I turn in a circle in the kitchen, scanning, assessing. Then I check the bathrooms, and the common areas, creating a mental list of things to get at the Piggly Wiggly. I change into boots and grab a thick coat from my closet. I won't need it unless something goes wrong, but I've been a firefighter for too long. The chances of something going wrong when the streets are iced like they are? High.

Tori's in the hallway when I emerge from the bedroom. She smiles up at me. "Hey, grumpy bear."

I raise an eyebrow.

She gestures at my face. "You're all up in your head. Going somewhere?"

"Store."

She brightens. "I'll go with you. We—"

"No." I see her deflate, but I can't do it. There's too much in my head and I just need *away*.

"Oh." She's trying to rally, searching my face for any indication that I'm anything but an asshole, but I don't think she's going to find it. I want to take myself outside and kick my own ass, but honestly, this is exactly what was going to happen.

"Can we talk for a minute?" she asks, tipping her chin to the bedroom and walking that way before I can tell her no.

I shouldn't follow.

I go anyway.

The second I close the door and turn to her, she shoves me against it, pressing her body to mine and threading her hands through my hair to yank me down for a kiss. This woman. She fucking sets me on fire. I kiss her back, wrapping my arms around her and lifting her for better access. She's so soft, and she tastes like coffee and cream, and, *fuck*.

When we part, I let her slide back down off her toes. She cups my cheek, her eyes boring into mine. "What you're doing, Will? I get it."

I close my eyes, wanting to keep her from seeing whatever it is that she sees.

Her laugh is soft, but she doesn't speak.

When I finally open my eyes, damn if she isn't right there waiting. Seeing. *Knowing*. But she doesn't know everything. She may think she knows me, but she doesn't. There are certain parts of me that never need to be seen. "I need to go."

"Let me go with you."

I shake my head. I've told her no already. There's no need to repeat myself.

"Fine. But I bet you don't know everything that we're out of." She purses her lips playfully.

I absolutely know everything. "Yes, I do."

"No, you don't."

"You can't possibly know everything that's on the list."

"The list that you never create in physical form? The one that's always in your head? You're right. But I'm willing to bet that you're forgetting something." She stays close to me, still touching me, as if she knows how much her touch grounds me.

"Then tell me," I bite out.

"Agree to let me go with you," she pushes.

"Woman," I say, exhausted with this. I straighten off the door and move us.

She meets me step for step, walking backwards. "I'm beginning to see why Price likes to mess with you," she says and grins. "It's fun to get a rise out of you."

Heat flaring inside my chest, I stop, pivot, and walk out the bedroom door.

"Will!" she hisses, following me into the hall. "Will, fine! I'm sorry!"

I whirl back on her, feeling every inch the Hulk that Price calls me as I glare down at her. There's no reason for me to be this angry, I know that. But just like the Marvel character, I'm too far gone to be reasoned with. "I am not a play thing, Tori. Price may not ever understand that, but I'm sure as fuck hoping you can."

Surprise flickers across her face as she takes a half-step back. "Will," she says.

"Don't do that," I say. "Don't sound all soft and like you feel sorry for me. I don't need your pity."

She straightens, her eyes flaring. "Who said anything about pity?"

"I need to go."

I walk away, half expecting her to follow and torn between wanting her to do it and wanting her to leave me alone. But she doesn't. Instead, I get a text as the truck warms up.

> TORI
>
> We're out of tampons and pads in the guest bathrooms.

I drop my head. I'm an asshole.

> Thank you. I had them on my list.

TORI

Seriously? Impressive.

I don't know what to say to that, so I don't answer. A moment later, another text pings.

TORI

I guess I always figured that sort of stuff was Price's realm.

I clench my jaw. Everyone always does.

I make my way to the grocery store, tires crunching on ice that isn't showing signs of melting anytime soon. By the time I return home, I'm as calm as I get, with the irritation of earlier having been washed away by soothing comfort of the grocery store. I enjoy the order of the store, the logic of it. No one talks to me. They never do, and today was no different. It helped that it was the middle of the day during an ice storm, but still.

Tori meets me at the truck, bundled up and wearing slippers. Which are entirely unsafe out here.

"Go back inside," I say, grabbing the plastic bags and starting to load them onto my arm. "I don't need the help."

She waves me off. "Take the help, Will."

"You're wearing slippers."

"And they're fine," she says, right as she begins to skid on the ice.

I expected it, and I'm close enough to reach her, so I grab her flailing arm to steady her, then pull her to me. I let myself enjoy the way her chest heaves before meeting her eyes. "You were saying?"

She extracts her arm from my grip and takes a step back. "It was a slip. I wasn't going to fall."

I fight a smile. "Keep telling yourself that."

A grin spreads on her face. "Are we done fighting now?"

"We weren't fighting."

She leans past me, her curves pressing against my chest as she grabs the remaining bags from the truck's back bench. "Yes we were."

I sigh. "Tori. We're not going to fight about whether we were fighting."

"So you're apologizing?" She uses her hip to shut the truck door and nearly loses her balance again.

I grip her arm once more and stare down at her. "Do you have a death wish?"

She grins. "No, but I gotta say, you're really hot when you're mad at me."

I turn us toward the door, still maintaining my hold on her. "I'm not mad at you. I'm mad at your choice of footwear."

"Tomato, tomahto," she says, shrugging.

The rest of the day goes by without a hitch, and I can't decide if it would have happened that way with or without Tori.

But watching how she smiles and talks to everyone, and how every head swivels toward her the instant she walks into a room, I suspect that she's the reason for all of it.

TORI

I HAVE NEVER been happier to see ice melt in my life. Nearly three full days of so many people was…intense. Dinner last night got a little feisty thanks to everyone's cabin fever, and I was pretty certain the inn was about to go all *Lord of The Flies* on us. Of course, Will would have won, and then he'd be in jail for murder with a kitchen utensil, and then I wouldn't have his fantastic dick, and *then* where would I be?

I laugh to myself as I get the studio ready for classes. I may be glad the ice is gone, but where would Will and I be without it? I'm grateful for how it forced me into his room. By the end of every day, Will was a wound-up mess, and I was more than happy to let him get out all that frustration on me. That man's mouth and body, the things he said and did to me…he was wicked and controlling and *addictive*.

It's more than that, of course. His heart is something else entirely. He's not given me all of it, and I haven't given him all of me, either. Maybe this is what it's like when grown folks fall in love. I've never felt anything like this; not even close. What-ever it is, the emotions that pour off of him are weighty and relieved, as though he's carried them for so long and finally has a place to put them.

Price had shown up at the inn this morning for the shift change, bringing with him the happy news that power to the area had gotten fully restored overnight, and we could start checking people out as soon as they wanted to leave. The whole house had erupted in cheers, and I swear I'd never seen Will look that happy outside of an orgasm. And since he knew I'd planned on coming to the studio to give some classes for any who wanted to get out of their houses today, Will had insisted on driving me. He also made certain to tell me about the tires he'd ordered for my car.

Whatever. My tires are fine.

But I'm starting to understand Will a lot more, and my tires are just the tip of a very, very large iceberg of anxiety. I think he could benefit from some therapy, but I'm fairly certain he'd laugh so hard he'd hurt something if I suggested it. And not because he's anti-therapy; more like because he would think that's something he doesn't need. It literally would not occur to him that something like therapy could help.

I roll mats out and set foam blocks next to them, lost in thought. Based on what I'd learned from Jodi and Devon, the Joseph brothers' relationship with their mother is…complicated, and that's putting it lightly. I don't quite have the full story, but piecing together what I remember from growing up, it sounds like Will bore the brunt of things back then. What I don't know is how much. He didn't give me everything in high school, that much I know.

I also don't know if it's my business. I mean, the way he'd balked at just the idea of me going to the grocery store with him was proof that I had a long way to go to get him to really open up to me.

"Is this where I can escape my kids for hours?" Ceci's voice calls from the door.

I turn, smiling. "It's a sixty-minute session, but you tell Rick whatever you need to tell him."

"Perfect answer. Jodi and Devon will be up here, too."

Over the next ten minutes, the studio fills for an introduction to Pilates session. I've been offering classes for a few weeks now, and it seems any remaining ice isn't keeping anyone away. In addition to Ceci, Jodi, and Devon, Mrs. Withers shows up in a sweatsuit and assures me she's done this before, and then a few of who I've learned are the "Mom Crew" from the coffee shop. It feels good to have them all here. I might actually be able to make this whole running a Pilates and yoga studio thing work.

I take them through an easy warm up, and then a basic series of poses, reps and holds. Hilariously, Mrs. Withers hangs in there, but Ceci moans and complains throughout class, the same way she has at every other session she's come to. I suspect Ceci doesn't really want to be here for the fitness, but uses it to get away from her kids.

After the class wraps, everyone leaves but the trio of women I've come to think of as my best friends. I'm not even sure how that happened, but here we are.

Devon's blue eyes sparkle as she says, "We're here for the goods, Tori."

"Spill it," Jodi adds on.

"Or don't, and we'll just harass you mercilessly until you give in and tell us anyway," Ceci says.

"Or wait until I get a hug, and *then* she can spill whatever it is you're trying to pry out of her," comes a deep voice from the door.

I look up and squeal. "Oh my god, Conner!"

He throws his arms open. "Get over here, Trouble."

I sprint the distance to him, ignoring the wide eyes from Jodi and the looks of suspicion from the other two. In moments, I'm wrapped in one of his amazing hugs and breathing him in. Finally, we let each other go and he gives me the once-over.

"Small town living looks good on you," he says.

"What are you doing here?"

He raises a brow. "You asked me to come. Last week. And the week before that. Basically, you have been a bit unrelenting, and I thought now was as good a time as any." He flicks his eyes to the women behind me and back. "Is this your personal army?"

I grin and thread my arm through his, walking him to meet the crew. "Ladies, this is Conner. He adopted me when I moved to Atlanta and showed me all the best places. Conner, this is Jodi, Ceci, and Devon."

"You're cute," Ceci says, giving him the stink eye. "I don't like it."

Conner laughs. "I like you," he says, then he looks at Jodi. "You own the shop downstairs, right?"

Jodi nods, her smile growing. "And you're here to meet Darius."

"Wait. What?" Devon asks.

"So you're not some ex-boyfriend trying to whisk our girl back to Atlanta?" Ceci asks. When Conner shakes his head, she says, "Then I take it all back. I love you. You're fantastic."

Conner laughs, his hazel eyes lit with amusement. "Tor, these three are amazing."

"What do you mean, he's here to meet Darius?" Devon presses.

They all keep talking, explanations and questions moving over each other so fast that no one can possibly hear anything. I put my thumb and finger in my mouth and issue my signature ear-splitting whistle.

"Holy *shit,* that was impressive," Ceci says. "Remind me to get you to teach me how to do that."

"Conner is here because he's my best friend."

"Liar," he teases.

I roll my eyes. "Fine. I thought he and Darius might hit it off.

And I missed him. So I've been asking him to come visit." Then I look at Conner. "What I didn't know is that you'd show up today."

"I texted you. *Multiple times*," he says.

"You did?"

"So what you're saying is, you still check your phone as regularly as before," he deadpans.

"Oh my gosh, so that's normal?" Devon says. "Thank god. I was getting a complex."

"Same," Jodi says.

"We've gotten way off track," Ceci says. "Conner, do you know about Will?"

Conner looks like a kid at Christmas as he turns to me. "Who. Is. Will?"

I hang my head. "There's a lot to talk about," I mutter.

"She's banging the oldest and grumpiest Joseph brother," Ceci offers helpfully.

"I'm engaged to the youngest brother," Devon says.

Jodi waves. "And I'm with the middle brother, Price."

"And Tori's staying at the bed-and-breakfast that Will and Price run when they're not being firefighters. Also Devon's fiancé is a paramedic," Ceci continues.

"I have so many questions," Conner says.

I wave him off. "All in good time."

"And *I* think that Tori's gone and caught feelings for Will," Ceci smirks.

"You'd know what that looks like," Devon elbows her. "Miss I-just-wanna-bang-the-company-mechanic-and-make-daddy-mad-and-oops-I-love-him."

"Mmm," Ceci replies. "Guilty as charged."

"So in addition to wanting to know if she's admitting it's more than sex—because you know, they literally made a deal that it was only sex for three months—we're also super curious how three days of being iced in with Grumpy Gus went." Jodi's flushed from how excited she is, and if I weren't ready to throttle all of them for how they've cornered me, I might think it's cute.

"Tori doesn't catch feelings," Conner says.

Devon coughs. "You haven't seen Will Joseph."

"Nope," Conner says. "Not possible. I don't care how cute he is."

"How do we describe him, ladies?" Jodi says, really getting into this now.

"Hottest Joseph brother," Ceci starts.

"Agree to disagree," Devon says. "But he's big. Like, spends hours lifting weights big."

"Yum," Conner says. "Not my kind of thing, but I can appreciate the look."

"He glares a lot," Jodi says. "I call him Mr. Scary."

Conner laughs. "This is amazing. Keep going," he urges.

"I've caught feelings, okay?" I yell it.

They all stop and look at me.

"I fucking *knew* it!" Ceci says.

I point my finger at her. "Somehow, someday, I'm going to figure out how this is all your fault."

She blows a kiss at me. "Continue."

I sigh and walk to a mat, sitting on it cross-legged. Everyone follows, and in moments we have a little circle of mats for my own personal story time. I blow out a breath. "I caught feelings. I'm pretty sure I caught them the second I saw him again, and I'm not proud of it, but there we have it." I don't tell them I'm pretty sure I've loved him since high school but it scared me so much I've never gone that deep again. I can't see the sense in giving them that kind of ammunition; I'm not a glutton for punishment.

"You—wow," Conner says. "I don't even know where to start."

"Oh, it gets better," I say.

"How can it possibly get any better than this?" Devon says.

"Because we're together."

All the women issue squeals while Conner stares at me, mouth agog. I hold my hand up to quiet them, then explain. "We've agreed to...be together. I don't really know what it means yet, only that there's a long way to go, so if you could *not* post about it on the town's social media feed, I'd appreciate it."

"So..." Jodi starts and stops.

"Does this mean..." Devon begins, but doesn't continue.

"I knew it," Ceci repeats.

I laugh. "Glad to know I've rendered most of you mute. But, honestly—this is so, so new. I know you're going to tell your guys. I get that. Please keep it contained." I don't know how to tell them that he doesn't even want to touch me in front of others. Or that he asked me not to say I love him. Or that I'm pretty sure he loves me. Or that what we have is something so primal, yet so fucking delicate, that I'm afraid to examine it too closely.

"You know, the only way this day could get any better is if it weren't a Sunday," Jodi says, then looks at Conner. "I'm half tempted to open the shop and call Darius just so we could watch you two meet."

"In that case, I'll forever remain grateful that I showed up on a Sunday," Conner quips.

Tori

W HEN I WALK into the kitchen the next morning, I'm surprised to see Conner's beaten me downstairs.

Price smiles at me from where he leans against the counter. "You didn't tell me you and Conner went back so far."

I shrug. "We do."

"Or that you and my brother were dating."

I nearly choke on the surprised laugh that manages to escape out of me, then glare at Conner. "I asked for discretion, and this is how you repay me?"

He grins mischievously, then takes a sip of coffee. "I figured Jodi would have spilled. Not my fault."

Price laughs. "Tori, I'm joking. I've known about you two. I'm happy for you."

I grab my mug from the cupboard and pour the extra-strong brew that only Price makes, courtesy of Jodi's teaching him the "proper" way to make a basic cup of coffee. Obviously, no one can tell Will anything, so his coffee is different.

My mug? I catch myself. Since when did I have a mug?

I should move. That's the only way to save myself from

entire extinction, but I can't do it. Maybe my sense of self-preservation is broken. I love seeing Will's grumpy growly face on the mornings he's here, love waking up wrapped in his arms despite his protestations that he's not a cuddler, and I love being the only person to make him smile. I feel safe here, and more at home in this house than anywhere I've ever lived. Not to mention the fact that Will's room is basically a sex den...

"What's on our agenda today?" Conner asks.

"I'm taking you to meet Darius," I respond. "I have some classes to teach, and after that, we'll do whatever you want."

Conner nods thoughtfully, his brown hair already brushed perfectly into place. He's wearing a pine-green sweater that I'll bet anything is cashmere, with dark jeans that I know are at least five hundred dollars, and driving loafers. When I glance back up, he's narrowed his eyes at me.

"What?"

"Why are you inspecting me like I'm a piece of meat?"

"Why are you fully dressed at seven a.m.?" I retort.

"Well, this has been fun, but I'll leave the two of you to it," Price says, pushing off the counter and nodding at us. "See you later."

As he leaves, I grin at Conner. "He's cute, right?"

Conner waves at his face. "He should come with a personal fire extinguisher. He's not real life. He's like Firefighter Ken or something."

"His job is fire," I say, waggling my eyebrows.

"Makes me even more interested in meeting *your* man," he says.

The smile on my face is almost too much for even me to bear. "He's..."

"Aw, you like him," Conner says softly. "Come sit and tell Daddy Conner all about it."

We settle at the kitchen table with coffee and slices of Will's apple cake and some fruit, and I tell him everything. How we dated in high school and I stupidly broke up with him, how he'd put me in some kind of sex-induced haze, and how that sex turned out to be a hell of a lot more intimate than I'd bargained for. "I love him," I confess.

Conner gasps, his face comically distorted and his hand pressed to his heart. "Really?"

"That was *way* more dramatic than it needed to be," I say, grinning.

"Sorry, I've just never heard you use the L word," he answers. He leans forward, his elbows on the table. "I wasn't kidding yesterday. You have never caught feelings. Ever. You're my impulsive little tornado. So to hear this—that you *love* someone—it's wild."

I nod. "I know. But I do. I love him so damn much. He's grumpy and moody and I swear he communicates more in grunts than words, but…" I sigh. "He's *my* grumpy, moody, grunty guy."

"Wow. You really do love him."

The warmth that spreads over me is comforting, not panic-inducing, and it's such a relief. Telling Conner makes it real. "I really do."

"Then take me to meet him," he declares.

"Before Darius? Because I gotta tell you, Darius is way more talkative."

He chuckles. "I need to meet the man who tamed my tornado."

I poke him. "Hey. There is no taming me."

An hour later, we've parked my car in front of the coffee shop —with fresh tires, because of course Will made that happen— and head down the block to the station.

Chief is sitting on the bench outside with Buck, the two of them gabbing away like old hens while they soak up the late January sun. As we near, Chief looks up and smiles. "Good morning, Tori. Who's this?"

"Hi, Chief. This is my friend Conner. He's visiting from Atlanta."

Chief makes no secret of inspecting him. "Hi Conner. This is Buck."

Buck nods a hello.

"Is Will busy?" I ask.

Chief nods toward the open bay. "He's in there somewhere. Knowing him, he's in the weight room. You know where that is?"

I don't, but I nod. "Thanks, Chief!"

We make our way into the engine bay and I angle us toward the back. I hear music, so I move us toward its source, and sure enough, we find the weight room.

And I skid to a stop.

Because Will is in there, all right, and he's defying gravity.

"Oh my god," I whisper, clutching at Conner's arm.

"That's...holy *shit*," Conner whispers back.

It's hard to describe the absolute insanity that we're witnessing. Will is laying on his back, gripping the bottom legs of a weight bench for stability. And he's lifting his entire body, legs, hips *and* torso, off the ground. But it's not just a straight up-and-down lift he's doing. No, this fine-ass man is snaking his body up, twisting and turning, practically dancing to the beat, pulsing his hips one, two, three times before twisting them back down to the ground and starting over. It's mesmerizing. And the filthy thoughts I'm having right now are...wow.

"I think I just got pregnant," I say.

"I'm beginning to understand why you love him."

"I'm not telling him we're here."

"I'll kill you if you do. We are watching an angel of God."

I snort. "More like a devil, but I get where you're going."

Will is in one of those barely-there shirts that allows us to see all his beautiful oblique muscles, and those fucking tree trunk legs are on display thanks to the almost indecent shorts he's wearing. A sheen of sweat covers his lickable skin. After a few more reps, he stops and sits up.

"You enjoying the show?" he asks, turning to me and almost —*almost*—grinning.

It's official. I'm head over heels for this man.

Conner inhales and mutters under his breath, "I will fight you to the death for him."

"Pretty sure I've heard Darius has dibs if Will switches teams," I respond.

"Never said I wouldn't share."

Raising my voice, I say, "Will, this is my best friend, Conner."

Will rises and a tiny whimper comes out of Conner.

"Same," I whisper and giggle.

As he gets closer, Will says, "Nice to meet you."

"Until yesterday I'd heard exactly nothing about you," Conner says, "but it's good to meet you, too."

I elbow Conner as they shake hands. "He came in yesterday from Atlanta."

Will nods, then turns his attention to me. "How are the tires?"

I roll my eyes. "You're ridiculous, you know that?"

He leans forward and pulls me to him, turning us just enough to give Conner a clear hint.

Behind me, Conner clears his throat and says, "Right. Well. I'll go…somewhere."

As I hear Conner's steps retreat, I raise my eyebrows at Will. "I thought you said no touching in public?"

He doesn't answer. He's overpowering like this, sweaty and brutally intense, muscles popping, eyes nearly black. His scent is intoxicating, singularly Will, and I nearly swoon as he slides my jacket off and lifts me like I weigh nothing. I wrap my legs around his waist, and he kisses me deeply. I give myself over to him, not realizing we're moving until I'm pressed against the cold of a mirror and Will pushes his hips against my center.

I grip him hard, groaning at the sound he makes as we ravage each other. My hips gyrate against his of their own accord.

He stops kissing me long enough to stare into my eyes and growl, "I've missed you," then takes my mouth once again.

My heart. I'm not going to make it out of this alive. "I missed you, too," I say. "But I can assure you I'll be using that visual from a moment ago to take care of myself tonight."

His eyes flare. "Absolutely not."

Still rolling my hips slowly, I say, "What do you mean, absolutely not?"

He nips my lower lip. When he speaks, his voice is deep and commanding. "I mean you're not coming unless I say so. The next time you come, I'm in the fucking room. Whether I'm getting you off or I'm watching you get yourself off. *That's* what I mean."

"Fine," I pout. "But I'm going to need to come a lot."

"How many times do you need, sweetheart?"

I take my time considering, luxuriating in the feel of him holding me. His eyes are almost pure silver now, the way they get whenever he's aroused. "Five," I decide.

The grin he gives is positively sinful. "Six it is."

He slides me down, deliberately running every bit of my body possible over his hard cock, and I palm it as my feet hit the floor. "Can I do anything about this?" I ask, my mouth watering at the prospect. We could get caught.

Will shakes his head. "No."

"That's a yes," I say. I drop to my knees and yank his shorts down as I go, and have his dick between my lips before he can say another word. He's sweaty, but I'm too far gone to care.

"*Fuck*, Tori," he breathes. "The door—"

"Is wide open," I say, looking up at him as I trace my lips with the head of his cock.

He groans out a wordless, quiet plea, his eyes locked on my mouth.

I chuckle. "I know. But I need you to understand how fucking hot it was, seeing you do that earlier. And," I take him all the way to the back of my throat and then back out, "I also know I can make you come in two minutes. So let me." I close my eyes and give him a show, one hand working the base of his cock and the other on his balls. I take him as far back as I can, sucking in and out, over and over, working him.

His hand goes to the back of my head, and it's almost tentative, as though he's asking permission.

I'm too busy sucking his cock to speak, so I nod.

Instantly, his hand fists my hair and he starts to control my rhythm. He shoves my head back and forth, and my eyes water as his dick hits the back of my throat. All I can do is let him fuck my mouth, and in mere seconds, his legs stiffen and he unleashes, his release pouring into me.

I take it, take *him*, all of him, and the act of it is more trusting and more intimate than I expect.

He curses softly as I swallow, then loosens his hold on my head. I pull up his wonderfully tiny shorts as I stand, and he tilts my mouth to his, kissing me deeply. His fingers stroke my cheek, the rough callouses gentle against my skin.

I flutter my eyes open as he pulls away, and can't stop the smile that spreads. Because his face is smooth, unlined with any of the worry that usually plagues it. The dusting of crow's feet at his eyes are still there, of course, making him that much more handsome. And to see him, even for a moment, set down the endless concerns that must cycle through his head and know that I'm the cause of it? Amazing.

"Will, I—"

"I love you," he says.

I squeak.

He gathers me even closer to him, his forehead bent to mine. "I love you," he repeats, "and it turns out I can't make myself not say it. I can't stop wanting to touch you every time I see you. Wanting to be around you all the time. I can't get you out of my head."

Every last piece of resistance I might have had against this impossible man crumbles in the face of his words. I open my mouth, but he's rendered me speechless, and he knows it. He chuckles, and then he smiles, and I swear I hear angels singing from on high while sunshine breaks through the clouds.

"Will," I finally manage to say. My heart twists at the sight of him, how bright his eyes are, how *happy* he looks. And it's because he told me he loves me. *Me.* I am ruined. This big-hearted, loyal, incredible man has decimated every last defense I ever had a hope of mounting in the best way.

He kisses me again, and I melt.

When we finally come up for air, I tell him, "I love you, too."

He stares at me, and his lips quirk. "I know."

I swat his chest. "Seriously? Did you just Han Solo me?"

"You're cute when you get angry," he says, squeezing me tight.

"Is it safe to come in here?" Conner calls. "I hear you talking so I hope so, because I'm coming in." He rounds the corner, his eyes covered. "Can I look?"

I giggle. "Yes, you can look."

He lets his hand fall and takes us in. "You two are adorable. But can we go? I need more coffee, and I think Chief has gotten it in his head that *he's* somehow responsible for coming up with the idea to introduce me to Darius?"

"Sounds about right," Will says, grabbing my hand and walking me to Conner.

And I'm trying to be calm here, but after a minute, I give up and turn to Will. "Catch me," I demand, then jump him. He takes me into his arms and I squeal, wiggling like a puppy against him as I plant another kiss on his lips. He chuckles quietly, and even *that* is so damn amazing that I almost can't stand it. I'm like a geyser, my emotions erupting all over the place with nowhere to go except all over Will. What even is my life right now? The big, grumpy man of my dreams just told me *he loved me,* and he said it *first,* and he's smiling and *chuckling* and, and, ah! Giddy bursts of serotonin are practically oozing out of my pores. I squeeze him tightly, literally on him like a spider monkey, and his chest rumbles as a deep laugh bursts out of him.

Naturally, that laugh tips me over the edge and I burst. "Oh my god I love you so much," I say, peppering his cheek with kisses. "I love you, I love you, I love you." I keep loving on him, squeezing as hard as I can and planting smooch after smooch, absolutely delighted in the way Will keeps laughing.

Conner taps me on the shoulder. His own smile is genuine as he says, "This is seriously cute, but can we go now?"

Will releases me and I slide down his body, not even trying to be subtle about the way I press against him until the very last second. I bask in the look of adoration on his face, taking a mental picture and filing it away for inspection later.

Conner hands me my jacket and turns to go. I back out of the room, feasting on the hunk of man who's looking back at me. My dark-haired broody man. Who loves me.

Finally, I turn to Conner. "Ready to go meet the love of your life?"

He quirks a grin at me. "I think the pheromones are getting to your head, sweet pea. Just because you've tripped and fallen into la-la-land doesn't mean I'm coming tumbling after you."

I wink at him. "We'll see."

Tori

I'M PRACTICALLY HYPERVENTILATING as we walk into the coffee shop, and can't begin to determine if it's because I'm on a Will Joseph high or because Conner and Darius's lives are about to change.

I am convinced these two are it for each other. I want time to slow, and I need a second set of eyes to watch Darius. Because right now, it's taking everything I have not to squeal and jump up and down.

"You need to relax," he says.

I glance at the counter, and only Jodi is there. "*You* need to get hyped," I shoot back. The words don't even make sense, and the way Conner slants his eyes at me tells me he agrees. I huff and grab his arm, pulling him to the front.

"Where's Darius?" I say.

Jodi's eyes widen, and finally I have to admit that maybe I'm being a little too aggressive. Is this what matchmakers feel like? It's heady.

"He's gone to pick up lemon squares from Mrs. Withers," Jodi says. "She said her arthritis was flaring up in this weather. He'll be back. What can I get you to drink, Conner?"

Conner looks up at the board behind her. "I'll have a latte, please."

When she presents it to him a few minutes later, his moan is audible. "Did you put something in here?"

Grinning, Jodi says, "Just Talladega water, Conner." Then she leans forward. "And something just as delicious has arrived."

Sure enough, Darius is approaching outside. His hands are full with a stack of lemon-square-filled Tupperware and he's wearing black jeans with a rip in one knee, Doc Martens, a black sweatshirt that says Y'ALL MEANS ALL in rainbow font, and a leather jacket.

In other words: Conner Catnip.

My best friend whimpers for the second time this morning. "Really?"

I laugh. "Yes, really."

The bell dings as Darius enters, and he does a little stutter-step thing when he looks at Conner. He recovers, throwing a smile on his face as he nears us. "I've got the goods," he announces as he walks past us.

"Yes, he does," Conner mutters under his breath.

"I'll take those," Jodi says, holding her hands out for the Tupperware stack.

Darius hands them over and turns to me and Conner.

"Darius, this is Conner," I say. "Conner, this is Darius."

Conner doesn't hesitate. "Join me?" he asks, nodding towards the overstuffed chairs in the back.

Darius opens his mouth, then closes it, and about a million different expressions seem to cross his face. Finally, he says, "Let me put my jacket up." He whirls away and into the storage room behind the counter, and I give Conner my sternest look.

"Don't scare the poor boy," I warn him. "I want this to work."

Conner's eyes darken as they focus on the doorway Darius

disappeared into. "Don't worry your little heart about it. Daddy's got it from here."

I cough out a choked laugh. "Oh god. What have I just done?"

He glances at me. "You've done well," he says. Darius reappears, and Conner's voice lowers. "So very, very well."

Darius comes out from behind the counter, his gaze trained on the man beside me, and he doesn't say a thing.

Conner tips his head, and Darius leads the way.

As they walk away, I look at Jodi. "Did that seem—"

"Like something out of the plots from one of Price's MM romance covers?" Jodi finishes. "Um, *yes*."

"Good. Not just me, then," I respond.

"As for you," Jodi says, her eyes narrowing playfully, "what's going on? You look...flushed."

I grin. "With good reason."

She starts making the latte I don't even have to tell her I want. "And? You just going to leave me in suspense?"

I'm about to tell her, then decide I want to keep it to myself for just a little longer. I sigh happily. "I will. After my classes."

"Fine, but if you don't spill the story when you come back here, no more coffee. Ever."

"Yes, ma'am," I laugh. I take the latte and head upstairs to get the studio ready for the day. By the time I return, three hours later, the guys are gone.

"Conner said you'd understand," Jodi says, a wide smile on her face.

"Did they *leave* together?" I say. I'm almost scandalized.

"Yep," Jodi says. "I joked that I'd fire Darius if he left, and Conner literally said, 'Perfect. Then Darius could come home with me.'"

"Damn," I breathe.

"Exactly." She points at me. "Tell me what happened with you."

My grin widens. "I'm still trying to believe it."

Jodi claps and squeals. "Tell me, tell me, tell me!"

I lower my voice and lean in. "I went down on Will in the weight room and then we traded I love yous."

"Oh my *god!*" she says, and the women from the Mom Group turn our way. She waves at them. "All good. Sorry!"

I wave sheepishly at them before looking back at Jodi, the smile on my face still so big it feels like a freaking beacon. "I know. I *know.*"

Jodi swoons dramatically before righting herself. "I'm telling you, those Joseph boys are nothing to be trifled with. The instant they set their eyes on a woman, poof. It's game over." She leans forward and lowers her voice to a conspiratorial whisper. "Sure hope you're up for this being a forever thing. Our men don't do anything half-way."

Twin spikes of euphoria and dread bolt through me, but I manage to keep the smile on my face. "Don't get ahead of yourself, Jodi."

Raising her hands in mock innocence, she says, "I'm not. I swear."

I twist my lips. "I don't think I believe you."

My phone vibrates in my tights pocket, so I pull it out. And I promptly swoon.

Will I can't stop thinking about you.

"Did he just text you?" Jodi asks. "Oh my god. Is this even *Will* we're talking about anymore? What did you do to him?"

I giggle and show her the message.

Jodi gasps and whispers, "If Ceci were here, she'd probably say you'd whipped him with a magic pussy."

I slap a hand over my mouth in delight, watching Jodi's face and neck splotch red with from what she just said. Then another text comes.

Will I can't wait to get my mouth on you and pay you back for what you did to me.

Will Then I'm going to fuck you so hard you see stars.

My core clenches. Holy shit.

"Ooh, what'd he just say?" Jodi asks.

I turn the phone to my chest, unwilling to show it.

She smirks. "Sounds like *all* the Joseph men have a dirty streak in them."

All I can do is smile.

WILL

S HIFT CHANGE TAKES too long to come. I need out of here. I don't know how much longer I can take being a firefighter. There's too much to handle at the inn. The guests, the baking. Tori.

I stop. *Breathe.* I can't explain why, but the panic spirals are getting worse, like they used to when I was a kid. I need to remember that everything is mostly okay. It's not like when we were young, when my making a crappy frozen lasagna was the only thing between my brothers and I going hungry because Dad was on shift and Mom was passed out.

I'm not the only one who can handle things anymore. Intellectually, I know that, but tell that to my brain. Tell that to my hands, which are shaking with urgency to get the fuck out of here at—I check my watch—five in the morning.

And Tori. I can't wrap my mind around what happened, can't quite believe she loves me and I love her. What kind of insanity is that? I need to see her, touch her, remind myself that she's real.

I roll out of the too-small bunk and throw on pants and shoes before making my way to the dimly lit kitchen. The station is as quiet as it ever gets right now, but in another half-hour it'll be bustling with activity.

I start a pot of coffee and inspect the contents of the fridge for something to pull together for breakfast. There's some asparagus and red and yellow bell peppers that look like they're on their last legs, and of course plenty of eggs, cheese, butter, onions. Pounds of potatoes are in the old-school wooden box in the corner, so, casserole it is. This is usually Aaron's domain when he's on shift, but he's not here, and the guys will appreciate more than a pile of muffins and a giant plate of scrambled eggs.

My mind quiets as I work, like it always does, soothed by the steady rhythm of chopping and slicing, and the knowledge that what I'm doing will benefit people. I'm self-aware enough to know that I may have started cooking and baking out of necessity, but that I do it now for a whole host of reasons. Maybe it's still out of necessity, only the word has a totally different connotation than it did before.

It doesn't matter. I just need to finish making the casserole and be ready to leave when Price shows up. Guests are happier when I'm in charge, even if they are intimidated by me. Food is better, bathrooms are cleaner, beds are better made, everything is a little tidier.

I hear Chief's footsteps on the wooden floors in the hall before he enters the kitchen. "Good morning, Will." His voice is quiet, and I know he relishes this brief moment of peace just as much as I do.

I slide the casserole into the oven. "Morning, Chief."

He gives me a sly smile as he pours a cup of coffee. "Two words before six a.m. from Will Joseph? It's gonna be a banner day."

I grunt and fight the twitch of my lips.

Chief chuckles as he assesses me. "You've been a lot happier lately. Glad to see it."

I don't really know what to say to that, so I shrug and keep cleaning.

"You know I'm always here for you, right?"

The words catch me by surprise. I turn the water off and squeeze the sponge out before putting it in its holder, adjust the holder so it's perfectly aligned with the sink, then swivel to face Chief. "I know."

His face is inscrutable, but then again, I'm typically shit at reading most anyone's expression. "Is there anything we need to talk about?"

My throat goes dry. Does he know that I don't want to do this anymore? Who told him? But I dismiss that, because *I've* not told anyone, which means no one knows.

He continues, more used to my silence than most. "Because I get the feeling your…interests are changing." He holds up a hand at whatever he sees on my face. "I'm not saying anything else. But let me know if you want to talk."

Another one of the guys walks in, and Chief drops it. But the whole thing leaves me flustered. I've told exactly no one that I'm ready to stop working at the station and dive full-time into the inn, so I don't understand how he's figured it out. Or maybe he hasn't, and he's thinking of something else entirely.

By the time Price shows up a few minutes past six, I'm ready to bolt. "You're late," I growl at him.

He waves me off like he always does. "Relax, broseph. All is well at the inn, and your girl wasn't even awake when I left."

I raise an eyebrow. "Who said she was my girl?"

He grins and gestures between us. "*Our* girls talk, Will. I probably know a hell of a lot more than you want me to."

My jaw clenches. "I need to go."

Laughing, Price hollers as I retreat, "Yeah you do. Don't do anything I wouldn't!"

I pull into the back driveway and barely keep from running inside at a dead sprint. I tell myself it's because I need to make sure the guests are doing okay, but it sounds hollow even to me. I make it into the kitchen without seeing anyone, and pluck up the little note cards we leave for the guests to help themselves to coffee and pastry during my and Price's shift change. I tuck those into the drawer and scan for what to do next, fighting every instinct I have to run upstairs to Tori's room and bury my face in her hair. And then, once I've managed to battle away the nagging doubt that won't pull its claws out of me for more than half an hour, bury my face in her thighs.

"Good morning."

I whirl around, caught off-guard by whoever's behind me, and relax when I see Conner. "Good morning." Then, because he's a guest, I keep talking. "Coffee? I can make you breakfast, too."

"Coffee sounds amazing. Do you have any idea how good you have it with Jodi as a local barista?" He accepts the cup I pour for him. "It's ridiculous. I'm buying up as many bags of beans as she'll send me home with."

Nodding, I continue my path around the kitchen, tidying and straightening, inventorying what needs to be done and bought and cleaned as I go.

"She likes you, you know."

I freeze, turning to meet Conner's eyes and trying not to cling too desperately the hope his words give me.

He's smiling at me. "I've never seen her like this. Like, *ever*. And don't worry, this isn't a 'hurt her and I'll punch your face' kind of talk—I'm pretty sure you can break me with one hand— but I want to be certain you understand something."

I lean a hip against the island and cross my arms, waiting.

"You really don't talk much, do you?" he says thoughtfully. When I stay silent, he continues. "Tori's special. I think you know that. I've never seen her like this about anyone, and it's not like we're spring chickens. Whatever this is between the two of you, she's feeling it deeply. Like, *really* deeply," he says, as though he wants to make sure I understand his meaning.

"I love her, Conner." I don't know why I confess to him when it didn't occur to me to tell my own brother, but the words come easily.

His eyes widen. "That's—really?"

I nod.

He breaks into a wide smile. "Amazing. Just…you've made me the happiest best friend on the planet."

I let a small grin out, then get a mug and pour him a coffee. "Creamer is in the fridge and sugar is here." I gesture to the set-up of various sugars on the counter behind me.

He lifts the cup to his lips. "And ruin this delicious coffee? No way." After a few minutes of amiable silence, during which I want him to tell me everything he knows about Tori but I can't bring myself to ask, he speaks again. "I need to check out."

I raise an eyebrow. "Thought you were staying longer."

He smiles. "I am. Just…not here." His cheeks get a little pink and he looks at the floor.

"Darius?" I ask.

His eyes pop. "Oh. Wow. Who told you?"

My lips curve as I move past him and head to the desk in the foyer. "Lucky guess. Come on."

He follows and we get everything settled up right as a flash of light brown skin comes bounding down the stairs. *Tori.*

My chest tightens as I glance up at her, and when she smiles at me, all sunshine and light, I almost lose my breath entirely.

She leaps down the two remaining stairs and is on me before I have a chance to realize what she's doing. But in seconds, this glorious woman has literally jumped into my arms and wrapped her legs around my waist, forcing me to hold her up by her butt.

I take the kiss she plants on me, inhaling her shea butter scent and sinking into her while trying to understand how this is the life I have right now. How this incredible woman is wrapped around me and pouring herself into this kiss.

"Ahem." Conner's tone is amused as he says, "Seriously, Tori. Let the man breathe."

She giggles as she eases up on the kiss, but she makes zero effort to get down as she smiles at me. "Good morning, big guy."

I smile at her, willing myself to punch through the doubt. "Good morning, Chaos."

Her grin gets even wider. "Chaos, huh?"

"You've met yourself, right?" I tease.

"Seriously, you two?"

Tori sighs and unwraps her legs to slide down, taking care to rub right over my crotch and toss me a mischievous smile before facing him. "Ugh, *fine* Conner. Good morning, and what the hell are you doing?" Her voice pitches up as she clocks Conner's bag.

"Checking out."

I lean down and put my mouth near her ear. "He's going to Darius's."

"You're going to Darius's?" she repeats, her voice even higher.

He nods. "I'm going to Darius's."

Tori rushes him and engulfs him in a bear hug, knocking him back a few steps. "Oh my god tell me *everything*."

I tune them out as I check the day's list of guests, happy to see that the inn is almost entirely full. We may be a small town, but we're a small town with a NASCAR race track and access to some great hiking and lakes. After a few minutes, Tori lets Conner go. Then she turns to me, all smiles and happiness.

How am I supposed to get used to having someone look at me like this? Because I sure as hell have done nothing to deserve it, other than a lifetime of surliness and grunting. "Go out with me tonight." The words are out before I have a chance to really think about it.

"Really?"

I nod, holding her gaze. "Really."

Her skin darkens in a blush and she says, "I'd love to."

WILL

THERE'S FAR TOO much noise coming from the floor above me, and I know without question that it's coming from Tori's room. Not that she's in that room a lot these days. Ceci, Jodi, and Devon have been here for at least an hour, and I'm fairly certain I saw Ceci trying to hide a couple bottles of wine in her coat as she sprinted up the stairs when she got here.

I text Rick.

> Did your wife drive over here?

RICK

Do you really have to ask that question?

Don't answer that.

I dropped her off. Twins and I are grabbing pizza and will pick her up in a bit.

> Thank you.

Rick doesn't respond, and I don't expect him to. My next text is to my brothers.

Your women are loud.

AARON

And this is a surprise?

PRICE

Jodi's even louder when she's under me.

AARON

Really, Price?

PRICE

shrug emoji

AARON

Are they at the inn helping Tori get ready for
your date?

I didn't think she needed help.

AARON

Of course she doesn't. And yet, she does.

What the hell does that mean?

PRICE

It means you're fucked. Completely and totally
fucked. When they pulled that shit with Jodi, I
nearly swallowed my tongue when I saw her.

So this is a thing?

AARON

This is a thing.

Seems ridiculous.

PRICE

You're ridiculous.

AARON

Just sit back and enjoy the ride.

PRICE

That's what she said.

I roll my eyes and click my phone off. And then, because I can't help myself, I go up to see what all the fuss is about. The door is open, but I hear a hiss and a giggle seconds before I get there and it slams shut.

Feeling like a total fool, I knock.

Ceci's head pokes out. "Yes?"

I stare at her.

She rakes her eyes up and down me, then raises an eyebrow. "Are you here to offer snacks? Last time I did this, snacks were offered."

I have no idea what she's talking about.

"So *this* is what it feels like," Jodi says, her voice muffled behind the door.

"Fun, right?" Devon responds.

Ceci's head disappears, then Jodi's head appears. "No snacks? Price had snacks. We didn't take them, but snacks were offered."

I can't take it anymore. "What snacks? When?"

She smirks. "When Price took me on our first date." She looks over my shoulder, her eyes getting hazy. "What a night that was. Anyway, why are you here?"

I shift on my feet, suddenly uncomfortable. Which is stupid. This is *my* inn. I have every right to be here. "Tori," I grit out.

Jodi is jerked back, and Devon's face appears. "Hey, almost brother-in-law."

They all have the same shit-eating grin on their faces. I'm beginning to think Price wasn't kidding when he said I was fucked. "Devon."

"You can't see Tori until it's time for your date. *Especially* since you didn't bring snacks."

"Hi, Will!" Tori's voice calls from the room.

My damn stomach clenches at the sound of her voice like I'm some kind of hormonal teenager.

Devon laughs. "Oh, Will. I gotta say, this looks good on you."

I growl. "What does?"

She waggles her fingers at me. "Whatever this is. But you should change."

I sigh. "No shit."

She laughs again. "God, this is fun. See you later!"

The door is shut in my face, and I stare at it as I hear the four of them cackling.

Thirty minutes later, I've set out the evening's snacks for the guests—of course there are snacks, but snacks belong in the kitchen—and I'm showered and changed. It's not easy to find clothes that fit me, so I have on the one pair of tailored dress slacks I own, and one of only two dress shirts. I feel foolish dressed up like this, and I know the entire town will talk about it later, but I'm taking Tori to a nice place. I want to look good for her.

The front door opens and Rick and the twins come in. We exchange silent nods as Eva and Luke head straight for the kitchen.

"I told them you probably had cookies," he says.

"I do," I confirm. "Homemade chocolate chip. Kitchen table."

He lopes after them, and then Ceci, Devon, and Jodi come down the stairs.

"Where's Tori?" I ask, because I'm an idiot.

They all give me the same shit-eating grin as earlier. "She's coming," Jodi says.

"You cleaned up nice," Ceci says, then turns to Rick as he reappears. "Not as hot as my husband, but you're a close second."

Rick chuckles and accepts the hug Ceci gives him. "Did you have fun?" he asks in a low voice.

"It's about to get even more fun," she says.

Tori appears on the landing at the top of the stairs, and now I understand what Price meant. Because my brain just emptied.

I take in every inch of her as she descends. Her feet are in strappy gold sandals, and her legs seem to shimmer as I follow them up to her knees, where a Christmas-red dress clings to every bit of her thighs and hips, dipping into her tiny waist and wrapping back up and around her breasts. It's strapless, leaving her chest bare except for a delicate gold necklace. Her hair fans out from her face in a halo of tight, dark curls.

I fist my hands to maintain my composure, fighting the urge to throw her over my shoulder and take her to my room.

"See? Fun," Ceci stage-whispers behind me.

But I only have eyes for Tori, who's smiling almost bashfully at me as she takes the last few steps to the floor. I move to her, unable to resist. "You are stunning," I say. My voice comes out scratchy.

She trails a finger down my chest and follows it with her eyes. "You, too," she murmurs. When she looks back up, her gaze is heated. "We should leave before I drag you into my room and have my way with you."

I clench my jaw, images of all the dirty things I could do to her flashing through my head. "Agreed," I manage to get out.

"It's getting hot in here," Devon says gleefully.

"Definitely," Jodi agrees.

I ignore them. "Please tell me you have a coat."

"She's borrowing mine," Ceci says, producing a long wool coat from seemingly nowhere.

The twins run back into the room, cookies in each hand, and Ceci stops them right before they try to hug Tori. "Whoa there, gremlins. Let's say hi to Miss Tori from a safe distance."

"Hi, Miss Tori," they say, then turn to hug Devon and Jodi in turn.

I help Tori into her coat and look at the rest of them expectantly. "Well?" I ask.

"Well what?" Ceci asks. "This is my evening entertainment. I'm not leaving until the two of you are safely on your way." Then she steps forward. "Unless you want to just skip the dinner and go straight to dessert. I wouldn't blame you."

"There are *children* present," Tori says.

"So?" Ceci counters.

I hold my arm out for Tori. "Shall we?"

She takes it and glances up at me, and her expression—heated, longing—sends a wave of goosebumps down my spine. "Lead the way."

We leave to a chorus of catcalls.

I walk Tori to the side of my truck and help her in, then get settled and start the ignition. I can feel her looking at me as I back out of the back driveway, and I glance over at her as I put the truck into drive. "Something wrong?"

She shakes her head, smiling softly. "Something is right. Very right."

Well, damn. A smile creeps over my face, and she brightens.

"I love your smiles, Will," she says.

"Never had much to smile about until now," I say truthfully.

"I don't believe that," she responds, reaching over to put her hand on my thigh. "I also don't believe how fucking good you look in this outfit."

I bark out a laugh. "I love you," I say, and it's almost effortless.

"I love you, too," she says.

The restaurant is in the adjoining town, fifteen minutes away. The hostess seats us, and we order, and I'm fairly certain we eat, but I don't pay attention to any of it because I'm too busy watching this gorgeous woman in front of me. Taking in all her different laughs: the husky, low-pitched ones that are sexy as hell, the giggles when she's teasing me, the full-bodied ones when she's truly amused. The way she licks her lips. The way her tits look in that unbelievable red dress.

"Would you like any dessert?" the server asks.

"No," I say, my eyes pinned on Tori's.

She smiles at me and looks up at the server. "I think he's trying to ask for the check," she says.

I pay and we walk out, my hand on her lower back because I can't help but touch her. We get to the truck, but instead of opening the door for her, I whip her around and crowd her until her back is pressed against the door. She sucks in a gasp, her eyes going wide as I palm her hip and rake my hand up her side possessively.

"Will…" she whispers, looking up at me.

Mine. It's all I can think as I cup her cheek and tilt her chin up, taking her lips and drinking her in. She feels like heaven and tastes exquisite. She arches up, pressing her soft curves against my chest. I growl and deepen the kiss as she wraps her arms around me. I move my hand to her chest and run a thumb over her breast, loving the way her breath hitches in response.

"Take me home," she says. "I need you."

I don't speed, but it's hard not to. At the inn, I throw the engine into park and whip my head to hers. "Stay."

Her eyes flare, and I can tell she's about to snark at me.

"If you move, I'm putting you in your room alone for the night," I warn.

She snaps her mouth shut.

Satisfied, I get out and round the truck, then pull her out into my arms in a bridal carry.

"Will!" she squeals.

"Your shoes are completely unsuitable for nighttime," I say.

"You're joking."

"I would never joke about your safety. Your heel could catch and you'd trip," I gruff.

"So you're going to carry me?"

I don't answer, kicking the door shut and walking to the house. We cross the threshold and she wiggles.

"Will, put me down."

I grip her tighter, exasperated. "Woman, will you just let me hold you?"

She stills, a soft "aww" escaping her. "You're really sweet, you know that?"

"I'm not sweet," I growl as I walk us into the kitchen and survey the area. Everything looks good, nothing is out of place, and I can see the guests have helped themselves to the rest of the cookies. I walk us back out, turning to keep from hitting Tori's feet against the door frame, and head to the bedroom.

Once there, I let her down. "Take off the coat. Nothing else," I direct, shutting the door softly behind me.

She obeys, a miracle in itself, tossing the coat on the chair in the corner.

I start to unbutton my shirt, but she holds her palms up. "Absolutely not."

"No?"

"No." She closes the distance and puts her hands on my chest. "I've been dreaming of unbuttoning this all night long. If you deny me, I might cry."

A soft laugh escapes me. "I'd hate to see you cry."

Her hands work to undo my belt and yank it off, letting it clatter to the floor as she untucks my shirt. With her fingers on the top button of the shirt, she looks up through her lashes and says, "It's not pretty. My eyes get all puffy and the snot is disgusting."

Grinning, I say, "You're something else, Tori."

She smiles as she undoes the first button, then the second, and pushes the fabric apart to expose my skin. She sucks in a breath. "You are so fucking sexy, Will." She presses her lips to the hollow of my neck, then kisses down to my chest. She follows every inch she reveals with her lips, and I stop her as she begins to kneel.

"No way, baby. I'm the one getting on my knees tonight."

She straightens and pushes the shirt off my shoulders. "Fine," she pouts, "but you better make it good."

I raise an eyebrow. "Challenge accepted." Then I whirl her around and pull her to me, her back to my front. I band one arm around her waist and drift my fingers up her arm and over her chest. "So silky," I murmur. I keep skimming her soft skin, sweeping down her other arm, then back up to the front of her neck and around the back, before tracing her collarbone and dipping to the top of her dress.

"This dress," I growl, "has driven me crazy all night."

She sucks in a slow breath as I dip my fingers between the hem and her skin. Then I lower my mouth to the curve of her neck, taking the skin between my teeth and biting it while I unzip the fabric.

She shivers, her ass pressing against my dick.

I push the dress off, revealing nothing but a tiny red thong underneath. My mouth waters as she steps out of the dress and kicks it to the side. She bends to take her heels off, but I stop her again.

"You're keeping those on, Tori. I want to feel them digging into my ass when I fuck you. Understand?" I grip her hips and pull her ass to me, grinding her against my cock through my pants.

She sucks in a breath. "Yes, sir."

I nuzzle her hair, breathing her scent in deep and dropping into the quiet refuge of her body. Then I kneel before my queen and prepare to worship her.

TORI

AFTER A SUCCESSFUL day of classes, I head down to the coffee shop to meet up with Ceci, Devon, and Jodi. It's time to launch Operation Get Devon and Aaron Married, and I am absolutely here for it.

Then I see the piles of wedding magazines and sticky notes and highlighters in front of Jodi's seat. "What is that?" I say warily.

Ceci waves it off. "Jodi's under the misimpression that we're planning a big wedding. We're not."

Devon nods vehemently. "Exactly. The wedding is next week, Jodi."

I whirl to her. "Seriously? Why?"

"I told you, Aaron is threatening Vegas. It took me a while to want to do this again, and I swear the man wants to lock me down before I change my mind," she laughs.

"I think she's pregnant and doesn't want to tell us," Ceci says.

Jodi yelps. "Ohmygosh, are you?"

Devon holds her hands up to shut us down. "I am not pregnant. We're just doing it quickly. So," she pushes the magazines over to Jodi, "this is *my* wedding and we will do it *my* way."

"Devon," Jodi wheedles.

"It is my second wedding. You of all people should give me a break—I was married to your brother first!"

I blink, having forgotten this little part of the story. Then I smile. "Wait. This means you two were sisters-in-law, then you weren't, and…eventually you might be again?"

Jodi blushes a deep red and Devon winks at me. "That's the plan," Devon says. "But what's *not* the plan is for all those magazines and stuff to be used. That's all you, Jodi. Not me."

Jodi huffs, but smiles as she does it. "Fine. Do you at least have a dress?"

Now it's Devon's turn to blush, and I poke her. "You got a dress, you got a dress," I sing-song.

She pulls out her phone and shows us the picture, and I sigh at how cute it is. We talk some more about the plans, how Rick will walk her down the "aisle"—which is really going to be the sidewalk—and guests.

"Wait," I say. "What about Aaron's mom?"

Devon takes a breath. "It's…complicated. But getting better. She knows the wedding is happening, but I haven't called to give her final details."

"I'll do it," I say, wanting to help and figuring this is an easy thing to do. "I've got her number."

Devon worries her lower lip. "Are you sure?"

I wave it off. "Of course!"

She nods. "Thank you. That's nice of you."

"Piece of cake," I say, sliding out of my chair and pulling up her number, dialing and walking outside as I go.

The phone rings and rings, but eventually she picks up. "Hello?" Barbara's voice is tentative, thin.

"Barbara?" I prompt.

"Who is this?"

"It's Tori. Tori Welch. We met at Christmas, remember? And I got your number?" I'd forgotten how unlike her sons she was.

"Oh, of course!" she says, seeming to warm up.

When she doesn't say anything else, I plow ahead. "Okay, so I'm calling because Aaron—"

"Oh god, is he okay?" Barbara interrupts.

"All three of your sons are okay," I say, realizing I should have started with that bit of news, given that they're all first responders and she barely knows me. "And since Aaron is getting married next week, I'm calling with the final details."

"Next week?" She sounds unsure.

"Yes, next week," I say, worry clenching my gut. Was this a bad idea? "Can you get up here?"

"Yes, yes of course. I'm sorry." She lets out something that might be a laugh, but it sounds so choked and unnatural that I'm honestly not sure. "I'm just trying to process this. Married. My baby boy is getting married. Do you—are you sure he wants me there? Why didn't he call?"

"Oh, you know, they're busy with all the wedding preparations. Takes a village!" I cross my fingers and hope this is all going to be okay.

"Of course," she says, but she doesn't sound convinced. Then again, I'm not sure what *would* convince her.

I clear my throat. "So anyway, next Saturday at two o'clock, at the fire station."

"The fire station?" she repeats meekly.

I grit my teeth. "Yep! You'll be there?"

"Yes," she says.

"Can't wait to see you. Bye!" I disconnect, eager to get off the call and shake off the feeling of unease the entire thing put in my stomach.

Back in the coffee shop, I smile broadly and wave the phone. "All done!"

Jodi returns the smile. "This calls for a round of smoothies!" She hops up as I plant my butt in the chair and stare at Devon.

"That was the most painful conversation I have ever had," I say.

Devon bites her lip again. "I'm sorry. Like I said: complicated."

"Yeah," I say, worried that I've somehow really messed up. But that's silly. It has to be. It's a wedding, and if she's still around, a person should have their mother at their wedding. "You're going to let them know she's coming, right?"

Devon nods. "I'll tell Aaron."

That's not what I asked, but it's as good as I'm going to get, and I don't want to push—it's not *my* wedding, after all. Unbidden, an image of Will in a tux flashes into my mind, and I nearly lose my breath. I blink rapidly to dispel the picture, focusing instead on Jodi as she comes back with the smoothies. Whatever Will and I are, we are *not* marriage material. Right?

We finish up the planning, and as I bundle up to head outside and make the short drive to the inn, I can't manage to shake the feeling of unease.

TORI

THE MORNING OF February 14 dawns crisp and bright, but that's not what I notice first. Instead, it's the feeling of Will's thick fingers blazing a trail down my belly and right onto my clit. His cock is against my ass, and as I moan softly, his voice is low and deep.

"Good morning, gorgeous."

I wiggle my butt against him. "Hell of a way to wake up."

It's the way I've woken up every morning Will was home the past week. It turns out that Will is *very* creative when it comes to ways to test how limber I am. I can't convince him to have sex in the kitchen—he's far too worried about guests or potential guests, no matter the time of day—but I've managed to go down on him in the laundry room, and I'm pretty sure my body has been on every available flat and not-flat surface in his bedroom.

His fingers move lower and push into my pussy. "How about this?" he growls softly.

I shift onto my back and spread my legs, giving him all the access he needs. Then I grab his cock with my free hand, stroking it languidly. "Careful. A girl could get used to this."

"That's the idea," he says. He curls his fingers and I gasp, already so close to coming. "Stay here. At the inn. Give up your room upstairs and stay with me."

I can't think about anything except the way his fingers fill me up and press right against my g-spot. "Not...the time...to ask," I pant.

He moves his thumb up to my clit, circling it as his fingers continue to work me. "Come for me, baby."

It's too soon, but on his command, I tip over the edge and into the abyss, shuddering as an orgasm breaks across me. He soothes me down, then says, "Open."

I do, and he puts the fingers that just made me come into my mouth. I suck, tasting myself on him even as I shift to better grab his cock. His eyes slam shut as I swirl my tongue around his fingers, and as soon as he withdraws them, I straddle him. He snaps his gaze to mine as I position him at my entrance, and as I sink onto him, he reaches for my breasts and squeezes.

"Damn, baby," he says. "Ride me. Make me yours."

"You already are mine," I say, even as a small voice reminds me I don't know if that's entirely true.

"Harder," he says. "Need it."

My big guy woke up needy this morning. I'm happy to oblige, leaning over and getting some leverage to piston my hips against his. "You're so fucking big, Will."

He growls, then pushes me up and off him, turning me so that my stomach is against the mattress and yanking my hips up. Immediately he shoves into me, and I scream into the pillow.

"There we go. That's what I need," he says, thrusting mercilessly into me. "Tell me you like it."

"*Fuck*, Will, I love it."

"More," he demands.

And the more he wants, the more I want. "I need to be filled, Will," I gasp. "I need more. *Please*."

His thumb pushes into my ass, and I groan. "Yes," I say, drawing it out. "But more." He pulls his thumb out, still fucking my pussy hard, and a moment later I feel his fingers push into me.

"Is that what you want, Tori?"

"It's what I want," I answer, breathless.

"Good. Because it's what I want, too. I need to fuck you there. Can you take me?"

I nod.

His other hand comes around to my clit, and I'm almost overloaded with sensation. In moments, I'm almost at the edge again. "Don't come yet," he growls. "Wait."

"I'm...trying," I bite out.

He pulls out of my pussy and positions himself. "Relax," he says softly, running his hand down my back to arch me up where he needs me.

He pushes in and I groan. "Fuck, baby," he says, withdrawing and going a little farther. "So tight. Look at you taking my cock. You're so beautiful. Such a good girl."

His hand returns to my clit, his cock thrusting in and out of me, and it's only moments before I start to shake. "I can't hold off," I say, feeling the wave of pleasure starting to crest. "I need to come."

He speeds up, and the euphoria is too much. I come, screaming into the pillow, knowing I have to be quiet and barely able to contain myself. Behind me, Will thrusts into me one last time, stiffening and holding still through his own release.

After a moment, he pulls out and rests his forehead on my back. "Fuck," he breathes.

I let myself fall onto the bed and giggle, my fingers and toes tingling with leftover sparks of pleasure. "Precisely." I roll over and smile up at him. He looks thoroughly debauched, his chest heaving, his eyes glassy, his hair mussed, his five o'clock shadow moving into beard territory. "You look like you just had a really nice orgasm."

He gives me a wicked grin. "Because I did." Then he leans down to give me a kiss, and climbs off the bed. As he holds his hand out for me, he says, "You ready for a wedding?"

My heart skips a beat, then settles. *He's not talking about ours, for god's sake. Get a grip.* I take his hand and let him pull me to him. "I am," I say, my head tilted back for the kiss he lays on me.

In the shower, we lather each other up and rinse, and I can't help the need I have for his cock. So I kneel down to take it into my mouth, sucking him all the way in and delighting in the way his legs stiffen almost instantly.

"I want you to come on my tits, Will," I say, looking up at him as the water sluices down his chest.

"*Fuck*, Tori, I'll do whatever you want," he growls, his voice reverberating on the tiles.

In moments, he grits out a "*now*" and I pull away, watching him come all over me. "Good boy," I say, then smirk at the way his eyes flare at the term.

He pulls me up and pushes me against the tile, then sinks to his knees. He hikes my leg over his shoulder and descends, licking and sucking my pussy like his life depends on it. His fingers push into me again and I grab onto his hair, unable to keep my moans quiet as he feasts. My legs shake and I feel my knees begin to give out.

"Will," I gasp. "I can't..."

"You absolutely can," he demands, shifting his arm to hold me up even as he pushes a third finger into me.

I stare down at him, taking in the way this beast of a man is bent before me, water beating onto him as my leg is thrown over one wide shoulder. The power that emanates from him is effortless, as is the way he pulls yet another orgasm from me. It arrives like a bullet train, speeding through me, relentless in the pleasure it brings. The sound that comes from me as I come is guttural, feral, nothing I have ever heard.

And when he looks up at me, the heat in his eyes is enough to brand me. "Good girl."

I can't help the laugh that escapes. "Are we trading good boys and good girls now?" I quip.

He kisses my belly, then pulls a nipple into his mouth as he straightens. I hiss, the pleasure almost too much to bear, and he growls against my skin. He continues his path of kisses and bites until he's at my lips, plunging his tongue into my mouth as he grinds against me. Because of course he's hard again. The man is insatiable. He hikes me into his arms and I hook my heels at the base of his spine. I wiggle against him, already feeling empty and desperate for him to be inside me.

"You want my cock again, Tori?" he asks, scraping his teeth over my neck.

"Fuck yes," I breathe out.

Without another word, he positions us and brings me down onto him. I swallow another scream of pleasure as he covers my mouth with his and fucks me.

"Holy. Shit." My jaw is on the floor as Will steps into the kitchen.

He stares at me. "What."

Silently, I gesture at him. At his large body swathed in his uniform. At the way the dress blues seem to make him appear even bigger and more darkly handsome. He's completely clean-shaven, and even his hair seems to be on its best behavior, slicked back into a Superman-as-villain style that I immediately want to muss.

He looks down, inspecting himself and checking his zipper.

"Babe. You look *incredible*," I say.

He jerks his head back to mine, surprise evident in his eyes. "You're the gorgeous one, Tori."

I shake my head. "You know you're the hottest Joseph brother, right?" I say.

Confusion streaks across his face. "I don't know what you're talking about."

I snort a laugh. "Your brother was a romance cover model, Will. Surely you're aware that the three of you practically make women weep when you're in a room together."

He shrugs. "I don't really think about that stuff."

I step to him and run my hands over the crisp lines of the uniform, already plotting what I can get him to keep on and the playtime we can have later. "Well, trust me when I say that angels sung the *Hallelujah* chorus in my head when I saw you. And that women around the world will despair to know that one of the Joseph brothers is officially off the market."

"If you say so."

"I say so." I tip up to give him a kiss, and immediately sense something is off. The sexy, confident man I'd shared a shower with is gone, and a different, more worried man is in his place. Is it me? As he glances around, I keep up a steady stream of talking. "I've already set out the cookies and a sign for the guests about you and Price being gone for a longer portion of the day than normal, and your cell is on there for them to text or call with emergencies. Even though I'd rather put mine because it's your brother's wedding, but there's no way you'll actually let me do that. *And* there's a different sign on the desk with your number if anyone shows up needing a place to stay."

The tension around his eyes doesn't ease. "Thank you."

I smile teasingly at him, hoping to pull him out of the strange place he seems to be heading to. "But you're going to check anyway."

He looks at me, impossible to read. "I'm going to check anyway."

I step back for him to make his regular path, watching as he tidies everything just so and nods to himself as he goes along. Maybe he's realizing that he doesn't want anything long-term. Maybe in the face of this wedding, he's starting to regret starting something up with me. I try to ignore the doubt, but it takes root as I follow him into the foyer and wait as he reads the sign, then adjusts its place on the desk.

Finally, he straightens and turns to me. "Thank you for…" he clears his throat. "For setting all of that up."

Needing to touch him, to reassure both of us that he's okay, I close the distance between us. His mouth is tight, but when I misstep and nearly fall, he reaches for me.

"You okay?" he asks, gathering me to him.

"Yep." Heat stains my cheeks. For once in my life, I'd like to not be in danger of falling every thirty seconds.

"Then let's go."

He doesn't say another word, and even though I know something is off, I lean up to kiss his cheek, adjust my hold on his arm, and we head into the sunshine.

We park behind the station and walk around the building to the sidewalk. Will needed to be here a little ahead of time for photos, but before he peels off to find his brothers, I say, "Stop."

He halts, and I move in front of him. I put my hands on his chest and wait for him to look at me, which takes longer than normal. When his eyes finally meet mine, they're distant, almost cold. I inhale a shaky breath. "You're okay, right?"

He blinks and looks away. "I'm fine."

It's a gut punch. "Talk to me," I urge.

He takes a step back, his hands clenched at his sides. "I need to go."

I watch him retreat, my stomach a ball of knots. I don't understand what's going on. It's supposed to be a happy day, but that's the last emotion I feel right now.

My phone buzzes with an alert.

Will Aaron says you should go to the coffee shop since you're here early.

Sighing, I do exactly what he says, only to realize by the sign on the door that the shop is Devon's home base. I nearly weep when I see her. She's in the center of the room in a knee-length cream lace dress that hugs her up top and fans out at the waist, showing off her legs and the blue suede heels donning her feet. Her blond hair hangs just below her shoulders, and the front half is pulled back and secured with a barrette of blue flowers. She's beaming, laughing at something Miss Betty and Mrs. Withers are saying as Jodi and Darius fuss over the bouquet at another table. Ceci appears to be giving the twins a stern talking-to, and the photographer is snapping photos.

Devon looks up and waves. "Hi, Tori!"

"You look beautiful, Devon," I say, my throat tight with emotion.

"Don't you dare cry," Jodi says. "I cry at nearly anything, and I'm already going to be a disaster when the ceremony actually starts."

"Yes, ma'am!" I laugh, sniffing back the tears and forcing myself to be in the moment. Whatever is going on with Will is something that I can't control. But this? Being here with my friends as one of them prepares to be married? I can do this.

"I need to get over to the guys," the photographer says, checking the image on her camera as she speaks.

"Thank you so much," Devon says. "I know these are going to be incredible."

The photographer smiles. "It's my pleasure. The Joseph boys are always fun to put in front of a camera."

Everyone laughs, and Jodi turns to me and says, "This is Lisa. She's shot Price a bunch of times, and did the station's fundraising calendar."

I cock my head. "Fundraising calendar?"

Ceci whistles. "You've not seen their calendar? The one where they're bare chested and oiled and delicious?"

My eyebrows raise. "No, and I can't believe we've been friends for two months and you haven't said anything."

"We'll show you later," Jodi says.

"Now that you're here, it's time for my homemade limoncello," Mrs. Withers announces.

Devon laughs. "Of *course* you make homemade limoncello."

"The way Jodi keeps ordering my lemon squares, I've got to do something with all those lemon peels," she says haughtily, tossing a satisfied smile at Miss Betty as she does.

Miss Betty sticks her tongue out at Mrs. Withers and I can't help but giggle. I've heard that the old women have only recently become friends again after decades of animosity, but that they still argue over whose lemon squares are the best.

Mrs. Withers motions to Darius, who disappears into the back and returns with a tray of glasses and a bottle full of bright yellow liquid.

The two of them set to pouring out the drinks, and we toast to the bride. The liquor is cold and soothing as it goes down. Soon after, Rick appears, looking dapper in a dark gray suit that seems to have been tailored to fit his bigger frame. His expression softens as his eyes find his sister's.

"Time for us to go," Darius declares, bustling all but Rick and Devon out of the coffee shop. He motions at me to stay back, and as we walk down the block, he gives me a wide grin. "Have you talked to Conner?"

"I haven't, but you look pretty happy," I say.

His eyes glitter. "Happy doesn't really describe it."

My heart squeezes at the dreamy look on his face. "Yeah?"

"He's...everything," Darius sighs.

I squeal and grab his hand. "So I was right."

"You were *definitely* right," he confirms.

One of the engines is parked on the street to make room for

the ceremony, but there aren't any chairs in the area that's been cleared out. Instead, there's a small wooden arch interlaced with ivy set about halfway back, and Chief wanders around it, a piece of paper clutched tightly in his hand.

I see Will's mom off to the side, doing her best to blend into the background, and my heart squeezes again, this time for a different reason. She shouldn't have to feel so separate, and since I'm not one of Devon's two bridesmaids—the honor for that goes to Jodi and Ceci, to match up with Price and Will—I decide it's my job to take care of it. Ignoring the twinge that pings through me at the idea that maybe this isn't the best move, I beeline for her.

She smiles as I approach, with no tentativeness or hesitation to be found. "Hi, Tori," she says softly.

"Hi, Barbara," I say, immediately feeling better. "It's so good to see you! I'm glad you made it. How was the drive?"

"It was fine," she says. "You look beautiful."

I glance down at the maroon velvet jumpsuit I'm wearing, then back to her. "Thank you. You, too. A perfect mother of the groom outfit."

"Oh, thank you," she says. "You wouldn't believe the things I can find in the Goodwill down where I work. Lots of people leave perfectly good things in the rental units, and those find their way to the thrift stores."

"Well, it's beautiful." And it is. She's in a powder blue skirt and jacket, and though it seems like it might be more suited to a woman in her seventies or eighties, it works on Barbara.

"Everyone, if you'll please gather around," Chief says. "We're about to begin."

"Come on," I say, holding my hand out for her. She takes it, and as we move to the right of the wooden arch, I try to let all my worries about Will drift away for now.

WILL

MY STOMACH PITCHES into overdrive the second I leave Tori's side, and my head floods with a relentless spiral of *what ifs*. I'd gotten a text from Mom yesterday asking me if it was okay that she came, and I didn't know what to do with that. Why should I be the one to give permission?

Because you were the one to make her leave in the first place.

Sure, she needed help, but did I have to kick her out of her own house? I remind myself that I was a kid and doing what I thought was best, but honestly, *was* it? For years, Aaron believed Mom abandoned him, for Christ's sake. I couldn't be a shittier brother if I tried.

Last night, looking at her text, the roil of guilt nearly brought me to my knees. All I could do was reply Yes, and bury myself in Tori's embrace. It wasn't until I was dressed this morning that I realized my final text to her didn't show as being read, and that was all it took.

What if she didn't come? Would Aaron think it was my fault? Did she have enough money to make the trip? I should have offered her gas money. What about her car? Is it in good shape? I should know these things about my own mother. What if her tires are just as bad as Tori's were, and she has a blow-out on the interstate?

I pat my suit pocket for my phone and check the messages and call log. Nothing. She must be okay.

But is she here? Did she come last night? She should have driven up last night and stayed at the inn. But I didn't invite her. Did she stay with Price? Price is her favorite, anyway. He's everyone's golden boy, always has and always will be.

Which is fine.

Shit. If she isn't here, I'll never forgive myself.

"Broseph!" Price's voice booms from the station's kitchen, where we're gathering in advance of whatever ridiculous pictures we'll have to pose for.

I accept the hug he plasters on me, managing to pull my head out of my ass long enough to give him one back. He's always been one for human contact, and the tighter I squeeze him, the happier he is. Today is a day I should aim to make my brothers happy, so I go for broke.

"Ooh, good one," Price says, tucking into the hug. "Aaron, get over here. I need a Price sandwich!"

I meet Aaron's eyes over Price's shoulder and catch the eye roll he delivers, even as he strides over and embraces Price from the other side.

Price, the weirdo he is, wiggles like a damn puppy. "So good. Sooooo good!" he enthuses. "Need these all the time."

"All right," I say, releasing him and stepping back. "It's not about you today, Price."

"Yeah," Aaron says, a big grin on his face. "Give me one day, man. Just one."

"I can't help it if I like hugs," Price says. "Sue me."

"Where's your photographer?" Aaron asks.

"*Your* photographer," Price corrects. "Lisa. You remember her from our calendar photoshoot. She's just finishing with the girls and will be here in a minute. We should head downstairs."

Aaron takes the lead and I bring up the rear, and I nearly stop dead in my tracks when we round the apparatus in the bay and I see Mom talking to Chief. *Thank god.* She turns, smiling broadly at Aaron and Price. The smile dims when her eyes meet mine.

Lisa's waiting on us, and she takes us through what feels like an interminable amount of poses outside in front of the ladder apparatus. When we're done, it's just about time.

Rounding the rig, my gaze finds Tori like a magnet. She's got her back to me, looking incredible in the jumpsuit she's wearing. She shifts, and I realize she's been talking to my mom. I don't have time to have an opinion on it, though, because Chief is directing us as though he's suddenly a concertmaster, getting Aaron into position and motioning Price and I out of the bay to meet up with Jodi and Ceci.

Aaron and Devon's dogs, Daisy the brindle pit and Samson the raggedy white mutt, sit patiently on the sidewalk as if they've somehow been trained for this, but that can't possibly be true. My guess is that the twins have treats in their pockets, or maybe even under the rose petals. The twins themselves are in the front of the pack, both of them holding onto a basket full of petals, and Jodi takes Price's arm to get behind them. Ceci and I are next, and behind us are Devon and Rick.

"Devon," I say.

She swings her gaze to me.

"Thank you for loving my brother. I know I did some things that probably fucked him up, and I'll never be able to apologize enough for that."

Her eyes water. "Will…"

"But you made him whole," I said. "You gave him the happiness he deserves. He's the best of us, always has been. He couldn't have found a better person than you."

She sniffs. "Dammit, Will," she says, her voice cracking. "Why do you never speak, and when you do, you let this kind of stuff fly?"

I shrug silently, figuring it's best if I keep my mouth shut before I beg for her forgiveness for things she has no business knowing. It's not as though she can offer me salvation, anyway.

No one can.

Price checks his phone, then pockets it. "Chief says it's time. You ready, kids?"

"Go, Daisy! Go, Samson!" Eva and Luke say, and damn if those dogs don't trot forward and head into the station. The twins race forward without a second glance, rose petals bouncing out of the basket as they go.

"So much for my instructions," Ceci mutters beside me.

Price and Jodi go, and a few moments later, Ceci and I follow. I take my place next to my brothers, noting the look of pure peace on Aaron's face. It's almost enough to make me calm, and I take a deep breath, forcing myself to settle. Like I just told Price, today is about Aaron, so I need to focus, get my act together, and quit spiraling like an asshole.

Aaron's jaw slackens as his expression changes to one of awe, and I know that Devon must have rounded the corner.

Sure enough, she's walking towards us with her brother, her eyes locked on Aaron's, a broad smile on her face as she giggles at something Rick says.

Beside me, Price clears his throat. I glance at him, but of course, he's only got eyes for Jodi.

I can't bring myself to look at Tori.

Rick and Devon get to us, and the ceremony begins as Rick steps away. Aaron mentioned that he and Devon aren't doing the usual vows, which is probably for the best, because Chief is launching into a soliloquy about how he brought these two together.

"I remember the day I told you to reach out to her," he says, his chest puffed out beneath the uniform. "And here we are now."

A collective groan rises, because we all know that Chief is convinced he's the town matchmaker. Chief ignores us and the ceremony continues.

As Aaron says his vows, my gaze falls once more on my mom. She's watching with this look of pure wonder on her face, as though she can't believe what she's seeing. Or maybe it's that she can't believe she's here. Maybe both.

I can't shake the guilt. And it hits me that even though Aaron and Price have managed to rise above the clear fuck-job I did of raising them, I'll never be where they are. I'll never manage to be good enough for anyone, let alone Tori.

Unbidden, I look at Tori, only to find her deep brown eyes waiting for me, shining with love I don't even remotely deserve. She smiles and dips her chin a bit, and I fight the urge to turn and run. Run from the way she makes me feel, and run from the way I'll inevitably screw it up. Because how can I not? I'm too controlling, too set in my ways.

Devon begins her vows, and I blink to force my attention back to the ceremony. I can't even *listen* right, for fuck's sake. I see the love in their eyes, the absolute devotion they have for each other, and it's something I'll never know. All I can do at this point is focus on what's next, and for me, that means diving full time into the inn. Maybe now that at least one brother is married, I can let myself turn the page and stop being a fire-fighter. I never did it because it was something I was passionate about; I did it because I didn't know what else to do, and I knew I needed to stay in Talladega. But running the inn, for as much as it can send me into anxious spirals, also gives me a sense of purpose that firefighting never did. Besides, if I run it full time, that means Price can step away, and the anxiety is bound to lessen.

"You may kiss," Chief intones happily.

I snap back to attention as they embrace, and then Aaron pulls her tight against him and dips her. The women all seem delighted, but all I can do is worry he'll drop her. He doesn't, and when they straighten and finally part, they're both flushed and happy.

Focus, Joseph. Today is not the day, and this is not the time.

The photographer swoops in to take a million more pictures, then says, "Let's get a picture of Mom with the boys."

My spine goes ramrod straight, but I follow Lisa's instructions and stand in front of the apparatus with Price and Aaron. Mom approaches tentatively, like a dog that's been chastised, and I know it's because I'm here. Tori stands off to the side, and when I allow myself to look at her, she's staring back. She's more than I deserve, and it's never been more apparent.

Again, I watch Mom as she smiles brightly at Aaron and Price, only to falter as she turns to me. "My boys," she says, but it's soft and uncertain.

I force my version of a smile at her, hoping she can read in there that it's okay. That she should be here. That she shouldn't have had to ask for my permission. What kind of shit son—shit *person*—must I be to have turned my own mother into this?

Mom blinks, and I can't read the look on her face. Relief? Terror? Who knows.

"Get in here, Mom," Price says, guiding her in front of us. Lisa gets her shots, and when she calls for the inevitable separate shots of each of us with Mom, I'm ready.

"I'm glad you came," I murmur as we get into position.

"You are?" she asks, surprised.

"Of course I am. It's your son's wedding. You should always be here for the happy things."

"And the unhappy ones?"

The question catches me off guard, but I understand what she's asking. "Yes," I say, holding her gaze. "Those, too."

The smile she has goes all the way to her eyes now, and instead of it being a relief, all I feel is guilt.

WILL

I WANT TO escape and go lift weights, over and over, until my body goes numb, but there's no way anyone's going to let me get away with that during the reception at the coffee shop. I don't like all the feelings that are raging through me. I'm a complete fuck-up. It's all I've ever been, despite all efforts to the contrary.

A first-born son is supposed to be the one everyone can look up to. Who makes sure that everything goes the way it needs to. Looks out for his little brothers. I never kept them from hearing Mom and Dad argue, even though neither of them seem to remember it. And I sure as hell didn't keep them from realizing that Mom wasn't interested in being a mother with the way she holed up in her room those last few years.

"Will?" Tori reaches for my arm, and that's when I realize I've been frozen at the front door, hands clenched, scowling out at everyone as they celebrate my brother's marriage.

I'm fucking up again.

"Hey, big guy. Talk to me."

I look at her, and her mahogany eyes are pinched, worried. It's my fault. She's so beautiful and kind and soft. I don't deserve her. I don't deserve any of this. How can she even stand me?

I shake my head. "There's nothing to talk about."

She laughs softly. "Oh, there's definitely something going on. Come upstairs." She tugs gently on my hand, and I let her lead me to her studio.

A sign on the door says *Get Bendy With It*, and it's so perfectly Tori that it makes it hard to breathe. Because I didn't know it. How could I not know the name of her studio? We cross the threshold and she shuts the door behind me, locking us into a eucalyptus-scented haven of quiet and calm. Sunlight streams in through the windows, showing off the two torture devices against the far wall that I know have something to do with Pilates. The walls alternate between a creamy white and a light yellow. It's nice. And I'm an asshole for not coming up to see it.

But that's standard for me: always in my head, always focused only on what I need, and never bothering to see what others need and give it to them.

"I'd tell you to have a seat, but something tells me that uniform doesn't lend itself too well to crisscross applesauce." Tori tries to joke.

I grit my teeth. "It's fine."

"Will—"

"I can't do this," I say.

"I get it. There are a lot of people down there. What can I do?"

It's such an innocent question, and of course she asked it. Because that's what she does, looks out for people without a thought to how it impacts her. And it rips me apart.

"Unclench your fists, Will," she says, reaching for one and pulling it into her.

Since I'm a selfish prick who will do anything for her touch, I let her pry my fingers open and thread her own through them.

She runs her thumbs across my palm, going deep into the muscle and massaging.

We're quiet while she works one hand, and then the other, and instead of making me feel better, all it does is confirm that I have no right loving this woman. That I need to let her go. Because I'll never be worthy of her, never be the kind of person who should be beside her. She's sunshine and rainbows, and I'm nothing but darkness and growls.

After a few minutes, she says, "I'm sorry."

I glance at her sharply. "You, of all people, have absolutely nothing to apologize for."

Guilt and worry cloud her face. "I'm the one who called your mom and invited her. Well, not exactly—I volunteered to call with final details. I thought I was doing the right thing, but seeing you...I messed up, didn't I?"

I swallow thickly. Mom is here because of Tori? I turn away from her and spear a hand through my hair. It's worse than I thought. I screwed up my family so badly that Aaron couldn't even bring himself to talk to her? *Tori* had to do it?

"Talk to me, big guy."

I whirl back around, the ever-present vise around my chest starting to squeeze tighter. "It's worse than I thought. You're not even family, Tori."

She jerks back, her eyes going glossy. "Right. Like I'm just a guest." Her voice is calm, even. Like she's trying to contain me even as she fights through her own pain.

Her reaction confirms what I need to do. "I can't do this," I repeat, hoping she understands what I'm saying. Because the words themselves won't come. Because I'm a coward. Just like I couldn't tell her I loved her at first, I can't say the words to let her go. "I'm not the man I need to be. I need to focus on the inn and getting better."

"Getting better? Will, you're perfect," Tori says.

I scoff and back up. "Far from it. If I'm perfect at anything, it's at messing things up. Messing *people* up."

She steps closer, grabbing onto the lapels of my jacket and shaking her head. "Fine—you're not perfect. But guess what? I don't want perfect. I want *you*. I love *you*." She searches my face, her tone beseeching.

She's not going to let this go, and I can't ruin my brother's wedding. I close my eyes and take one breath, then another. I need to do the right thing for once in my life, to think about people other than me. Act like Price and Aaron. Coming to a decision, I open my eyes and find that hers are filled with tears.

I reach up and wipe them away with my thumbs, caressing her silky skin as I do and knowing it's the last time I'll touch her. "I'm sorry, Tori. Please don't cry. I shouldn't have even let you bring me up here, because it's my brother's wedding and we should be down there, celebrating." Then I take a deep breath and lie to the love of my life's face. "We'll talk later, okay?"

She studies me, a riot of emotions flitting over her face. But finally, she nods and releases me. "Okay."

I gesture for her to lead the way out, but she shakes her head. "Not this time. You first," she says.

Downstairs, it appears that no one noticed we were gone, so at least I have one thing working in my favor. I find an unoccupied table and sink onto the tiny chair, praying it doesn't collapse beneath me. Damn thing feels like it was made for a doll. Tori doesn't follow, opting instead to go over to where Ceci and Jodi stand. I watch them lean into her, clearly asking her what's wrong, and then Ceci glares over at me, followed by Jodi.

Can't blame them.

A little while later, Chief comes over and takes a seat beside me, sliding a plastic cup of water in front of me. Technically, I'm on duty, but he knows I rarely drink, anyway.

"Wanna tell me why you're over here scowling like someone kicked your dog?" he asks.

"I quit."

He chuckles. "Quit what? Quit trying to make sense of people? Smart move."

I pull my gaze away from watching Mom with Price and Aaron and look at Chief. "I want to stop being a firefighter. I can't do it anymore. I'm not—I just need to stop," I say. No need to dive into an extensive explanation.

Chief's eyes flare in surprise. "I knew it wasn't your calling, son, but are you sure?"

I flinch at the term of endearment. He's certainly treated me and my brothers like we were his kids, and I'm grateful as hell, but right now it just makes my skin crawl. "I'm sure."

He nods thoughtfully. "Can you give me a little while to sort some things out? Maybe a month?"

"Of course," I answer. "I want to do this right, for once."

He stands and claps my shoulder. "Will, the day I see you do anything *wrong* is the day the world stops spinning."

He's lying, and we both know it.

Tori

GUESS I'M GETTING drunk.

Because whatever Mr. Scary is up to, it ain't good, and I can't focus on it or I'll ruin the wedding. So Will can sit over there and stew and look all hot and broody with a cup of water, and I'll just be over here pounding shots of limoncello.

"Another."

Darius raises an eyebrow from where he stands behind the counter, a barista turned bartender. "Tori, I—"

"*Another*, and I know you're not going to be one more man to tell me what he thinks is good for me. You know who my mother is, and let me tell you, I will go Southern Black Mama on you and you know it won't be pretty."

He pours me another shot and pushes it forward. "I'm only saying there's a lot of sugar in these and—"

"Shut up." I pound the shot and chase it with a gulp of Pinot Grigio. Darius sucks his teeth in disapproval and I glare at him.

"I will always love you for bringing Conner into my life, but whatever this is," he circles a finger up and down at me, "it's tragic. And you're better than this."

"Whatever," I mumble. "It's necessary, is what it is."

"And I don't have to stand here and watch it," he says, and walks away.

I turn, wishing this was a bar so that I could lean against it instead of the pitiful butt-on-counter move I've just done, but again: whatever. The celebration is in full force and random strangers are popping in to offer their congratulations and get a slice of cake. It's lemon cake, because of course it is. But I love that. And I love the cake. Tangy, but sweet as soon as it melts on your tongue.

Kind of like Will, when he's not being...whatever it is he's being. Obstinate. Obtuse. Obliteratingly sexy as fuck in that uniform.

A whine escapes me at the realization that he is most definitely not going to play with me tonight. And isn't that some shit? My legs are shaved and *everything*. But noooo. No, Mr. Scary has to go and get all up in his feelings, and they're not the good feelings, and I know without question that whatever is going on with him is bad. Super bad and it's super not good news because...ugh, I'm drunk. Guess I'll stay here with my ass on the counter.

Ceci saunters up to me, her sharp gaze assessing me in two seconds flat. "You're getting drunk on limoncello?"

"Incredulous and judgy is not a good look on you," I snap.

"That bad, huh?" She looks at Will, then back to me. "You love him, don't you?"

I whine again. "Yes, and it's not fair, because he definitely isn't in love with me. I mean, he's said it—I love you—but now? I don't know. All I did was call his mom with final details, Ceci. And suddenly I'm the bad guy. Was it really that bad of me? I don't get it. Fucking Joseph men and their mommy issues, I swear."

Ceci chuckles, then gets serious after I glare at her. "Sorry, but you're awfully cute when you're limoncello drunk."

"Fuck you." My words have zero bite.

"Aw," she coos, "look at you trying to be mean. It's adorable. And listen, I get it. Aaron and Price are pretty straightforward guys, right? What you see is what you get, and all that. But Tori, no one's ever gotten behind Will's gruff exterior. You're the only one who has. So take comfort in that and have some patience. He'll come around."

I heave out a sigh and take another gulp of room temperature wine. "Whatever." It's my line right now, and I guess it's my mantra. Blow up my life in an effort to reset and find some meaning because it turns out being a pill peddler ain't all it's cracked up to be? Whatever. Come home and see old man ass on my mom's couch? Whatever. Run into my only regret in life on my first night home? Whatever. Fall in love with him even though I knew better? What. Ever.

"Oh, honey," Ceci says, pulling me into a hug.

Huh. Guess all that wasn't in my head.

How much of that limoncello have I actually had?

"I should go," I say, pulling out of the hug. "I'm tired and hungry for more than lemon cake."

"You can't drive," Ceci says. "Let me get Rick."

I'm already shaking my head at the offer. I don't want to break up the party. "I'll walk. It's nice outside." It really is, sunny and in the upper fifties. It's still very much daytime, even though it feels like I've lived about twenty years since I woke up and had delicious morning sex with Will.

Again: whatever.

I angle for the door, nodding and smiling at anyone who makes eye contact with me and generally pretending like I'm the happiest fucking person on the planet, all in hopes that Will sees me and thinks he hasn't affected me. Hasn't completely pulled my heart out, showed it to me, dropped it on the ground, and stomped on it. Because screw him. Screw him and his big, stupid heart and his big, stupid muscles and his big, stupid dick.

I'll just...buy a vibrator. A really big one. Lots of speeds and definitely one with the little rabbit ears. Those things are great. I threw my last one away when I packed up to move home.

And wasn't that stupid? Moving home, that is.

Maybe I'll move back to Atlanta. Call Conner and beg him to let me crash on his couch while I get a new job slinging pills, and I'll just go back to the way my life was before. Because I was fine before Will, and I'll be fine after him.

Digging in my clutch for my ear buds, I pop them in, turn on some girl power music, and take off. It's too bad I'm in these tall-ass wedges because half the time I'm like a damn baby giraffe in them, teetering on the edge of a fall, but whatever. *Whatever.*

I'm only half a block down from the coffee shop when I spot a blur of white fur and realize Samson is walking with me, his little body quivering as I squat down to pet him. "You're such a good boy," I say, giving him pets and basking in the easy love of a dog.

I'm half tempted to stay here with Samson, but I need to pee and it's chilly in the shade, so I surge upright and shoo him back to the shop. He ignores me, planting his butt on the sidewalk and cocking his head to the side to study me.

"Your choice," I mutter. As I turn to step off the sidewalk between some parked cars, I lose my balance, and the last thing I see is the chromed, rather pointy edge of an old car surging up to meet me.

WILL

I HEAR A tapping on the shop's window and glare over at the noise. Samson's pawing frantically at the glass, and something about it doesn't sit well with me, especially since I saw Tori flounce out of here a few minutes ago as though she didn't have a care in the world.

It hurt, not having her warm gaze on me as she walked by. But I'm the one who put her in that mood, so I absolutely deserve the ice I felt flowing off her.

Samson's pawing doesn't stop, so I pull myself up to standing. Price catches my attention as I head to the door, his eyebrows raised in a *what's up* question. I point to the little dog and go outside.

Instantly, Samson is circling me and yipping. Feeling a bit foolish, I say, "What is it, boy?"

He runs ahead, then stops, comes back and circles me, then bolts again like he's Lassie from that show from the I don't even know what decade. Old show. Sixties? Doesn't matter, because I'm trotting after Samson like he clearly wants me to.

He's dancing in circles in front of some parked cars, and my pulse kicks up. *Fuck.* I sprint the rest of the way, then skid to a stop at the sight before me.

"Price! Aaron!" I bellow.

Samson's feet tap-dance on the sidewalk, as though he knows it's bad.

"Go get Aaron," I tell the dog, hoping to hell he understands, and the white ball of fur takes off.

I turn my attention back to Tori, and an anguished growl comes out of me. No. *No.*

She's sprawled on the ground between the cars, a small amount of blood trickling down her temple, her legs and arms thrown in a way that tells me she lost consciousness before she hit the ground. Her neck might be bent oddly, but I can't tell because I'm too fucking big to get in there in a way that won't move her.

I don't recognize the sound that comes out of me. Running around to the back of the vehicle, a giant Buick from the eighties, I'm seconds from turning into my own version of Hulk and moving it when I hear a shout.

"Will!"

Thank fuck. Aaron and Price are here, with Chief pulling up the rear, a medical bag in his hand.

"I can't—" I manage to choke out when Price pulls me away.

"You're damn right you can't," he says, his expression stern. "Let Aaron in there."

"I can't breathe," I wheeze, turning around in a panic. "She's —*fuck.*" Then I hear the telltale *whoop* of the ambulance siren that's suddenly twenty feet from me and feel faint.

"Jesus, Will," Price says, backing me out of the road up against one of the cars. "Get out of the road. Sit down before you pass out."

I'm distantly aware of my ass hitting cold metal and watching Mike jump out of the ambulance and round it to open the back. This cannot be happening. *How* did it happen?

Me. It's all my fault. I watched her pound the wine and some kind of yellow booze. And those damn shoes. Why did I let her leave by herself?

I surge off the car, needing to see her.

Immediately, I feel a hand lock on my arm. "Whoa there, buddy. Hang on." Price pulls me back, his jaw locked and expression fierce when I turn to glare at him. "You know how this works. Let them do their job."

"Let me go, Price," I warn.

"Not a chance," he says.

I'm swinging my fist at him before I even realize it's happening, but he ducks and head-butts my stomach, shoving me back against the car.

I recover, pushing him to the ground and leaping over him to run to the rig.

"Mother *fucker*," he swears, scrambling off the street to hustle after me. "Aaron!"

Aaron's ready for me, his arms out to keep me from jumping into the back of the ambulance. "*No*," he says.

I'm having none of it. Her face looks pale, too pale. But before I can land a punch on Aaron, more hands are pulling me back.

"Easy," Chief says from one side.

"You're a strong mother fucker," Rick huffs from the other.

Aaron hops into the back of the rig, his dress blues stark against the scene behind him, and locks eyes with me. "I've got her, Will. I promise." And with that, he shuts the doors.

A second later, the rig speeds off, siren wailing, and Chief and Rick let me go.

I sink to the ground, gulping in air, unable to take a deep breath. What if she's not okay? I should have been with her. I'm never going to forgive myself for this. "Fuck!" I yell. Then I yell again, again, again, my fists pounding the pavement, and I'm spiraling, punching and yelling until I can't feel anything except the rage that fills every single part of me, and I let it take over. I let myself turn into the exact person everyone thinks I am, because that's all that's left. Rage, fury, and the darkest of angers.

Because that's been my constant all these years. The cold caress of loneliness, the icy embrace of solitude, the cruel spike of control, all of them wrapped and warped together to form the shield that's only ever been pierced by her. Who I pushed away. Because no one wants the monster. Not really.

I don't know how long I'm there on the pavement, only that when I finally stop punching and yelling, I open my eyes to find a circle of people have formed around me. I blink, taking in the sight of Chief, Price, Rick, Ceci, Jodi, and Devon. Even Mom is here.

Devon steps forward with a wet cloth. "Hey," she says softly, her blue eyes catching mine as she kneels in front of me. "This might sting," she warns as she wraps the cloth around my bloodied hands.

I don't feel anything.

"You're kind of a mess, Will," she continues, "but I'd like to think I know a little about how you're feeling."

I jerk my gaze to hers, immediately assuming the worst.

Her eyes soften. "She's okay," she says, then looks over her shoulder.

Jodi approaches and shows me a phone. There's a text from Aaron.

AARON

She's stable.

I choke out a sob and lower my chin to my chest, relief washing over me. *Stable* isn't enough, but I'll take it.

"You want to go see her?" Devon asks, still speaking softly, as though I'm some kind of wounded animal.

I nod.

She squeezes her hands around the cloth that's still draped over my hands. "Let's get you cleaned up, and I'll drive you."

"I ruined your wedding," I manage to get out.

"Oh, Will," she sighs. "You didn't ruin anything."

I don't believe her.

Price steps forward and holds out his hand as Devon moves to the side. "Come on, Hulk."

I don't want to take his hand, but I don't think I have it in me to get up otherwise. So I lock my palm against his and let him haul me up.

"You're fucking heavy, bro," he says, slapping my back with his free hand.

Numbly, I let Devon and Jodi lead me back into the coffee shop and behind the counter to clean my hands. My knuckles and fingers look like they've been attacked by a cheese grater, and somewhere in my head I know they probably hurt. But I'm empty of everything.

Before long, I've been shuffled into Devon's car on the way to the hospital. It's just the two of us, the only sound that of the engine and the tires on the road. No radio, no talking, and I'm grateful for it. When she pulls up to the Emergency entrance, she puts the car in Park and lays her hand on my knee. I meet her eyes.

"Earlier today—before the wedding," she starts. "What you said about doing things that may have messed Aaron up? Will, it's not true. You've been an incredible brother to him."

I scoff and look away.

"I'm serious," she insists. "He's told me the stories. I know the sacrifices you made."

"They weren't sacrifices." I look back at her as I speak, my voice hoarse.

"What would you call them?"

Without hesitation, I reply. "Fuck ups. He thought Mom left *him*. He doesn't know—"

"Yes he does."

An emotion finally manages to stir inside of me, and of course, it's anger. At myself. "No, he doesn't. *I'm* the one who made her leave. *I'm* the one who fucked him up. *I'm* the one who—"

"Kept your family together through thick and thin," she interrupts. "Trust me, I know a little about that, too. And you didn't make your mother leave. She knew she needed help. So did your dad. They were already planning on it."

I shake my head. "That's not true."

Devon shrugs. "You'll have to talk to your mom. But Will, my point is that you have nothing to feel badly about. You deserve just as much happiness as your brother. As *both* of them."

I deserve no such thing. But instead of saying anything, I clench my jaw and look away from her, opening the door and stepping out.

Aaron's waiting on me when I walk in, and his face betrays nothing.

"How is she?" I demand.

"She'll be fine."

"That's not what I asked," I say, angling towards LaToya at the desk. "Where is she." I don't bother making it a question.

LaToya arches her eyebrow. "You're not family, Will."

I growl, but she's unmoved. I turn to Aaron. "Please."

"Her mom is here," he says. "Do you have her number?"

I push my hand through my hair, frustrated. "Aaron."

He pulls me away from the desk, walking us farther into the hospital and away from LaToya's view. Tossing a glance over his shoulder, he guides us to the left and to a set of stairs. "She's on the fourth floor. That's all I know."

I nod curtly and open the metal stairwell door.

"Will."

I look back at him.

"You should let me bandage those hands, man."

It's his version of saying he loves me, and it's too much. I sprint up the steps without another word.

The fourth floor is quiet. Too quiet. I stride the halls, looking for any clue for where Tori is and feel the panic start to take hold again. I force air into my lungs, over and over, absolutely refusing to be a victim twice today. Finally, I see a cluster of people outside a room, two nurses and a doctor with the town librarian.

Tori's mom. Thank god.

I beeline for them, only for Mrs. Welch's eyes to widen as I get close.

The doctor turns around, her gaze narrowing as I slow to a stop in front of them. "Can I help you?"

I don't know this doctor, and I don't recognize either of the nurses. I take a breath to steady myself. "I'm here for Tori."

The doctor looks at Mrs. Welch, who nods and steps forward.

"Will," she says. "Good to see you."

I stare at her, unable to tell if she means it or not. Is she sad? Angry? Does she blame me? She should. "How is she?" I finally manage.

Her brow smooths. "She's okay, Will."

I hear the words, but it's hard to believe them. I need to see her.

Mrs. Welch's focus falls to my hands. "Are *you* okay?"

"Please," I grit out.

"Sir," one of the nurses says, her hand darting out to touch my arm.

I flinch. "Please," I repeat. "I just—"

"Let's come sit down," the nurse says, trying to guide me away from the room.

"I need to see her." The words come out in a growl, and I feel my vision narrowing. My heart rate is through the roof. Fuck. This isn't good.

"*Sir.*"

Everything goes dark.

TORI

T HE FIRST PERSON I see when I wake up is Mom, her head bent as she reads. "Mom?"

She looks up, breaking into a warm smile as she closes the book and scoots close to take my hand in hers. "There you are. Gave us all a good scare," she says, her eyes scanning my face.

I wince. "Sorry." I go to sit up, but groan as pain shoots through my head. "Ow."

Mom chuckles. "You have a concussion, and had some internal swelling on your brain. You'll be fine, but you're here for a day or two."

"How long have I been out?"

She checks her watch. "It's seven in the morning, so…fourteen hours?"

Damn. I wince again.

"Wanna tell me what happened?"

"Water," I say, spying the plastic cup and pitcher just out of my reach.

Mom presses the button to raise me up, stopping when I squint, and then pours me the water.

I drink and try to recall what happened. Will changed his mind about me, about *us*, which is exactly what I'd been afraid would happen. And in response, I got drunk in an effort to salvage whatever sliver of my heart wasn't owned by Will Joseph. Except he has it all. So really, my response was perfectly reasonable. "Who are you texting?" I ask.

She finishes the text and sets the phone aside before answering. "Your friends. I had to promise to keep them updated so they could tell Will." Then she smiles and says affectionately, "That poor man."

"That poor man?" I repeat, unable to keep the incredulity out of my voice. "Says who?"

She waves a hand and tsks. "He passed out, right in front of your room," she says. "Came charging up here like a bat out of hell and then got so panicked he just went splat." She grins. "Tell you what, it really is true: the bigger they are, the harder they fall. Took a fleet of nurses to get the man onto a gurney."

I can't quite compute this. "He was here?"

"For the three minutes he had consciousness," she says wryly, her gray dreads swinging. "Now, will you please tell me what happened?"

"I tripped."

She purses her lips. "You *tripped?*"

I shrug. "You know how clumsy I am: small feet, tall body. I tripped. Not the first time, won't be the last." No point in detailing how I was wasted on wine and limoncello and was all up in my feels with Beyoncé when it happened. I can go to my grave with those details, thank you very much.

Mom sits back in her chair and harrumphs like I've disappointed her. I probably have, but she'll get over it. She always does. What I'm more interested in is that Will actually bothered to come. Could I be wrong? Could he still care about me?

"Tell me more about Will," I press.

Her brown eyes assess me. "What's going on with you and that boy?"

"Wish I knew," I answer honestly. "And he's no boy and you know it."

"I'll be the judge of that."

I roll my eyes and whine softly at the pain it causes me. Ignoring Mom's satisfied chuckle, I ask, "Is he still here?"

Mom's phone pings and she looks at it. "He's outside." It pings again. "And—"

The door swings open and Will comes striding in, black hair wildly unkempt and deep smudges of purple beneath his eyes. His hands are bandaged and he's in a white undershirt and dress pants. Even like this, he's beautiful. He stops halfway to the bed and I'm pretty sure I stop breathing. His jaw muscles flex, and I swear I see his shoulders tense as he studies me head to toe. By the time his gaze lands on my face, it's as if he's made of stone.

The man may be one of few words, but he's got to make the first move here. A girl's got *some* pride, after all.

But he doesn't speak, just swallows hard and stares at me like he's trying to memorize me.

My heart sinks. Because I know that look. That's the look of a man who's finished with me.

A doctor comes in, breaking the silence with a happy, "Well, look who's awake!"

Will visibly recoils, finally looking away from me and stepping back as the doctor moves toward me. "How are you feeling?" she asks, brandishing a pen light before pressing it on.

"Like I have a concussion," I deadpan, submitting to her inspection.

"Yes, well, that would make sense," she says, "seeing as that's what you have."

She prattles on and I tune her out, noticing only that Will's no longer in the room. Finally, the doctor finishes and leaves, and I turn back to Mom.

"Do you have my phone? I need to talk to Will." Because it turns out, I actually have no pride. None.

Mom's eyebrows raise. "Excuse me?"

I sigh. "Mom. I just woke up and I have a concussion. The man I lo—care a lot about was here and now he's gone. Could you maybe not worry about manners for once? Just once? I'll make it up to you."

"You *love* him?"

Of course she caught that. I make myself meet her eyes and confess. "Fine. Yes. I love him. Can I have my phone now?"

Mom's eyes light up. "Oooh, y'all's babies would be so pretty!"

"Mom!" I admonish. Never mind that I've totally had the same thought, and never mind that we're both thirty-seven. *And never mind that I'm pretty certain he wants nothing to do with me.* So yeah, pretty babies aren't really in the plot right now.

She hands me my phone and I open it, ignoring the texts from Conner and going straight to my chain with Will.

> I'd really like to talk to you.

I watch the ellipses start up, then stop.

> Please, Will. Can you come back?

Like I said: pride go bye bye.

My text shows as read, but no dots. Finally, an answer comes.

HOTTIE MCHOT FACE

> You should spend time with your mother.

I growl and barely keep myself from throwing my phone across the room. Does this man not understand what it takes for me to ask this?

> She said she's tired. She'd appreciate the
> break.

More ellipses start and stop, before finally stopping. I wait for something, for freaking *anything*, but nothing comes.

My stupid heart squeezes and my brain begins a chorus of *I told you so* and *This is exactly why you've never gotten involved with anyone this deep before*, and I squeeze my eyes shut. My head may be the thing that's physically hurt, but my heart is utterly broken.

WILL

I'M CHECKING A couple out of the inn when the door opens and Tori walks in. Her eyes immediately find mine like the damn magnets they are, and I can't help but meet them and want to sink into their dark depths.

But I don't. Instead, I hand the husband his receipt and thank them for staying, even managing to plaster a semblance of a smile on my face and point to the QR code that asks for a review. The couple smile back, and Tori steps aside to let them pass. While she's preoccupied with shutting the door behind them, I take the opportunity to assess her. She's in sneakers and sweats I've never seen before, and her skin is still too pale. A tiny white butterfly bandage is nestled against her hairline, making her normally brown skin appear yellow. Her cheeks almost look sunken, too, but that has to be a trick of the light. It's only been twenty-four hours since I saw her in the hospital bed.

Really, it's been thirty-seven. But I'm trying not to focus on that.

Just like I'm trying not to focus on how small she looked in that bed, how fragile. And it doesn't matter that Tori is as far from fragile as it gets, because there's no stopping the way my head works. There's no denying that she was in that hospital bed because of me. I should have walked her home, but I didn't, and she got hurt.

"Will."

My eyes snap to hers.

She strides purposefully toward me, her gaze intent on me. "Why the fuck did you abandon me in that hospital? Huh?" She's rounded the desk and is crowding my space, and beneath the smell of hospital I catch her shea butter scent. "You said we'd talk. Remember? You said we'd talk, and when I'm in the *hospital*, asking you to come, I don't know, *talk to me* because I'm *in the hospital*, you bail!"

I close my eyes, the familiar refrain of *I can't do this* bouncing in my head.

"Oh the fuck no you don't," she snaps. "Open those eyes, Will Joseph. Don't you be a coward now."

Gritting my teeth, I open my eyes and find her glaring at me. "Fine. We're talking."

"You're damn right we're talking. Because this?" she seethes, gesturing between us. "This is absolute bullshit. This is exactly why I ran away in high school, you big idiot."

"What?" I cock my head, not understanding.

"What do you mean, what?"

"You broke up with me because you wanted to go out with dickbag Drew."

"No," she laughs sadly. "No, I broke up with you because I wasn't prepared for the way you made me feel. It scared the shit out of me. So I bailed."

My chest breaks apart, and all I can do is gape at her.

She rolls her eyes. "We aren't built for this. What did you call me—Chaos? Yeah, Will, guess what? I'm chaos and you're control. And for one tiny millisecond, I thought we could do this. You—you told me you loved me—" she chokes on the last part.

"I do," I say.

"*Ha,*" she scoffs. "You don't even fucking know what love is. And guess what? Neither do I!"

"I loved you in high school!" I roar, finally done with being yelled at.

She shrinks back, and I see the fear flit across her face. Fear. Of *me*. Did they tell her what I did when she was taken away? Of the way I lost all control?

I step around her, needing out from the confines of the desk and her fucking scent. When I'm a safe distance away, I turn. "Look at you," I say helplessly. "I don't deserve you. I didn't deserve you then, and I sure don't deserve you now. All I do is hurt the ones I love. I love you, and I hurt you. And apparently I scare you."

Her face softens. "You don't scare me."

"Bullshit. I saw it happen just now. I thought—" I break off. *I thought she was the one person who wasn't scared of me.*

She raises her chin, stepping around the desk. "I'm not scared of you, Will."

Intent on proving her wrong, I stalk back, forcing her to sit on the desk as I tower over her. Her eyes flash as I growl, and when I raise my hand to her neck, she sticks it out.

"Don't threaten me with a good time, big guy," she taunts, her eyes searing into mine. "You wanna squeeze? Do it. That doesn't scare me. *You* don't scare me."

Cursing, I pull my hand away and retreat. Tori stands. "I flinched when you yelled because you've never done that before. You're loud. I was surprised. But scared? No." Her voice softens. "I'm sorry for yelling at you."

"I'm sorry, too," I say. "But it doesn't change the fact that I can't be what you need."

She sucks the corner of her lip in, studying me. After a moment, she speaks. "So after…everything…we're really done."

I sag in relief. She gets it. She understands that I'm not worth it. "We're done."

She nods, then presses her lips together and looks away. "I figured. I'll get my things."

I swallow the knot in my throat as she ascends the stairs, too much of a coward to watch her go.

An hour after she leaves, Price and Aaron appear in the kitchen, where I'm deep in pastry prep. I glance up from the dough I'm kneading to take in their grim expressions, and sigh. I know exactly what this is.

Price wastes no time. "Just how dumb are you, asshole?"

"Devon and I are supposed to be packing for our honeymoon," Aaron says. "But instead, my wife is at the coffee shop with the rest of the women, trying to make sense out of whatever bullshit you've just pulled."

"Seriously. What. The. Fuck. Happened?" Price demands.

I cover the dough and put it in the proving drawer beneath the oven, then stand and lean against the counter to glare at them. "What happened is none of your business."

"See, that's where you're wrong," Aaron says. "Because you're our brother—"

"—and you've fucked up," Price says.

I pull at my hair and growl, completely done. "Of *course* I fucked up, Price! It's what I do! It's all I have ever done—look at him!" I point at Aaron. "I fucked him up from the jump! What kind of brother does that, huh? What kind of selfish prick kid tells his mother to get the fuck out of the house so that he can have some peace and quiet? What kid is fucking *gleeful* that his mom is finally gone? And then I go and become a firefighter because it's the only thing that makes sense, saving every fucking penny in the hopes you two can leave this town and do something with your lives, and I can't even do that right because you both follow me like I'm some kind of hero, when I'm the farthest thing from it."

Both of them stare at me, but before they can say anything, I keep going. "Do you have any idea what goes on in my head? The scenarios I go through, running over every single fucking thing that can go wrong and then doing everything in my power to head it off at the pass—and it still doesn't work? I still think it's my fault Jason died in that fucking fire, because he didn't listen to me. I should have been more forceful, *made* him listen, but I didn't, and he died."

"Will—" Price starts.

I wave him off. "All those years that Mom wasn't around, do you know why?" I ask. "Because I wouldn't let her. I decided it was better for her to not be here because she couldn't stay sober. But where the hell do I get off making that decision? What kind of asshole move was that? To the point where it's Tori who calls her about the wedding, not you?" I ask Aaron. "And then—*then* Mom texts me to ask if it's okay that she comes." I spread my arms wide. "What kind of fucked-up shit is that? She barely spoke to me during the wedding, too. I'm pretty sure my own mother is scared of me. I'm the one *everyone* is scared of. Jodi and Devon call me Mr. Scary, for fuck's sake. So yeah—" I whirl to Price. "Yeah, I fucked up. I fucked up good. I am not worth anyone's time, and I know it. All I am is a controlling asshole who demands excellence from everyone while managing to be entirely ruined on the inside." My voice catches and I realize I'm crying. Fucking *crying*. I heave breath after breath, unable to stop the tears, and for a long moment, no one speaks.

Then Price huffs a sad laugh. "You big-hearted mother fucker," he says, wiping at the tears in his own eyes.

Drained, and not knowing what else to say, I slide down the cabinets until my ass hits the floor. I bring my knees up and drape my arms around them, letting my head hang.

Price joins me on one side, while Aaron sits on the other.

"I don't even know where to start," Aaron says.

"I don't think I've ever heard you say that much in my life," Price says, making a half-hearted attempt at a joke.

I'm still crying. "I'm sorry," I manage to say. "I'm sorry for all of it."

"You're wrong about so many things," Aaron says.

I shake my head. "I'm not. It's all right there."

Price grips my neck. "Broseph. It's really not. Why haven't you said anything? We could have cleared a ton of shit up."

"Let's start with the fact that Mom was leaving anyway," Aaron says.

I turn my head to look at him, and that fucker isn't crying. "Because I told her to."

He shakes his head. "No. She let you think that because she thought it somehow made you feel better."

"How do you know that?"

"Because we've been talking. There's a long way to go—but Will, none of that is your fault. She made her choices, and a lot of them were really shitty. But she's an addict. We can't punish her for that."

I grunt and Price squeezes the back of my neck again. "Do you have any idea how many times she relapsed?" I ask.

"Do *you* know how proud she is of you?" Price counters. "How proud we all are?"

I grunt again.

"None of that," Aaron says. "Not when we know you have allll the damn words in your head, apparently."

"I don't understand why Tori needed to call her," I say, because I can't get my head around the rest right now.

"You misunderstood that, too," Aaron says on a sigh.

"So is all this because Tori called Mom?" Price asks.

"No," I mumble.

"Then what is it? Because I gotta tell you, man, you will never find a woman like the one who walked out of here."

I don't say anything, but I at least manage to stop crying. Price produces a blue polka dot handkerchief from his pocket and hands it to me. I raise an eyebrow.

"Jodi likes polka dots, okay?"

I raise my other eyebrow.

"Just shut up and blow your nose, asshole," Price says.

Chuckling, I do as he says, and we all get up off the floor.

"Is everything okay?"

I whip my head to the phone that Aaron's holding out, and Mom's face is staring out at us.

"Did you three get into a fight?" she asks. "Price, you know it's your responsibility—"

"—to keep the peace," he finishes on a smile. "I know, Mom. Don't worry, we're all fine. But we need you to clear some things up, okay?"

She nods.

"Did I really kick you out, or were you already planning to leave?" I blurt it out before either of my brothers can start down some kind of path I'm unwilling to follow.

She blanches. "That's such an ugly time in our lives. Do you really want to discuss it?"

It's nearly comical the way all three of us nod at the screen. I'm glaring, Aaron is studiously neutral, and Price is encouraging.

"Well," she sighs, "I knew I needed help. It was obvious. I was a terrible mother to the three of you, and I couldn't function without a drink from the second I woke up. Your dad and I fought constantly. You know that, Will."

"I do."

"But I don't think the other boys truly realized it."

"Not really," Aaron says, and Price shrugs noncommittally.

"So I knew I needed to leave and go somewhere. And when you came into my room that day, the fury in your eyes, Will…it was time. So you didn't 'kick me out,' per se. You were the kick in the pants I needed."

A tightness in my chest loosens by a fraction.

"See?" Price says. "Told you."

"Um, no," Aaron says. "*I* told you."

"Did you really call me just to ask about this?" Mom says.

We all nod again.

"It'd be good if you told Will none of this was his fault," Price says.

"None of what?"

"This," Price says, gesturing between the phone and the three of us. "He's got a complex over here that he's screwed all of us up somehow, and it all goes back to when you left."

Mom puts her hand over her heart. "Will. My strong boy. Of *course* none of it is your fault. I'm an addict, and I'm the one who messed it all up. I'm trying to get better."

"You need to stop asking me permission," I interrupt. "Quit texting and asking me things."

"You're right," she concedes.

"And the way you look at me," I say, deciding if we're doing all this touchy-feely shit then I'm going all in. I've already cried. What's a few more things?

"The way I look at you?" Mom asks, confused. Even my brothers are looking at me weird.

"You look at these two like they hung the moon. But when you look at me, your eyes dim. Like you're scared of me, or disappointed."

"I could never be scared of you," Mom says.

"So you're disappointed."

"I didn't say that, either. You just—Will, you look so much like your father that sometimes it hurts. I see you and I see him.

I see all my failures, and how we fought, and how I never got to tell him I loved him before he died because I was on a bender." She tears up and sniffs.

Well, fuck. My eyes are watering again.

"I am so proud of you. I'm so proud of *all* of you," she says. "God knows I had nothing to do with any of your success. I think my leaving actually helped. But Will, if anything, *you* are the reason the three of you are thriving. *Your* hard work. *Your* sacrifice. *Your* endless love."

"Mom, you're killing us over here," Price says, producing yet another polka dot handkerchief and wiping his eyes with it. Then I look closer.

"Price," I pinch his leg. "Price, *get your girlfriend's panties off screen*," I mutter.

"Oh my word!" Mom gasps.

Aaron bursts out laughing, and even I can't help the chuckle that comes out of me.

Price pulls the panties away, studies them, then shrugs and stuffs them back in his pocket. "I'm not apologizing for that."

"Fucking hell," I say as I shake my head.

On the screen, Mom sputters, "I—I—*Price!*"

"Okay, Mom, love you, bye!" Aaron says, still laughing as he ends the call.

TORI

I AWAKE TO the sounds of Jodi and Price getting it on in the pre-dawn of the morning. But it's better than seeing my mom get railed on the couch, so I'll take the win. Tonight, I'll go to Aaron and Devon's place to take care of Daisy and Samson while they're on their honeymoon. I'll have the week they're gone to figure out my next moves.

Because I want to stay here. Despite everything. Even knowing that I'm going to run into the man who lifted me up only to smash me into a million little pieces. Even knowing the chances of finding another man in this small town are minimal. Not that I'll be looking, but I know myself. I'll need some vitamin D eventually.

Who am I kidding? The only man I'll ever look at and want sustenance from is Will. He ruined me, body and soul. I roll over and pull the pillow over my head, wishing my generous hosts would come already. Honestly, they're giving me and Will a run for our money.

Or they would have. Because Will and I are no more, and I need to get that in my head.

No.

And see, that right there. Rationally, I know it's over. The man literally looked me in the eyes and confirmed that we were done. Finito. And my brain has had a delightful time with this information, reminding me why we don't let our feelings get in the way, and why we've only ever kept things surface-level with boys.

But my heart? My simple, stupid heart is entirely not rational, swinging between gut-wrenching desperation, a righteous sense of anger, and a determination to fight. Mad *at* Will, mad *for* Will. It's my typical chaos, only it's the heart version. And it's confusing and painful. Physically painful. My face hurts from all the crying I did yesterday.

My alarm goes off and I grab my phone to silence it, noticing that the happy couple is also silent. I pull myself out of bed and head for the shower down the hall, even though I'll be sweaty after the morning Pilates session and will need another one by the time the day is through. I make quick work of things, and dress in my favorite red tights and top. My face may be puffy, but at least the ridiculous bandage is off my head.

I threw those shoes away. Not that it'll keep me from taking another tumble at one point down the road, but at least it won't be in the shoes that are costing me thousands of dollars in hospital bills.

I find a rosy-cheeked Jodi in the kitchen, and instinctively I look around for my half of the pastry that Will always splits with me. But all the delicious pastry is across the street at the inn. Not here.

Dammit, heart. Give a girl a break.

"Coffee?" Jodi hands me a cup that I take with a grateful smile.

"Thank you," I say before taking a sip. "So good. You should think about opening a coffee shop," I joke.

"Morning, Tori," Price says, swinging into the kitchen and planting a kiss on Jodi's head. He grabs a mug and pours himself some before turning back around. "I need to get over there. I'm already late."

Jodi laughs. "It's 5:45, Price."

He smiles adoringly at her. "Exactly. See you two lovely ladies later!"

Jodi watches him go. A moment later, he reappears through the kitchen window as he saunters to the street, looks both ways, then crosses it. He's inside the inn in seconds, and I know without a doubt that Will's griping about the time and how he's going to be late getting to the station, and Price is laughing and telling him to *chill out, broseph.*

It's not until I see Will's truck round the corner from the back side of the inn that I finally look at Jodi and force myself to not think about Will. "Someone had an orgasm or two this morning," I say as I take another sip of coffee.

She blushes. "Oh my gosh, you heard us?"

"Hard not to," I answer. And I try hard to smile, but I'm pretty sure it looks more like a grimace.

"I'm so sorry." Anguish is written all over her face. "Especially…"

"That I'm not getting any orgasms?" I finish.

"That's not what I meant," she says.

I wave it off. "I know. Don't worry. Don't you need to be at the shop?"

"I told Darius he was running solo for a little bit this morning. I wanted to make sure you were doing okay. Besides, he gave notice, so I've got to use him as much as possible for the next few weeks."

My eyes widen. "He gave notice? Why?"

Jodi's smile is huge. "Conner didn't tell you?"

A flicker of emotion that isn't sadness or anger comes awake in my chest, and I clutch my hands together. "Please tell me that Darius is moving to Atlanta to be with Conner."

She nods and squeals, "He is!"

"That's amazing!" And for a moment, I'm flooded with giddiness at the prospect of one of my best friends getting the happiness he so deserves. It feels good to be this happy, and I want it to stay, but the emotion recedes almost as quickly as it crashed into me.

"Oh, Tori." Jodi sets her coffee down and opens her arms.

I step into them and cry some more.

I know word has spread when my own mother waltzes in to the studio in yoga pants.

"Mom?"

She smiles warmly at me. "I hear Pilates is the new yoga."

"Pilates is Pilates. Lucky for you this session doesn't use the reformer," I say, pointing to the machines on the wall.

"Looks like something from medieval times," she mutters.

I smirk, then get her set up with a mat, ball, and blocks, but she stops me before I can walk away.

"Are you okay?"

My eyes immediately sting and my throat thickens. Blinking rapidly, I shake my head. "But I will be."

She grabs my hands in hers and waits until I meet her eyes. "You are a strong, generous, beautiful woman, inside and out. You will absolutely be okay. But Tori, it's okay to not be okay for a little while. You're allowed."

Her words are a punch to the gut, and I have to straighten my spine to keep from crumpling into her arms. Instead, I take a deep breath and let it out. And with that exhale comes clarity, stark and ringing in my head like a bell. Because I *am* allowed. I am allowed a lot of things, and I know what I have to do. For the first time in days, I manage a real smile. "Thanks, Mom."

She grins back. "Now go easy on me, will you? This is my first Pilates class."

"I will," I promise.

But I know who I'm not going to go easy on: Will fucking Joseph.

Tori

I T TURNS OUT that holding a grudge is great for my skin. I am positively glowing, and I credit my plan to tell Will exactly where he can shove it for how good I look.

Three days. I've had three days of house-sitting to stew and think and write lists and cry and yell and scream into a quiet house and plan my speech, all while trying to ignore the fact that my heart straight-up *refuses* to let go. Which means that I'm more pissed than anything. Pissed at Will for leaving, and pissed at my heart for not getting the memo. Clearly the twenty years between Will Experience #1 and Will Experience #2 have not taught my heart shit, and I'd really like it to get the memo, so that I can feel whatever sadness I need to feel and move on with my life. I can only hope that the speech I have planned for him does the trick.

Because today, February 20, is the day that William Franklin Joseph is going to get his ass handed to him.

After work.

And after I shower.

And dress in devastatingly sexy clothes and heels.

Because I plan to look good as hell while telling him off.

I realized this morning that we were exactly a month under our original timeline, and it makes me even angrier. We were supposed to have another month of earth-shattering sex, but I let my heart go and mess that up. I ended up being a jittery mess all day, more than a little distracted during my classes, but not enough that anyone really noticed. They just held poses a little longer than usual. When I bound down the steps, Ceci and Jodi are waiting for me.

"What are you up to?" Ceci asks. "Because that ashtanga yoga class of yours I took this morning was not ashtanga. You went *way* off-script." Then she narrows her eyes. "And you look…*really* good. Is this what a break-up does to you?"

Jodi waves her hand at me like I'm Exhibit A. "Exactly," she says to Ceci. "How does anyone look this incredible after getting their heart broken?"

"It better be a new skin-care regimen that I can buy," Ceci declares.

"Nope," I say. "I cried out all the toxins in my life."

"And the toxin was…" Jodi says.

"Will Joseph," I confirm. Meanwhile, in my head, I'm squishing a metaphorical stiletto onto the little part of my heart that's still squeaking about loving him.

"Hmm," Ceci says thoughtfully. "I'm not sure I buy it, but you do you, boo."

"What's there to buy? I'm telling the truth. We're done. *He* said so," I remind them. "We've been over this."

She shrugs and sips at her iced coffee. "If you say so."

"I do say so. Just like he said so. We allll say so."

Jodi studies me.

I sigh dramatically. "Look. It's over. *He* said it. *I'm* saying it. We have both said all the things that need to be said. Except for the part where I lose my shit all over him. That's coming." I rub my hands together. "And it's going to be so good. Seriously, the speech I have planned is epic. I'm going to give that man hell for making me love him and then leaving me."

Ceci narrows her eyes. "Yeah…no."

"What do you mean, no?"

"I mean I don't buy any of this. You're not acting like a woman with a broken heart. You still love him. My money's on you two getting back together."

It takes a ridiculous amount of control not to gape at how she hit the nail on the head. Because of course I still love him. But he doesn't love me back, and I refuse to wallow. My mom didn't raise me to wallow. So I ignore Ceci and hand Jodi my travel mug. "Can I have my caramel latte please? I have a speech to give."

"When Devon and Aaron broke up, they were both disasters," Jodi says.

"I'm not Devon," I say.

Without another word, but with plenty of meaningful looks at me and Ceci, Jodi makes the latte and hands it over.

I salute the both of them with it. "Thank you. See you on the flip side!"

Naturally, I trip on my way out. I ignore the snickers of the women behind me.

Two hours later, I pull up to the inn. I'm in three-inch red velvet stilettos that have pink ribbons crisscrossing up to tie in a bow at the back of my bare calves, and I'm wearing a white leather skirt with a red, skin-tight long-sleeve turtleneck. Underneath is an all-black lace panty and bra set. Not that he'll have the privilege of seeing them. My hair is down, skimming past my shoulders. I smell fantastic.

In other words: I am a goddamn siren and he's going to hear me scream.

I've timed my arrival to be in the window that Will tends to have the inn as closed as it gets: the two hours between check-out and check-in. If he's lucky, no one will be around to hear me take him down. Getting out of the car, I step gingerly to the porch, because I absolutely refuse to fall and ruin the entrance I plan to make.

At the threshold, I take a breath, fluff my hair, and fling open the door.

Except he isn't at the desk. Which, frankly, puts a damper on my entrance. But whatever.

I shut the door and head to the kitchen, but he isn't there, either. A fresh platter of cranberry scones rests on the table, along with a note for guests to help themselves.

Huffing, I head around to the laundry, but he's not there either.

Dammit.

One more shot. I stomp to our—*his*—bedroom and try my fling-the-door-open move once more. Except, yet again, the fucker isn't here.

Then I hear him talking in the bathroom.

Is he—oh, god, is someone else in there with him?

I will *kill* him.

I choke down an angered sob, throw some rage on top of it, then stomp across the room and prepare to confront him.

WILL

I'VE BEEN PRACTICING my apology speech to Tori. It's not going well, and all it's proving is that I'm a caveman who's spent too much time grunting and not enough time exploring my feelings. It's precisely what my brothers said right before they started texting a shitload of articles about the toxicity of American masculinity, how childhood trauma shows up in adulthood, coping with addiction as a family, learning to apologize, understanding anxiety, and a bunch of other things.

It's been...a lot. *They've* been a lot, the little shits. But I'm grateful, because it's made me realize that I have some major issues to sift through. I probably need therapy, the idea of which makes me itchy.

Stepping out of the shower and drying off, I don't bother wiping the steam off the mirror to see what I look like, because I already know: a sorry creature who doesn't deserve to breathe the same air as the woman he loves. But Aaron and Price insist that I need to be the one to make the first move; Price called it my "grand gesture," whatever that means.

I wrap the towel around my waist, take a breath, and grip the sides of the sink. I'm going to try this one more time, then I'm going to march across the street and say it. "I'm so sorry, Tori. I've got some shit to work through and…will you forgive me?" I hang my head. "Worst apology ever," I mutter. I really should have taken Aaron's offer of help. I wasn't kidding when I told Devon that he was the best of us.

"I need you to forgive me." No, that sounds demanding. "I'm an asshole." Better…maybe?

The door swings open and I jump, then blink rapidly.

Because I've died and gone to heaven.

That is the only explanation for why Tori is standing in my doorway like a furious goddess of love sent from above.

Why do my knees hurt?

Oh.

Because I've sunk to them.

Tori

W HAT THE FUCK is he doing?

"What the fuck are you doing?" I ask.

But he just stays on his knees, his towel wrapped around his waist, his chest still sporting droplets of water as if they couldn't bear to be parted from his incredible skin, his wet hair falling across his forehead in the exact deliciously sinful way that makes *me* wet, and says nothing.

"Will, answer me!"

His eyes are eating me alive, and I swear my skin heats in the wake of his ravenous gaze. Feet, legs, thighs, stomach, tits, neck, face. He swallows hard, and all I can wonder as I watch his Adam's apple bob is what it looks like when he swallows while he's between my legs. To say that the thought isn't helpful is a drastic understatement.

"Tori." His voice is rough, rapturous.

And it unravels me.

"No, nope, no," I say, shaking my head and clenching my fists to stay in control. "No. No, you don't get to act like that. I came here to tell you off."

His chest, that beautiful strong chest, *heaves*. And I cannot with that. "Victoria."

"Will. *No.*"

And then he moves toward me.

On his fucking *knees.*

Oh, god. What is happening? I back up, and he keeps following. "I had a whole speech planned," I say, my heels scraping lightly across the floor.

"Yeah?" He's still following on his knees.

I nod, but I'm having a hard time remembering what I was going to say. I'm mad at him. Right. Mad and mad and...mad. Right?

"Me, too."

Suddenly, my back hits the bedroom door, closing it all the way shut. I lean against it and try to process what's happening, but my head is completely scrambled. "You have a speech?"

He's mouthwatering, his chest moving up and down with every breath he takes as he gets closer. "Mine is shit. I want yours. Give it to me, Tori. Give everything to me." His eyes darken as he speaks.

God *damn.* I need space. I hold my hands out. "Will. Stop."

He does.

My brain short circuits at the sight of him kneeling in front of me, but I fight through it. I drop my gaze from his, and it's a mistake, because my hungry eyes simply rove his body, cataloging the wide set of his corded shoulders and the way they taper to his stomach, to the line of dark hair that leads to the best dick I have ever had the pleasure of welcoming into me. God, I miss him. It's not even been a week, and I fucking *miss* him.

And I remember: me missing him is why I'm pissed.

So I take a deep breath and meet his eyes again, noticing for the first time that they've lost the haunted look that was always in the background. They're clear. Wide open. Untroubled. "You broke my heart."

"I know." He lifts his chin as he says it.

"You know?"

He nods.

My heart squishes, then expands. But then I remember I had a speech. "And you lied. You said we'd talk, but we never did. You didn't come see me in the hospital, even when I asked you to." I straighten off the door, battling through the tears threatening to fall. *I will not cry.* "And on top of everything, you broke up with me like a fucking coward, and why? Because you 'couldn't do it,' whatever 'it' is. I don't understand. I have never in my life fallen for *anyone*, and you made me fall for you, you asshole!" I swipe at the tears falling and realize he's come closer, still on his knees.

"Is that it?" he asks, his voice low, his eyes holding mine through strands of inky black hair.

"No," I say, trying to keep my voice from trembling.

"Then tell me," he commands.

"You, you," I start. Then I sniff. "Goddammit. I *hate* that I'm crying. I'm so pissed at you! I love you, you asshole. I love you and I am so fucking mad at you, and if you think you can just break up with me and be done with me so easily, then you have another fucking thing coming." And as the words come, I realize I've landed about a million miles from where I intended. I was supposed to tell him I hated him and wanted nothing to do with him ever again. I was supposed to tell him that he wasn't worth my tears or my time, and that I didn't need him anyway. That I was a strong woman who didn't need him or his heart or his muscles or his dick to be complete. That I could go back to the way I was before, and that I'd be just fine.

But it's all bullshit.

Because while I *am* strong, I need him. And I *am* complete without him, but he is the missing piece to my life. He is everything, and it's terrifying and infuriating in equal measure, and... shit, what is he doing?

He's closed the remaining distance between us, looking up at me like a fallen dark angel, and all I can think to do is lift a heel and put it on his chest, digging the point of the stiletto into a solid wall of muscle.

His eyes close and he shudders. "Fuck, Tori. I missed you." When they open, they're on fire. "Harder."

I increase the pressure, watching the skin around the heel go white as his hands skate up to wrap around my calf and pull. "You deserve more than this," I say as he drags the heel down his chest.

"Yes, I do," he growls.

"You hurt me," I say.

"Yes, I did." His gorgeously clear eyes hold mine.

"You can't do that again." My voice is a whisper.

"I won't, sweetheart. I'm so sorry."

"You are?" I rasp.

He nods slowly. "I love you so much, Tori. I'm sorry," he repeats.

I don't speak again, transfixed by what he's doing. With a few more moves of my stiletto over his skin, he's finished, and my name is written across his chest in bright red welts.

He looks down at his work, then presses his lips to the shoe as his eyes meet mine. "These stay on until I say otherwise."

I raise an eyebrow. "Says who?"

He growls and nips at my ankle before guiding my foot to the ground. "Me."

"What makes you think I'm going to listen to you?"

He growls, then pushes a hand beneath my skirt and squeezes between my legs, eliciting a gasp of pleasure from me. "Because I may have been a bad boy."

"The worst," I breathe out.

"But I need to make it up to you. And you're going to let me do it the way you need me to."

I try to breathe normally as his grip tightens. "Is that your speech?"

He chuckles darkly. "It's a lot better than what I was practicing, so yes."

I rake a hand through his hair, holding it tightly away from his face and looking down at him. He hasn't shaved, and I know the scruff will abrade my skin when he takes me. A shiver of anticipation makes its way through my body. "Your eyes."

His brow furrows even as his thumb presses against my clit.

I moan. "They're...*fuck*, they're clearer."

"Ah. Yes." Without additional explanation, he undoes my skirt and lowers it to the ground. In a daze, I kick it to the side, and he leans his nose to where his thumb works me, still maintaining eye contact. He inhales.

Fighting to keep my knees from buckling, I force out, "So?"

"So what, Victoria?" He hooks his thumbs under my panties and pulls them down.

I step out of them, too. "What happened?"

His tongue darts out to taste me. He still hasn't stopped looking at me. "I quit the fire station."

The surprise that pushes through me is intensified by his tongue. "You...quit? *Shit*, Will." I groan his name, drawing it out.

"We're not talking about this right now," he says. "We're talking about this sweet pussy, and how I've missed your taste, and how I'm going to make you come right now."

I let my head fall against the door and let out a sigh of pleasure, utterly done fighting.

"Pull," he commands.

I grab the top of his hair and curl my fingers into fists, giving him the bite of pain he wants and holding him against me as he fucks me with his tongue. My hips swirl and buck, riding his face as he pushes one, then two thick fingers into me. It doesn't take any time before I'm coming, my orgasm cresting on his command.

WILL

I WILL NEVER let her go. Not ever again.

She shudders above me and I taste her sweet release. I work her down, and once I feel her go limp against the door, I finally rise from my position of supplication, kissing my way up her body as I go. I pull her shirt off and take my fill of her breasts, sitting so prettily on display in a lacy black bra.

I leave it on and seal my mouth to hers in a kiss. She melts into me, pliant for at least the time being, and I relish it. Her hands rise up to my chest, and she pulls away to study it.

"That might be there for a while," she murmurs, her fingers tracing the letters.

"That's the point," I say. "I'll fucking brand myself for you, Tori."

She smiles. "You would, wouldn't you?"

I nod, deadly serious. "I'm sorry for hurting you, Tori. I took my own fears and issues out on you, and it was wrong of me. I've got some things to work through, and I've started, but I'm not done. Not even close."

She pulls my towel off. "That's a better speech." Her hand wraps around my cock and I hiss. "Keep going."

I clear my throat. "Right. I, ah…what was I saying?"

She grabs my balls with her other hand. "You were saying you were very sorry for not coming to see me in the hospital."

"You're never going to let that go, are you?" I grit out.

"Nope."

I fight for control of myself. "Is now when I mention they tried to hospitalize me, too?"

She pumps my cock slowly and licks the hollow of my throat. "Is that so?"

I cough. "Yeah. Yes. I was so, *fuck, baby*, I can't…"

"You can, and you will." She bites my collarbone.

"I was so worked up," I gulp in some air, "that I kind of… lost consciousness once I knew you were okay." I exhale.

Pushing off the door, she walks me backwards to the bed and forces me to lay down. "Sounds serious."

"It wasn't."

"I think it was."

"Then you should forgive me for not coming to see you."

She quirks a smile. "Nice try."

I'm helpless to do anything as she straddles me, then moves her way up to where her pussy is above my mouth. She smiles down at me. "Eat up, big guy."

On a groan, I wrap my arms around her and pull her down to me, lapping at her, worshipping her, feeling her legs go taut. I will stay here till the end of my days if needed. Whatever my woman wants. But it doesn't take nearly that long before she's chanting my name and digging those phenomenal fucking stilettos into my sides and coming on my tongue.

She hums as she lifts off me, moving down to slide her pussy against my cock. Smirking, she uses her thumb to wipe herself off my mouth. "You weren't done apologizing."

I shake my head. This fucking woman. She can boss me around till the end of my days and I'll thank her for it every time. "I definitely wasn't."

"You were going to apologize for taking your fear out on me."

I unclasp her bra and watch as her breasts fall out. I pull one into my mouth, sucking hard as I grab her ass with my other hand. After I feel the nipple peak and pull it between my teeth, I pop off. "I do. I apologize profusely."

She continues to grind her wet pussy against my cock. "Will," she whispers, her dark eyes bottomless with need.

"Let me inside you, baby. Let me make you feel good."

She nods, and I lift her hips, watching her face as I guide her onto me, controlling her descent inch by hot, wet inch. Finally, she's fully seated on me, and I nearly come at the way she feels. "You are wondrous."

"I love you so much," she says.

"I love you, too."

"Don't you ever try to pull that shit again, do you hear me?" She arches a brow.

"Yes, ma'am," I grunt. I move my hands to her legs, feeling for the silk ribbons at the tops of her calves and threading my fingers through them. "These fucking shoes."

"You were supposed to regret not being able to have me ever again," she says, riding me slowly.

"I would have."

"We were supposed to be over."

"That's never happening," I say. "You were it for me from the minute I saw you, Tori. No one else was ever going to measure up."

She stops. "Will. We went to grade school together."

I lift my hips into her. "I know."

She begins to move again. "Didn't I punch you on the swings?"

I smile. "Yes, sweetheart, you sure fucking did. Explains my need for pain, don't you think?"

She laughs, then her face gentles. "*You're* wondrous," she

says. "Not me."

I flip us so she's on her back, needing more of her and unable to handle the lack of control. I pull her knee up and push into her, memorizing yet again the way her neck arches, the specific noise that she makes only when I enter her. "I'm not special."

She cups my face in her hands. "That's where you're wrong. You are incredibly special, and I'm the lucky woman who gets to have you. You are everything to me, Will Joseph. You are my heart. You are my beautifully stubborn, immovable North Star. Because no matter what, you are always pointed toward what is right, and good, and just. *Fuck* you feel so damn good."

I push into her, fighting the tears that clog my throat. I squeeze my eyes shut.

Her nails scrape down my back. "Give me everything, Will. I can take it."

I push again, my heart bursting apart as I bury my head in her neck. "Tori," I choke.

She gasps and crosses her legs behind my back. "I've got you, big guy. Let me catch you."

Nodding, I lean up and push deep into her. And as my tears hit her cheeks, she pulls my mouth to hers.

EPILOGUE
TWO MONTHS LATER

"GENTLEMEN, START YOUR engines!"

My chest thrums with the roar of thirty-eight NASCAR engines coming to life in front of me, and I squeal and bounce up and down on Will's lap. "This is *awesome!*"

Will laughs, his smile broad and indulgent. "Can't believe you've never been to a Talladega race," he says. "It's practically a rite of passage living here."

Surrounding us are Ceci and Rick, Devon and Aaron, and Jodi and Price. It's the April race weekend, and the sun is shining hot and bright as the pace car leads the pack out of pit lane and onto the track. Devon demanded we wear themed outfits, so we're all decked out in various forms of "1970s Racing Chic," whatever that means. All three guys are in baseball hats, seventies-inspired sunglasses, and haven't shaved in nearly a month in order to sport mustaches that are, quite frankly, horrific. But Price managed to find vintage bellbottom jeans, and my big guy gamely wore some jean shorts, bless him. I'm sporting a massive Afro and sunglasses, the other girls' hair is feathered back like the screen legends of the time, and we're all in various styles of fringed and beaded vintage-inspired t-shirts. What's funny is that no one has given us a second glance. The variety of people here is something I wasn't expecting. Little kids, grandmothers, every color human under the rainbow dressed every which way...humanity is here, and apparently humanity loves NASCAR.

And tailgating. Humanity most definitely loves tailgating, and it turns out that there is nothing quite like getting friendly with your neighbors and trading jello shots for sausage balls at nine in the morning. It's possible we were in the fields outside the track at eight this morning and indulged in a significant amount of food and adult beverages before coming into the track. It's also possible that the guys toted in some hard ciders and plenty of water and snacks in their coolers to keep us hydrated and on the road to sobriety for the duration of the race. Possibly.

I sigh contentedly and focus on the cars as Will's rough hands slip under my shirt and rest against my skin. The vehicles move like a brightly lit snake, light glinting off the roofs as they round a corner in a colorful clump and disappear from view. I lean back against him.

"Is this comfortable?" I ask.

His laugh rumbles through my body. "I've got the most gorgeous woman in the world wiggling on my lap. Doesn't matter if it's comfortable."

"Do you even fit in this seat?" I twist around to inspect. The plastic seats aren't exactly spacious, but we're in the first line of chairs and we're right in front of pit road, so we can see all the action.

"Barely," he answers.

I give him a kiss, not caring that the surrounding seats are packed with people. The likelihood that most of them aren't entirely sober is decent, anyway, so no one pays us any attention.

Until Ceci pokes me in the side. "Ugh, get a room, you two," she jokes.

I yelp and glare at her. "You've got an entire day away from your kids. Why are you being mean?"

"It's my love language," she shoots back. "Besides, you're my bestie. If you can't handle it, then no one can."

I giggle and turn my attention back to the track. The pace car pulls off into pit road, which signals the true beginning of the race. In seconds, the pack surges forward, their already-loud engines getting that much more powerful. All around us, the crowd stands and cheers, but I stay planted in Will's lap.

He leans up and brushes my hair back to put his lips to my ear. "Thank you."

I glance back. "For what?"

"Everything."

My heart squeezes. I take off both our sunglasses so I can see those amazing silver-blue eyes, and they twinkle back at me. "Who are you, and what did you do with Will Joseph?" I tease.

His arms tighten around me, warm and safe, as his lips tip into a smile. "This is all your fault. You swooped in with all your chaos and love and made me happy."

"What about Price and Aaron?"

"What about them?"

I giggle. "How many articles and links have they sent you by now?"

He groans. "Too many. Between them and the therapist, my way of life is being threatened."

"I kind of miss super grumpy Will," I say, running my hand up and around his massive chest.

"I'm still grumpy," he pouts.

"Says who?"

"I still don't like people."

"But you run a bed and breakfast," I point out. "By yourself."

"And that makes me grumpy," he huffs.

I grin. "It does no such thing. You love being the one in charge of everything. Folding those fitted sheets *just right*, even though no one but you sees them—"

"Because I'm not an animal."

"And making sure each bathroom is stocked with every type and size of feminine product and multiple toothpastes and extra toothbrushes and lotions—"

"People need *options*."

"But I thought you didn't like people," I tease.

He growls.

I laugh and concede, "I'll pretend that you're still a *little* grumpy."

Immediately, his frown disappears and a big grin is back on his face. "Thank you."

"You're ridiculous," I laugh.

"And you're the love of my life," he says.

My breath catches as the cars roar by. The man in front of me is so different from the man I ran into after the Christmas parade: wide open where he was once so closed off, all toothy smiles when it used to take a miracle to get the slightest grin from him, and telling me he loves me when he once was too scared to utter it. And as I sit in the warm sun with his arms around me, the two of us surrounded by friends and family, I know that this is the man I'll spend my life with. This amazing man, who may be *slightly* grumpy, but who loves with his whole heart. "I'll never get tired of hearing you say that."

He takes my chin between his thumb and forefinger. "Good. Because I plan on telling you that until we're old and gray."

"I love you so much, Will Joseph."

"And I love you, too, Chaos."

Thanks for reading The Grump's Guide to Chaos! I hope you loved it. I'd be grateful if you'd review it on Amazon and Goodreads!

Be sure to join my mailing list for news about upcoming books!

Can't get enough? Keep going for a sneak peek at Love Potion No. 69, which kicks off the Sacred River series!

Love Potion No. 69
Chapter 1: Clementine

Once upon a time, there was a princess…

Nope. Not accurate.

Once upon a time, there was a girl…

Scratch that. Everyone treats me like I'm far younger than my twenty-seven years, so let's try that again.

I hold the glass jar up, the sun's light refracting through the clear liquid, and hold my breath as I slowly pour the Elysian Blossom essence in.

"Please don't cloud, don't cloud, don't…son of a biscuit eater!" I set the jar down, put the vial of essence back in the refrigerator, and grab my notebook and pencil. Love potion number 68, bust.

Once upon a time, there was a botanist who was tired of her sisters treating her like a baby, so she decided to recreate the famous love potion her family was once known for. Except the potion was never written down, and the botanist's mother only remembered how it smelled instead of what was in it, which was supremely unhelpful. So the botanist toiled day after day in her greenhouse laboratory, her only exposure to sunlight the rays that came through the glass surrounding her, and definitely no prince to speak of.

Better. Except when would I actually have time for a prince? Also, it's the twenty-first century in America, and unless I'm aiming for the British guy who's living on the West Coast with his gorgeous wife and family after having told the crown to shove it, then no prince for me.

I finish my notes, then pull my hair into a bun and secure it with a pencil right as my sister Magnolia comes into the greenhouse.

"Hey, Clemmy-clem-Clementine!" she calls, her voice as bright as the Saturday sun outside. "Figured I'd find you in here." She holds out a mug of tea as she approaches, and I take it gratefully.

"Thank you." I inhale the aroma before sipping, because as grateful as I am for the tea, I also know my family's tendencies when it comes to tea. Granted, Magnolia is the second-oldest of us and generally behaves herself, but there's a lot of things growing on our land that can be put to mischievous use. All I smell is lemon and verbena, so I'm going to assume it's safe. After a small sip, I grin and take a larger drink.

She quirks a dark brow at me. "So suspicious," she chides.

"Do you blame me?" I ask, taking another deep gulp. It's the perfect temperature, and none of us have figured out how to keep a ceramic cup heated, so I need to drink it now.

Magnolia laughs. "No, I don't. But I'm here with a favor."

I sigh. "I swear, if you're here to ask me to call Hazel and beg her to come home for a visit—"

"No, not that," she says. "Not today, anyway."

"Then what?"

She hesitates, and instantly I'm on edge.

"Mags, out with it. You're freaking me out. None of you ever ask for a favor, unless it's to help play a trick on someone, and I'm really busy—"

"Could you come talk to my class on Tuesday?"

I stop mid-sentence, clamping my mouth shut and squinting

at her through my glasses. "I'm sorry. Did you just ask me to come speak to your class?"

She nods, a hopeful look in her amber eyes. "I thought I'd let them see what a career that uses chemistry looks like."

I sigh. "You know how much I hated high school. Why would I willingly go back there?"

"Because your favorite sister is begging you? Because I'm the only one who doesn't give you shit on a constant basis? Because—"

"Fine," I cut her off, knowing it's better to give in than endure the constant stream of reasons she'll come up with. "I'll do it. You owe me."

She jumps up and down and rushes me, wrapping me in a crushing hug and saying "thank you" on repeat. I manage to save the tea, but only barely. When she lets me go, I finish the tea and hand the cup back to her.

"You need to send me a calendar appointment. Otherwise, I can't be held responsible for missing it," I say.

She flashes me a wide smile. "You got it." Then she assesses my work station. "Now that I've gotten the boring stuff out of the way, how's it going?"

I let out a frustrated groan. "Horribly. I thought I was onto something, but the last batch clouded as soon as I put the Elysian Blossom essence in."

Magnolia's eyes widen. "You're using *Elysian Blossom*?"

I smile. "Yep."

She frowns. "But—but it only blooms once every hundred years. It's extremely rare. Our family is the only one that even has seeds, and you know how important it is to us, Clementine."

I cross my arms, instantly on the defensive. "Quit using your teacher voice on me, Mags."

She's not fazed. "Clearly someone has to. Does Mom know?"

I grind my teeth. This is exactly why I don't like my family to come in here. Never mind that I'm a grown woman with an advanced degree and plenty of common sense. All they see are the messes I made as a little girl with insatiable curiosity. The burn on my right hand and arm, the color of an over-ripe strawberry against my olive skin, doesn't let them forget, either.

"Well? Does she?" Magnolia prompts.

"She doesn't, and she doesn't need to," I shoot back.

Magnolia barks a laugh. "You're hilarious. Mom will kill you."

"Could you for once, just *once*, pretend that I might actually know what I'm doing?" I keep my voice calm and even, despite preferring to screech at her. "Pretend, for just a moment, that I have been doing this research for five years. Pretend that I'm the one who tends to our land. Pretend that I might have figured out a way to force the flower to bloom when I want it to, and that I've managed to capture its essence in a way that doesn't harm it."

She shakes her head. "You're begging for trouble."

"I'm not. I know what I'm doing," I repeat.

My phone pings from beneath my notebook, and we both turn in its direction.

"Who's that?" Magnolia asks.

I roll my eyes. "I don't know. I haven't looked yet. Also, it's none of your business."

"Since when has that stopped me?" she asks, angling her body to look at the screen with me. Then she snorts. "Who is 'Entitled Canadian Asshole'?"

I smash the phone against my chest. "No one."

"That doesn't seem to be the case."

I consider her eager eyes and the way they betray her carefully-presented patience. It wouldn't be a bad idea to have a sister on my side, and honestly, if I could choose the sister to go to battle with, it's always going to be Mags. She is the one who gives me the least shit, and in my family, that's saying something. "It's this man, Quinton Henry."

She gasps. "The perfume prince of Canada?"

The effort it takes for me to not roll my eyes at that ridiculous nickname should win me an award. "Yes."

"What does he want?"

"Christ, Mags—why don't you stop talking and I'll *tell* you?" I huff.

Properly chastised for a whole two seconds, she nods.

I continue. "He wants to buy all our Elysian Blossom."

Immediately, every part of her goes on high alert. "Absolutely not."

I smile wryly. "Yeah, no shit. And that's what I've continued to tell him, but it's not sinking in."

"So what's he saying now?"

I hold the phone so we can read it together.

ENTITLED CANADIAN

I'm certain I can convince you. Please send me
your address. I'll be there tomorrow.

Magnolia sucks in a breath. "He's coming here? To Sacred River?"

Forcing down the spike of anger at the man's audacity, I answer. "It would appear so."

"Does he have any clue what he's walking into?"

"Not even remotely."

She chuckles. "Well. Guess we'll have to show the perfume prince of Canada a good time."

* * *

Love Potion No. 69 releases on January 31, 2024.

Also by Valerie Pepper

Guided to Love Series

The Mechanic's Guide to Getting the Boss's Daughter (series starter novella; free to newsletter subscribers)

The Widow's Guide to Second Chances (Book 1)

The Barista's Guide to The Perfect Steam (Book 2)

The Grump's Guide to Chaos (Book 3)

Sacred River Series

Love Potion No. 69 - (Series starter novella, Book 1)

Novellas

Naughty All The Way (November 2023) - Part of the Twelve Days of Smutmas limited-time collection

To Have and To Scold in the *Holidays & Hook-Ups* anthology by The New Romance Cafe (June 2023 - limited edition)

Acknowledgments

Thank you, as always, to the people who make up my real life happily ever after: my husband and kids. I love you. Thank you for celebrating every milestone with me, and for your endless support and encouragement.

To The Cheeto Dust Crew: my amazing critique partners Alicia Wilder, Ivy Fairbanks, and Kat Saturday. Thanks especially to Alicia, who really carried this book on her shoulders.

SRE: The best damn group of writers on the internet. Here's to the Indie Chat, the Wet Henrys, and seasonal novella takeovers. SRE for life!

Thanks to my editor, Jennifer Sommersby. Thank you to Sarah Hansen of Okay Creations for another beautiful cover.

To my readers: holy cow. Thank you for the love you continue to show me and my books. My street team and ARC readers, Bookstagrammers, BookTokkers, reviewers and readers: Thank you, thank you, thank you. Thank you for giving me your time, your enthusiasm, your memes, your exclamation points, grabby hands, and hearts. You are why I keep doing this…well, that and the voices inside my head, ha.

xo,

About the Author

 Valerie Pepper is an incurable optimist and a firm believer in the girl getting the guy, or the guy getting the girl, or the girl getting the girl, or the guy getting the guy, or basically any way it needs to happen to make a real-life happily ever after, even if it takes more than one try.

When she's not writing, you can find her reading, hiking, listening to whatever music suits her mood, and hanging out with her family. She's fascinated with the idea of a capsule wardrobe, but loves clothes and shoes and boots far too much to make a real go of it.

She's currently living out her own happily ever after with her husband, kids, and dogs, and maaaaaybe too many shoes. She lives in Birmingham, Alabama, and is the recipient of the Contemporary Romance Writer's 2021 Stiletto Award. Learn more at www.authorvaleriepepper.com.